Murder at Haddonford Manor

A Charlotte Reinford Mystery

Irina McGrath

CAVEL PRESS

KENMORE, WA

A Camel Press book published by Epicenter Press

Epicenter Press
6524 NE 181st St.
Suite 2
Kenmore, WA 98028

For more information go to:
www.Camelpress.com
www.Charlottemysteries.com

This is a work of fiction. Names, characters, places, brands, media, and incidents are either the product of the author's imagination or are used fictitiously.

Cover design by Scott Book
Design by Melissa Vail Coffman

To my beloved children. You inspire every word I write and every dream I dream. This book is for you, with all my love and hopes for your brightest futures.

ACKNOWLEDGMENTS

I am deeply grateful to all who have supported me on this journey. First and foremost, I thank my children, Monica, Nicole, and Ahmed, whose belief in me and constant encouragement have been pillars of strength and inspiration. Their love and enthusiasm have sustained me throughout this writing endeavor. I also extend my heartfelt appreciation to Jean Wolph, who has supported my literary pursuits over the years. Finally, I owe profound gratitude to Jennifer McCord, Executive Editor & Associate Publisher at Epicenter-Coffeetown-Camel Press, who provided the opportunity to bring this book to life. Her guidance and support have been instrumental in making this dream a reality.

Chapter One

THE BUSTLING PLATFORM AT KING'S CROSS Station offered a captivating mosaic of sights and sounds. The rhythmic chugging of locomotives, interspersed with intermittent hisses of escaping steam, permeated the soundscape, overshadowing the hurried voices of commuters in their relentless rush to catch departing trains. Overhead, the platform announcements, delivered in a courteous yet authoritative tone, evoked a mix of relief and disappointment, confirming the punctuality of some trains while bluntly announcing unexpected delays.

In this organized chaos, Charlotte stood out, emanating poise. Her emerald-green eyes sparkled with a magnetic allure as they observed the frenetic ballet of the bustling crowd. At just eighteen, she displayed an extraordinary blend of qualities that spoke of her maturity: decisiveness, determination, and discipline. Her speech, thoughtful and distinct, was honed by countless hours in the seclusion of St. Helen's convent library. This sacred place, where she was raised as an orphan of the church, held a special spot in her heart. It was her only home, and although she cherished every moment spent there, Charlotte found herself intrigued by the endless possibilities that lay beyond the convent's hallowed walls. Driven by immense curiosity, she chose not to pursue becoming a novitiate, opting for the thrilling adventure of exploring the world and forging her own path. With the blessing of Mother Superior, Charlotte bid a heartfelt farewell to the nuns and proceeded to King's Cross Station, where her journey would commence.

Now at the station, she observed people swiftly boarding and disembarking from trains, focusing on specific individuals, such as the middle-aged gentleman who walked stiffly and wore an outdated bowler hat despite the fashion trend having died twenty years earlier. Charlotte couldn't help but glance down at her own outfit, a gray frock dress adorned with shabby lace trim on the sleeves, complemented by ill-fitting kitten heels. Both the dress and shoes were hand-me-downs from one of the sisters at the convent, doing little to flatter her youthful figure. Clutching a small, weathered suitcase, Charlotte carried a wardrobe mirroring her current attire. Nestled alongside her worn-out clothes was her cherished and tattered Bible, a symbol of her faith that the sisters had insisted she carry into the world.

Positioned by the wall, a newspaper stand drew Charlotte's notice. She paused briefly, contemplating her next move, before opting to buy the day's newspaper. The prospect of employment had been a persistent focus for her, and she had diligently kept an eye out for opportunities. Among the intriguing listings were a tutoring position for young children and a housekeeping role catering to a prominent businessman. Yet, on this day, fortune seemed to favor her, as she stumbled upon a curious new advertisement.

Personal Assistant to Lady Haddonford

Ideal candidate is a youthful and sharp female willing to accompany and assist the Head of House with daily tasks, including but not limited to writing letters, accompanying on business trips, and maintaining organization.

Prospective candidates report to Haddonford Manor, Chelmsford, UK.

While her initial intent was to secure a job within the city, Charlotte couldn't help but consider the potential hidden within this unexpected opportunity: the sight of a train bound for Chelmsford, scheduled to depart in about twenty minutes. This was Charlotte's chance to embrace the moment and explore a new path. As Charlotte ventured forward, her attention was captivated by a book prominently displayed at the newspaper stand: *Murder on the Orient Express* by Agatha Christie. Its intriguing title, an unconventional sight within a train station, sparked her curiosity. "A departure from my usual reading material," Charlotte mused, impulsively buying the book before resuming her path toward the ticket counter.

Once she boarded the train, she settled into her seat and immersed herself in the suspenseful narrative, occasionally looking up to appreciate the changing scenery—busy cityscapes transforming into picturesque rural countryside. The train's rhythmic movements acted as a soothing background to the captivating words on the pages.

Upon her arrival at Chelmsford station, Charlotte stepped off the train with a sense of excitement, still clutching the book firmly in her hands. Finding a nearby cab proved effortless, and armed with the newspaper displaying the address, she easily communicated her destination to the driver. Before she knew it, she found herself standing in awe before Haddonford Manor, a magnificent three-story mansion.

As Charlotte rang the doorbell, a surprisingly melodic sound filled the air. A young maid who appeared to be around Charlotte's age opened the door, dressed in a tasteful gray gown. Along with her attire, she wore a meticulously starched white apron and a delicate lace cap, resting gracefully on her blonde hair. With a sense of intrigue, her deep blue eyes carefully studied Charlotte.

"Good afternoon," Charlotte began, her voice filled with sincerity. "I am here in response to the advertisement for the position of Personal Assistant to Lady Haddonford, as featured in the

Daily Mail. Since no contact number was provided, I boarded a train this morning," she explained, her words reflecting her genuine enthusiasm. The maid courteously guided her into the grand foyer of the manor.

"Please wait here momentarily, and I will promptly inform Lady Beatrice of your arrival," the maid said politely before gracefully disappearing into a room down the hall.

Meanwhile, Charlotte became deeply engrossed in the stunning elegance and refinement of Haddonford Manor. The walls were adorned with rich wooden paneling, intricately carved with floral motifs and delicate scrollwork. The color palette was warm, with deep, polished mahogany and shades of burgundy. The floors were made of marble. An impressive chandelier, a work of art itself, was suspended from the double-height ceiling. A grand wooden console table stood against one wall, and an elegant, upholstered bench right next to it invited visitors to take a moment to appreciate the surroundings.

Charlotte's admiration was interrupted as the maid returned with a warm smile illuminating her face. "Lady Beatrice is expecting you in the Blue Room," she informed Charlotte, guiding her down the hallway to a sanctuary decorated in serene hues of blue. The room emanated a sense of tranquility, with its tasteful decor and peaceful atmosphere.

As they entered, Charlotte's eyes met the gentle gaze of Lady Beatrice, a woman who embodied elegance and grace and was somewhere in her mid to late sixties. Her refined features were accentuated by a kind expression, reflecting a depth of wisdom and life experiences.

"Please, take a seat," Lady Beatrice gestured toward a plush chair, her voice exuding warmth and genuine hospitality. "I am Lady Beatrice Haddonford, though you may simply call me Lady Beatrice. I understand you saw the advertisement and are interested in becoming my companion. Before we proceed, may I ask, how old are you?"

"Well, actually, I had initially thought the position was for a personal assistant. Nevertheless, I am incredibly willing and excited about this opportunity! I am eighteen, brimming with enthusiasm to serve," Charlotte confidently responded, her nerves gradually subsiding with each word spoken.

Lady Beatrice's smile widened. "Eighteen. Indeed, quite young," she remarked.

Curious about Lady Beatrice's reaction, Charlotte inquired, her concern evident, "Is there something amiss?"

"No, no," Lady Beatrice reassured her. "Nothing is amiss, my dear. Now, please do tell me a bit about yourself. You know, the sort of information essential for us to understand each other in such situations."

Taking a moment to compose herself, Charlotte began sharing her story. "Well, I am an orphan. Sister Margarite informed me that I was left on the steps of St. Helen's Convent when I was just a few months old, and it has been my home ever since. However, on my recent birthday, I made the decision that it was time for me to embark on my own adventure and start a new chapter in my life."

Lady Beatrice listened intently, her eyes brimming with empathy. She was fully engaged in Charlotte's story.

"The sisters took exceptional care of me. While I had everything I needed, it was through books in the convent library that I found solace and expanded my horizons," Charlotte expressed with heartfelt honesty.

Curiosity and gentleness intertwined in Lady Beatrice's tone as she asked, "Do you have any family members?"

"The nuns at the convent are my family."

Lady Beatrice nodded, acknowledging the deep bond Charlotte had forged within the walls of St. Helen's.

"Well," Lady Beatrice began, breaking the silence, "the role of my companion entails both secretarial duties and providing me with your company in social settings. Your workday commences at 6:00 in the morning and concludes when I retire for the night. I must confess that my bouts of insomnia may result in shorter sleep for both of us on certain occasions. You may have already encountered our maid, Margaret, and as you settle into your role, you will have interactions with other members of our staff, including our exceptional cook," Lady Beatrice explained, a warm smile gracing her lips as she mentioned her employees.

Interrupting gently, Charlotte sought clarification, "Forgive me, but did you just say, 'as I settle in'? Does that mean I have been offered the position? If necessary, I can provide references, although they will all be from the nuns at the convent."

"There is no need for references, my dear. It appears that you are more than suitable for this job," Lady Beatrice reassured Charlotte. She rang a small silver bell, and as the same young lady who had welcomed Charlotte half an hour ago entered the room, Lady Beatrice addressed her, "Margaret, please show Miss . . . I apologize, what was your name again?" she turned to Charlotte.

"It's Charlotte Reinford."

"Char-lotte," Lady Beatrice repeated, savoring the sound of the name. "Did the nuns give you this name?"

"No, my name was written on a card tucked inside my blanket," Charlotte explained.

"Interesting," Lady Beatrice remarked, before refocusing her attention on the maid. "Please show Miss Reinford to her room."

As Charlotte rose from her seat, suitcase in hand, Lady Beatrice bid her farewell from the Blue Room. "Welcome to Haddonford, Charlotte. Tomorrow morning, we'll continue our conversation, and perhaps discuss a wardrobe upgrade. I expect to see you here at six."

A sense of excitement and anticipation surged through Charlotte as she followed the maid down the grand hallway, ready to embark on this new chapter of her life within the magnificent Haddonford Manor.

CHAPTER TWO

CHARLOTTE PAID LITTLE ATTENTION AS MARGARET directed her down the hallway and up the stairs to her new bedroom. Everything had happened so quickly that it felt surreal. She had landed a job working on a fabulous and enormous estate with minimal background vetting. While she was thrilled to have a place to stay, she couldn't help but feel curious and a bit suspicious about the ease with which she was accepted into the household. The fact that Lady Beatrice only asked for her name at the very end of their conversation seemed a bit off.

"Your room, Miss," the maid opened the door and stepped aside, allowing Charlotte to enter. "Is there anything you need?" she asked, and when Charlotte shook her head, the maid left, leaving her to get acquainted with her new surroundings.

The room was a lavish setting, a significant upgrade from her quarters at St. Helen's. Charlotte's gaze wandered around the bedroom, taking in an ornate writing desk and a plush pinstripe armchair in the far corner next to wide windows offering a view of the front courtyard of Haddonford. To the left stood a four-poster mahogany bed covered with a light blue duvet and fluffed pillows.

Exhausted from her travels, Charlotte dropped her suitcase haphazardly on the floor, causing the buckle to burst open and the contents to spill out. She flopped onto the bed, hoping for a moment of rest, but her hopes vanished when she heard an abrupt knock on the door, followed by someone entering.

"Ah, there you are! I heard you're the new girl in town. Welcome, welcome! I'm Rachel Offley, the cook here at the manor," said the overweight middle-aged woman with a strong Irish accent. The dimples on her plump cheeks and the good-natured smile on her round face contrasted sharply with her tenacious and piercing gaze. Caught off guard, Charlotte scrambled to stand upright and greet the unexpected visitor.

"Don't you worry about looking presentable to me. I just wanted to introduce myself," Mrs. Offley announced as she strode over to the armchair, stepping over Charlotte's scattered belongings. She sat down, and the struggling springs in the seat made their protest known.

"Tomorrow's your first day, my dear. Me and my husband, Frank, we've been here many, many years. Well, Frank more than myself. He's the chauffeur, the groundskeeper, and security, among other things. Of course, he gets a wee bit of help from Samuel. He's about your age, not like Frank though," Mrs. Offley clarified. "No, no, Frank is an old codger like myself. So where was I? Ah, right, Frank . . . he also runs errands for Lady Beatrice. And I never know what he does or where he goes. Take today, for example, he left early in the morning, and when I asked where he was going, he just gave me a mysterious face and refused to tell me, his own wife, as if he was the blooming secret service! Not a word, can you believe it! Oh, my goodness," Mrs. Offley threw her hands up in the air. "Anyway, I think you need a good hot meal. I heard a bit about your journey today. You must be famished!" Mrs. Offley put her plump hands on the soft armrests and made an effort to lift herself up. "Follow me," she commanded after successfully separating herself from the fine piece of furniture.

Without any room to interject, Charlotte felt inclined to follow Mrs. Offley into the kitchen. Despite her stodgy appearance, the cook moved swiftly, and Charlotte had to quicken her own pace to keep up.

"Now dear, let me know if you're ever hungry or need help with anything here as you get used to things," Mrs. Offley said over her shoulder as they strode to the massive kitchen.

The kitchen's centerpiece was an attractive gas range with multiple burners and separate compartments for various baked items. Copper pots and pans adorned the wall beside the stove, while cabinets on the far wall held dishes of various styles and sizes. In the center of the room, a spacious wooden table doubled as a workstation and seating for the staff during their meals. On this table lay a cutting board with a partially sliced carrot and a knife, suggesting that Mrs. Offley may have paused her vegetable preparation to fetch Charlotte.

Taking a seat opposite the carrot, Charlotte eagerly anticipated the cook as she ladled lamb stew into a bowl for her. The delicious aroma alone hinted that this would be one of the best meals she had enjoyed in a while.

"Well, how do you like it?" asked Mrs. Offley after Charlotte took her first bite.

"Absolutely ravishing, I haven't had anything quite like it before," Charlotte expressed.

Mrs. Offley beamed, pleased with the compliment. "Ah, good. It's a family recipe, you see. Passed down from my dear old granny. She was a fine cook, she was," Mrs. Offley reminisced, her accent lending her words a touch of nostalgia. "You have no idea how happy I am that Lady Beatrice finally hired someone. She's been interviewing local women for some time now. She got tired of them and decided to run an ad in London to broaden the scope of the search. And boom, you show up, and you get the job. You must've had some grand references or something for her to choose you," joked Mrs. Offley with a mischievous twinkle in her eyes.

"No, on the contrary, I didn't have to say much at all! It is all so very curious now, knowing that she turned down others before me . . ." Charlotte ended her sentence inquisitively, as her suspicions and uncertainty about the day's events settled in her mind.

Mrs. Offley, who had noticed her abandoned carrot on the cutting board, began cutting an onion instead, tearing up as she spoke, "Eh, don't worry your head too much about it. Lady Beatrice, God love her, she's a quirky one. I mean, for crying out loud, the woman prefers coffee over tea! I guess that isn't too weird . . . how about the fact that she cuts her grapes before eating them? With a knife and fork! Anyway, the point is, you are the right one for the job, I can just tell," said Mrs. Offley.

It was a lot for Charlotte to take in, and perhaps too soon for her to admit that she herself preferred cut grapes to remove the seeds.

"Mrs. Offley, I want to start on a good note tomorrow, and you've been here a while. Could you please tell me if there is anything else I need to know about Lady Beatrice and Haddonford? Truthfully, I don't even know who lives here."

Weeping and sniffling from the onion, Mrs. Offley explained, "There are only six of us here, not counting the occasional visitor. That makes it Lady Beatrice, Frank, Margaret, Samuel, and now you. Lady Beatrice is a bit of a hermit. She rarely leaves the manor and spends most of her days in the Blue Room. She has a son named Richard who visits rather frequently. I'd say he's a bit of a mummy's boy. And then there's her long-time friend Lord Carrington. You'd think he didn't have a home with the amount of times he's over here."

"And what about her husband? How long ago did he die?"

Surprised, Mrs. Offley quickly sobered up from her fiasco. "How do you know that he's dead?" she asked, her voice tinged with curiosity.

"I don't. I just assumed he did since you did not mention a husband in her current life."

"Right, right, that makes sense. Yes, Lady Beatrice's husband died, but when exactly, I don't know. It happened long before I came around here. Okay, that's enough. It's getting late, and you have to get up early in the morning." And just as abruptly as Mrs. Offley had introduced herself, she made it clear that the conversation was over. She left Charlotte with only one option, and that was to bid her goodnight and leave the kitchen in search of her bedroom. The hallway was dimly illuminated, with only a single wall sconce casting a faint glow in the darkness, just enough to reveal the portraits of nobles framed in heavy gold lining both sides of the walls. Charlotte noticed a small plaque beneath one of the paintings, dedicated to Sir William Finch. Even though she knew nothing about Sir William, she remembered reading back at the convent about his son, Sir Thomas Finch, who was knighted for his role in the suppression of Sir Thomas Wyatt's rebellion against Queen Mary I. While somewhat interesting and providing minor historical details, the books available to her during her childhood were exceedingly dull. Charlotte longed for access to fictional novels and hoped she would find them at Haddonford. As she walked along the hall searching for the staircase, she stumbled upon an entrance that seemed to beckon her forward. Peering into the darkness, she could faintly make out the outline of what appeared to be a library.

Curiosity propelled Charlotte to step into the room. The absence of light created an air of mystery, shrouding the room's features in a mysterious veil. Charlotte extended her hand, carefully trailing the cold wall near the doorframe, in an attempt to locate a switch that would illuminate the room. But her efforts proved fruitless, leaving her to navigate the dimly lit space with only her senses as a guide.

With every step, Charlotte moved around the room with care, ensuring she avoided any potential obstacles. As her eyes adjusted to the darkness, she discerned the faint outlines of furniture, delicate vases, and statues that stood as silent guardians, evoking an atmosphere of antiquity. Charlotte slowly walked towards the tall bookshelves. Reaching towards the heights of the ceiling, these imposing structures seemed to embrace the wisdom of the ages. Charlotte stood in awe; her imagination ignited by the knowledge that lay within the grasp of her fingertips.

A voice from the dark hallway broke the silence, "What are you doing here?"

Charlotte jumped and let out a small scream.

The lights went on almost immediately. A stocky man stood in the doorway, studying her with a stern and penetrating gaze. His hand was still on the light switch that Charlotte had missed. The stranger appeared to be around the same age as Lady Beatrice. His thick dark brows were furrowed as he waited for Charlotte to respond.

"I'm looking for my bedroom," Charlotte said, realizing that her explanation did not make sense without further clarification. "I was hired today as Lady Beatrice's companion. Mrs. Offley, who I believe is your wife, considering the description she gave of you earlier, offered me dinner, and I followed her to the kitchen, thinking that I would find my way back easily. But I was wrong. I got curious when I noticed this was a library and had to take a look around."

The man's face softened a little, but his tone of voice remained stern. "You will get to know Haddonford soon enough. It is much easier to orient yourself when the sun is out. At the end of this hallway, you will find the stairs. Go up, and your bedroom is the second one on the left. And one more thing," Frank paused, directing his look at Charlotte, "Always remember to keep your windows and doors locked at night."

An icy shiver ran down Charlotte's spine as she hurried to her bedroom. She wasted no time in securing her bedroom door and making sure the lock was firmly in place. With trembling hands, Charlotte latched the windows shut, ensuring they were tightly sealed against any potential intruders.

CHAPTER THREE

THE PIERCING SOUND OF THE ALARM clock at 5:30 in the morning jolted Charlotte from her drowsy state as she reluctantly opened her eyes. It felt like mere moments ago that she had settled into her room, engrossed in the Agatha Christie novel from the train, hoping to fall into a deep slumber, and now it was already time to get up. Charlotte hopped out of bed, carefully stepping over her scattered luggage still cluttering the floor and pushed open the window. The garden of Haddonford was utterly beautiful, bathed in the tender embrace of the rising summer sun. The meticulously trimmed lawns, still adorned with the morning's glistening dew, showcased an array of vibrant greens, each shade harmonizing with the next in a breathtaking tapestry. Dewdrops sparkled like scattered diamonds on the petals of delicate blossoms. As Charlotte stood by the window, she felt calmness wash over her, easing the tension that clung to her spirit. Just below Charlotte's window, a black Rolls-Royce was parked in a horseshoe gravel driveway. Frank Offley emerged from the mansion, carrying a large manila envelope, and proceeded to the car with a secretive demeanor. Before entering the vehicle, he paused, examining the writing on the front of the envelope, and then threw it on the passenger seat and sped away, leaving a trail of dust behind.

Catching sight of the time, Charlotte realized she had wasted fifteen precious minutes admiring the view when she should have been preparing for the day. A quick look in the mirror revealed her tangled hair, a testament to her deep slumber. She rummaged through her belongings until she found another gray outfit and a hairbrush to untangle the knots she had unintentionally created. With her appearance hastily improved, Charlotte hurried downstairs and entered the Blue Room promptly at six o'clock.

Lady Beatrice sat at the elegant writing-table, her poised figure exuding an air of refined grace. In her hand, she held a fountain pen, its nib gliding effortlessly across the paper as she composed her thoughts. By her side stood a young man of about Charlotte's age. With impeccable symmetry, his flawlessly straight nose heightened the allure of his finely sculpted features. His curly hair emanated a captivating charm, evoking memories of the mythical beauty of Adonis, Greek God of beauty and desire. Both the young stranger and Lady Beatrice turned their heads at the sound of Charlotte's arrival, her heavy breathing giving away her recent jog.

Lady Beatrice addressed Charlotte with a hint of sarcasm, "Some morning calisthenics, I presume? This is Samuel; he was assisting me with the mail, but now that you're here, you can take over."

Samuel appeared visibly relieved as he excused himself from his secretarial duties, quickly leaving the room to attend to his tasks on the grounds.

"I must admit, he excels in his role. I used to rely heavily on Frank, but as he's grown older, I've assigned him more senior duties and brought Samuel in for the labor-intensive tasks," Lady Beatrice continued.

As if following a rotation, Margaret entered the room after Samuel's departure, carrying a tray with a small silver pot, two cups, a sugar bowl, and a creamer. She carefully placed the tray on a small table next to the sofa before leaving the room. The enticing aroma of freshly brewed coffee wafted through the air.

"Charlotte, my dear, please step away from the doorway and be so kind as to pour me a cup of coffee," Lady Beatrice requested.

Flustered, Charlotte obeyed, fetching the tray and bringing it to the writing desk.

Lady Beatrice sighed in relief as she took the porcelain cup in her hand. "Ah, I can never truly function without my morning coffee. You see, my father was an avid coffee drinker, and I suppose I inherited my love for it from him. He traveled extensively during my childhood, and I eagerly awaited his return, which always marked a special occasion. He never returned empty-handed, always bringing me unique gifts: a moonlight stone from India, an original Faberge egg from Russia, or a feather-light silk scarf from China. He would regale me with enchanting tales of his adventures, and I would sit by his side, mesmerized, imagining myself walking the Great Wall of China, encountering an old friend on the steps of the Taj Mahal, or conversing with a Russian ambassador in the magnificent rooms of the Hermitage." Lady Beatrice's eyes gleamed with nostalgia as she reminisced about her childhood.

"I apologize for my earlier grumpiness, my dear. Normally, I'm served my coffee in bed, but it seems Margaret has forgotten that detail today. Would you care for a cup?" Lady Beatrice inquired.

"No, thank you. I prefer Earl Grey tea," Charlotte politely declined.

"I suppose we all have our preferences," Lady Beatrice mused. "Our tastes are often influenced by our upbringing. I'm not sure I would have developed a liking for coffee if it weren't for my father. Whose influences have shaped your preferences?" Lady Beatrice asked curiously.

"Primarily books, but also many of the nuns I grew close to," Charlotte responded. "St. Helen had a wonderful library, and I spent most of my time there while growing up. As for the nuns, they came from diverse backgrounds and had different personalities, but they were united by their love for God, which brought them together."

"Intriguing," Lady Beatrice acknowledged, raising the cup to her lips. "When you mention different backgrounds, what do you mean?"

"Mother Superior, for instance, joined the convent in her late twenties. She didn't like to discuss her past, but once I overheard a conversation between her and a visitor who referred to her as Lady Hastings."

Lady Beatrice winced at the mention of the name but swiftly composed herself, offering a forced smile. "It's a well-known name with a rich history," she remarked.

"Yes, indeed," agreed Charlotte. "Although Mother Superior never spoke of her relatives, I came across some information about them."

"Were you and Mother Superior close?" Lady Beatrice inquired.

"Very much so," Charlotte replied. "She was like a mother to me."

"And did the nuns ever try to convince you to join when of age?" Lady Beatrice probed.

"They never urged me to join, only to live by their teachings and work for the greater good," Charlotte clarified.

"Very well. Now, let's move on to business. I need you to lick these stamps so I can have these letters mailed," Lady Beatrice swiftly shifted the conversation to work. "I also require your assistance in ensuring everything is prepared for Lord Carrington's visit. I've invited Henry for a short stay to discuss . . . well, some old matters. The reason for his visit is inconsequential, though. He'll be arriving tomorrow morning and likely staying for a few days. Now, there are a few things you should know about Henry. We met when I was around your age, and I must admit, he hasn't changed much since then. He and I are complete opposites: I'm an introvert who prefers solitude, while he exudes boundless energy and turns the world upside down wherever he goes. I possess better listening skills, but he surpasses me in his propensity for speaking. In other words," Lady Beatrice took a sip of her coffee, wrinkling her nose at its bitter taste before reaching for the sugar bowl, "he talks too much." She added a teaspoon of sugar to her cup, stirring it carefully.

"This coffee is far too strong for my liking. I attempted to drink it without sweetening, but unfortunately, the bitterness exceeds my tolerance. I usually try to omit sugar," Lady Beatrice explained, "but in this case, it's a necessity. Rachel does her best, of course. She's an excellent cook, but coffee isn't her forte."

While Lady Beatrice finished her coffee, Charlotte diligently licked the stamps and affixed them to the envelopes. As she worked, she couldn't help but notice the written addresses: some were destined for various ladies and lords, one was addressed to a law firm in London, and the final envelope was intended for a bank with which Lady Beatrice seemingly conducted business.

"Please ensure they are properly sealed and mailed," Lady Beatrice instructed. "By 'mailed,' I mean give them to Frank, and he will take care of the rest. Also, my dear, do me a favor and call the dressmaker. You'll find his number in the black book next to the telephone. Tell him we need him for a fitting later today."

Charlotte acknowledged, "Of course, Lady Beatrice. When would you like the dressmaker to arrive?"

"For you, Charlotte. It's time you had a fitting. I think we ought to incorporate more blue and reduce the gray in your wardrobe," Lady Beatrice suggested, offering a mix of critique and kindness that took Charlotte aback. Nonetheless, she warmly welcomed the chance to acquire custom-made attire in any hue. With her duties for the day clearly set, including arranging the mail dispatch and readying for Lord Carrington's visit, Charlotte excused herself to commence her tasks.

Chapter Four

With Frank absent from Haddonford, Charlotte chose to first focus on the necessary preparations for Lord Carrington's imminent visit. What initially appeared as a straightforward task quickly revealed its complexities. Unfamiliar with Lord Carrington's preferences, identity, and even the mansion's layout, including where to find fresh linens, Charlotte recognized her limitations. She reasoned that entrusting the task to Margaret would be the wiser choice. Yet, the challenge of finding the maid within the sprawling house presented itself as an unforeseen obstacle. As Charlotte ventured from one room to another, searching for Margaret, she found herself drawn again into the library. Bathed in daylight, the library revealed its grandeur with wall-to-wall shelves and inviting leather couches. It beckoned Charlotte to immerse herself in a world of imagination. Intrigued, she grabbed a pristine copy of *The Secret Garden* from the shelf and settled onto the sofa, contemplating the possibility of indulging in a brief read while awaiting Margaret's appearance.

Although Charlotte's intentions were noble and her plan seemingly foolproof, the combined effects of an early wake-up and the monotonous descriptions in the novel swiftly lulled her into sleep. Her next conscious moment arrived with the jarring ring of the doorbell, accompanied by a new, boisterous male voice exclaiming, "Margaret! Oh Margaret! It's always a pleasure to see you!"

Realizing she had dozed off while on duty, Charlotte scolded herself internally, acknowledging her lapse in vigilance. She swiftly rose from the sofa, carelessly leaving the book on the floor, and hurried toward the front door to greet the visitor and Margaret.

As she entered the front foyer, her attention was immediately drawn to a distinguished gentleman exuding geniality and charm. Standing tall and slender, with an oblong face and eyes radiating contentment, he displayed a captivating presence. Just as Charlotte was about to extend her greeting, her gaze caught her reflection in an ornate mirror, revealing a reddened mark on her cheek and slightly disheveled hair—clear evidence of her midday catnap. Hoping her mishap would go unnoticed, she mustered a composed reply, "Um, good morning, sir. I am Charlotte, Lady Beatrice's personal assistant."

"Splendid, splendid! I'm Lord Carrington," the gentleman responded with enthusiasm. "I am delighted to make your acquaintance, Charlotte. I was beginning to think I'd have to assume the role of an assistant myself if Beatrice didn't find anyone soon. But judging by your appearance, you seem more than capable! If only I had a team like you two at my own place, I might be inclined to stay there instead of visiting Haddonford so frequently!" he winked mischievously at the two young women, eliciting an eye-roll from Margaret.

"I would love to learn more about you, so please don't plan on going anywhere until we have a chance to talk," he warned Charlotte. "Let me just say hello to Beatrice. She's expecting me tomorrow, but circumstances have changed, and I'm here today."

Without further delay, he briskly walked into the Blue Room. From where she was standing, Charlotte could hear him saying, "Beatrice, don't be upset. I took an early train."

Realizing Margaret had already departed, Charlotte assumed she had matters under control, given Lord Carrington's previous visits and made her way into the Blue Room to ensure the well-being of both Lord Carrington and Lady Beatrice.

Observing Lady Beatrice's discontented expression, Charlotte discerned that Lord Carrington's early arrival had caught her off guard, causing annoyance and frustration over her unpreparedness for a guest. Finally, Lady Beatrice exclaimed, "Henry! What on earth are you doing here?"

"You make me feel unwelcome, Beatrice," Lord Carrington replied with a gentle kiss to Lady Beatrice's hand.

"Nonsense. Haddonford practically is your second home. But what prompted this sudden change of plans?" Lady Beatrice questioned.

"My desire to see you, Beatrice," Lord Carrington responded, his gaze briefly shifting toward Charlotte. "This must be coffee, right?" he asked, picking up a silver pot and pouring himself a cup.

"You detest coffee," Lady Beatrice reminded him.

"Indeed, I do. But, of course, I'm always willing to give this beverage of roasted beans the benefit of the doubt," Lord Carrington quipped.

"Henry, don't waste my coffee just to be funny," Lady Beatrice admonished him, but her words had no effect as Lord Carrington continued to pour himself a cup. He took a large gulp of the lukewarm liquid, which his taste buds promptly rejected, causing him to choke and gasp for air.

Shocked and concerned, Charlotte watched the scene unfold, while Lady Beatrice seemed unfazed, calmly observing Lord Carrington's struggle. A sigh of relief escaped Charlotte when Lord Carrington finally placed the cup back on the tray, his voice raspy as he exclaimed, "Bloody hell, this stuff is rancid."

"You know, Henry, I could have done without witnessing your failed attempt at aspirating your lungs today. Why can't you accept your preferences and move on?" Lady Beatrice scolded him.

Lord Carrington, still recovering, responded, "Beatrice, I know we have our disagreements, but I firmly believe that desires and tastes can change based on one's gained perspectives and experiences."

"Really?" Lady Beatrice said with a hint of sarcasm. "I can't recall a single instance that supports your claim. Did you happen to visit a coffee farm in the past two weeks since I last saw you, compelling you to try coffee today? Mind you, it's only been two weeks since your last visit. I seem to see you more often than my own son, which is quite unfortunate."

"Is it unfortunate that you see me often? For some, my presence might be a blessing!" Lord Carrington retorted, attempting to lighten the mood.

"What's truly unfortunate is that I don't see Richard as frequently as I would like," Lady Beatrice sighed.

"I thought you mentioned he might visit soon?" Lord Carrington inquired.

"Yes, but this time he's bringing that fiancée of his. What's her name? Lady Isabelle?"

"And what's wrong with that?" Lord Carrington asked.

"Everything about this situation feels wrong. I can't see them as a suitable pair, but what can I possibly say to him?" Lady Beatrice said with a scowl. "Henry, would you mind explaining why you've arrived earlier than expected and why you're squandering my time and coffee?"

Charlotte noticed the deep irritation in Lady Beatrice, a stark shift from her usual demeanor. The harshness of Lady Beatrice's words seemed to extend far beyond any issue with coffee or Lord Carrington's professed tolerance for it, hinting at a deeper discontent with his actions or perhaps his presence itself.

Lord Carrington turned his attention to Charlotte, issuing instructions, "My dear, could you please ask Rachel to prepare some tea? Today, I'm back on Team Tea, rather than Team Coffee."

Not waiting for the argument to continue, Charlotte quickly excused herself, leaving the room to fulfill the tea request. The bright daylight and the aroma of Mrs. Offley's cooking guided

Charlotte to the kitchen. Inside, Rachel Offley was tending to a boiling pot of water, her hair slightly puffed due to the humidity. A tray of freshly baked strawberry scones sat on the table, with one of them missing a bite, placed on a small plate.

"Margaret told me that Lord Carrington is here," the cook remarked in her unmistakable accent, the words rolling off her tongue with a touch of rustic charm. As she deftly pulled out a silver tray, a spitting image of the one Margaret had carried earlier, she placed a steaming teapot upon it.

"It's ready. I knew he would fancy a cup." Mrs. Offley reached for the milk and poured a little bit into a delicate porcelain creamer. "You know, it's unlike him to show up a day early. But then again, who knows? He's an inconsistently consistent man. The type who methodically follows the rules and then, all of a sudden, changes his course. I've always enjoyed the energy he brings. It's just what I need in a workplace. My last job was a proper fright . . ." Mrs. Offley caught herself in the midst of her sentence, considering her forthcoming words, and discreetly swallowed the thick scone.

"I'm sorry, I didn't catch that. What happened in your previous job?" Charlotte asked surprised to see Mrs. Offley, who seemed to enjoy chatting endlessly, suddenly halt her story.

"Sorry, deary. I think I'll deliver the tea to Lord Carrington myself," the cook muttered, heading toward the Blue Room.

Intrigued, Charlotte followed Mrs. Offley as she hurried along, carefully balancing the tray.

"Rachel! How lovely to see you!" Lord Carrington greeted her as he took the tray from her hands. Despite her protests, he insisted, "Let me handle this. Please, tell me how you've been. You look as radiant as ever."

Lord Carrington's eyes focused on the cook, his body language conveying genuine interest in her well-being as he poured himself a cup of steaming Earl Grey tea.

"You're quite the charmer, Lord Carrington," Rachel chuckled, smoothing her snow-white apron with her hands. "I'm doing very well, thank you."

"I'm glad to hear that. No news is good news, as they say," Lord Carrington chuckled. "Did you know that this expression may have originated with King James I of England, who allegedly said, 'No news is better than evil news' in the year 1616? King James had many shortcomings during his 23-year rule, but he successfully united the Kingdom of Scotland and England, and he . . ." Lord Carrington trailed off, lost in his historical anecdote.

"Henry," Lady Beatrice interjected. "Did I ever tell you that you have a knack for obfuscation? And you still haven't answered my question about why you're here early."

With a sly smile, Lord Carrington responded, "Well, thank you for the compliment. Some might say that I enlighten their lives with fascinating facts related to the topic at hand. As for your question, it was to see you, of course."

"It's out of character for you to show up unannounced," Lady Beatrice remarked.

Feeling uncomfortable with the conversation, Mrs. Offley took a few steps backward, edging closer to the door. "Strawberry scones," she mumbled under her breath. "I need to check on them."

Ignoring the cook's unease, Lord Carrington glanced at his golden watch and suggested, "How about we take a walk, Beatrice? We could all use some sunlight right now, and I promise I won't discuss history for at least ten minutes."

Interest flickered in Lady Beatrice's eyes as she considered the proposal. "Very well, Henry. However, let's keep the walk short. I have several issues I'd like to discuss while we're outside," she decided. Turning to Charlotte, she continued, "Charlotte, please let Margaret know we will be taking a stroll in the gardens."

"Certainly, Lady Beatrice. I will inform her right away," Charlotte assured, mentally noting the task as she set off to locate the maid. Wandering through the corridors, the intrigue surrounding Lord Carrington's sudden appearance and Lady

Beatrice's growing restlessness weighed on her mind. The subtle tension between the two cast a peculiar light on their friendship. Charlotte speculated that Margaret, with her longer tenure at Haddonford and closer bond with Lady Beatrice, might shed some light on the situation.

Chapter Five

NAVIGATING THE CORRIDORS OF HADDONFORD MANOR in her quest to find the maid, Charlotte aimed to lend a hand with the guest preparations. She believed that by engaging in this way, she might learn more about the complexities of her new residence and its occupants. Without a clear idea of Margaret's location, she made her way to the kitchen to seek advice from the cook.

"Mrs. Offley, would you know where Margaret could be?" Charlotte inquired.

"Ah, my guess is as good as yours. One thing I know for sure is she isn't in the West Wing," said Mrs. Offley, her hands busy rummaging through the kitchen supplies.

Charlotte furrowed her brow, "I'm not quite familiar with the West Wing. Could you please point me in the right direction?"

Rachel Offley let out an exclamation of surprise. "Ah, I keep forgetting that you're not familiar with Haddonford!" She paused momentarily, her eyes lighting up with an idea. Grabbing a bunch of turnips, she arranged them on the table, forming a U shape.

"Why didn't I think of this earlier. Now you see, we are here, in the East Wing," she pointed at the bottom right corner of the root vegetable formation, "And over here on the opposite side is the West Wing. Lady Beatrice, she stopped using the West Wing a while ago, so we shouldn't be expecting Miss Margaret to be over there."

Charlotte expressed her gratitude, appreciating Mrs. Offley's explanation.

"Thank you for showing me this. It's quite helpful. By the way, do you happen to know why Lady Beatrice stopped using the West Wing?" she inquired, genuinely curious.

Before Mrs. Offley could respond, the melodic sound of the doorbell rang through the manor, interrupting their conversation. The cook visibly flustered, began shuffling the vegetable rendition of the Manor toward her chopping station. "Jesus, Mary, and Joseph! Who could this possibly be?" she exclaimed, her voice filled with surprise.

Charlotte anticipated that the doorbell's ringing would summon Margaret, thus concluding her quest to find the maid. She walked briskly from the kitchen toward the front door, arriving just in time to witness Margaret opening it and revealing a young couple standing outside. The young woman, slightly older than Charlotte, was adorned with a beautiful silk scarf around her neck, complemented by diamond earrings that sparkled amidst her dark curls. She wore beige shoes and carried a small hand-made purse, radiating elegance. Beside her stood a tall and fit man in his mid-twenties, dressed in a tweed suit, his bright white smile catching Charlotte's attention. His handsome appearance struck Charlotte notably, presenting a stark contrast to the usual figures she had encountered previously.

"Good afternoon, Margaret," the man greeted cordially, flashing a grin. "You seem surprised to see us. Where's Mother?" he inquired, turning his attention to Charlotte.

Charlotte gracefully stepped into the conversation, eager to be of assistance. "Your mother and Lord Carrington are currently taking a stroll in the garden," she informed them. "Shall I notify them of your arrival? By the way, I'm Charlotte," she added, introducing herself.

"Lord Carrington is here already? My, Mother will be surprised; everyone seems to have arrived ahead of schedule," he said with a laugh. "Charlotte, a pleasure to meet you. You must be the new addition to the household. I'm Richard, Lady Beatrice's son, and beside me is Isabelle, my fiancée."

"Actually, I would prefer to be addressed as Lady Isabelle, and this is Lord Richard Wharton," Lady Isabelle corrected, her voice carrying a touch of coldness. She then turned to Richard, suggesting, "We should allow your mother and Lord Carrington some privacy. Now that we're here, we're not in any rush."

"For once, I agree with you, Isabelle," Lord Wharton chuckled, then turned to Charlotte. "Thank you for your offer, Miss Reinford. It seems we will settle in first before greeting Mother."

Charlotte's eyes widened in astonishment. She hadn't mentioned her last name to the handsome visitor. Before she could gather her thoughts, he was already walking down the hallway. Her first impulse was to chase after him and inquire about how he knew her name, but she restrained herself and turned to Margaret, who was still in the front foyer.

"This day is truly filled with surprises," Charlotte commented.

"I couldn't agree more," Margaret replied. "I could have sworn Lord Wharton and Lady Isabelle weren't supposed to be here until Friday. I need to make sure their rooms are ready."

"I can help," Charlotte offered. She felt sorry for Margaret, who seemed overwhelmed. She also saw this as an opportunity to learn more about the newly arrived guests and forge a stronger bond with Margaret. Together, they walked upstairs toward the bedrooms of the East Wing.

"So, how often do they visit? I heard Lord Wharton is here quite frequently," Charlotte initiated the conversation.

"Lord Wharton stops by to see his mother about once a month or so. Lady Isabelle only recently started accompanying him, especially since the engagement. It seems like she wants to keep a close eye on him, if you know what I mean," Margaret whispered, her tone tinged with gossip. "I mean, if I were engaged to such a handsome and wealthy man, I would want to be with him all the time."

As the two young women entered the room, they were met with the bold and lively sight of loud floral wallpaper covering the walls. Among the extravagant floral designs, an unusual portrait of an iguana stood out to Charlotte, its unexpected appearance striking her as odd. Margaret, while tidying up the room by plumping the pillows and straightening the duvet, shared her insights, "I affectionately refer to this room as the Lizard Room. It's the same room Lady Beatrice had prepared for Lady Isabelle's last visit, and frankly, it's quite fitting for her unique character. While she may not be the most amiable, she does have a certain allure that's rather amusing. You'll see what I mean in due time."

"Do you know the story of how Lord Wharton and Lady Isabelle met, and when they plan to marry?" Charlotte inquired, picking up a feather duster and starting to clean the furniture, all the while taking in the room's eclectic decor.

"I believe they encountered each other while skiing in the Alps. Lord Wharton accidentally ran into her, then offered to make amends over a drink. Regarding their wedding, I'd guess she'd want to tie the knot with him sooner rather than later," Margaret said with a slight blush. "However, just between us, it seems Lady Beatrice isn't exactly overjoyed with Lady Isabelle as her future daughter-in-law. There was a bit of a mishap where Lady Isabelle ended up offending Lady Beatrice, and things have been somewhat tense between them ever since. But please, let's keep this conversation between ourselves."

"Absolutely," Charlotte reassured her. "Do you have any specifics about what happened? What exactly did Lady Isabelle say?"

"Oh, I didn't actually hear it myself. It was something I caught bits of when Mrs. Offley and Mr. Offley were discussing it quietly. They cut their conversation short as soon as they noticed me coming closer. It's quite the pair they make, with Mr. Frank always seeming to be up to something, and Mrs. Offley, well, she can be quite scatterbrained and forgetful," Margaret shared.

"How long have you been working here?" Charlotte inquired.

Margaret took a moment, reflecting. "Well, this August will be my two-year mark at the manor! It's amazing how quickly time passes."

"That it does," Charlotte concurred. "Do you feel like you've become familiar with everyone here?" she continued.

"Absolutely! I've managed to get to know nearly everyone around. Samuel is the most recent person to join us, so I'm still learning about him," Margaret explained as she collected her cleaning materials, preparing to leave the room.

"Thank you so much for your help, Charlotte. I believe I can handle the rest, especially with Lord Wharton's and Lord Carrington's rooms. They aren't as meticulous as Lady Isabelle, and I genuinely enjoy attending to their preferences and arranging their rooms just so."

"I'm happy to have been of assistance," Charlotte responded with a smile, contented by their exchange. Unlike Mrs. Offley, who had been more evasive, Margaret seemed open, suggesting the possibility of a growing friendship between them.

Returning to the Blue Room, Charlotte welcomed its serene ambiance, filled with anticipation for Lady Beatrice's return. The distant sound of a piano echoed through the manor, its melodious harmony hinting at a hidden virtuoso within. The music, with its gentle yet complex layers, caught Charlotte's ear, evoking a deep-seated sense of nostalgia. She realized that the piece was one she had once devoted herself to mastering during her convent days. The afternoon sunlight streamed through the curtains, bathing the room in a soft, ethereal light that enhanced the beauty of the melody. Curiosity about the musician's identity grew within her, and considering the current residents of Haddonford Manor, Charlotte surmised that Lady Isabelle was the one gracing the air with Chopin's Nocturne No. 6 in G Minor. Her speculation was soon confirmed when Lord Wharton walked in, a glass of neat cognac in hand, now dressed in a dark red smoking jacket and coordinating loafers.

"Is the early rise demanded by Mother wearing on you?" he queried.

Caught off guard by his sudden appearance and concerned he might mention her apparent idleness to his mother, Charlotte quickly responded, "Um, I'm truly thankful for this role and the chance to reside in such a splendid manor, Lord Wharton. I'm actually fond of the 6 o'clock start; it's invigorating to begin the day so early."

Lord Wharton chuckled, settling himself into a blue chair opposite Charlotte. "Well, I must confess, I would have a hard time being up at that hour all the time. I'm more of a night owl, you could say. By the way, please call me Richard. No need for formalities with me. Unlike my mother and Isabelle, I don't pay much attention to the nitty-gritty details of status and pleasantries. So, I hear you are an orphan who was raised in a convent by nuns, giving you a unique story and background. And you may be wondering how I knew this and your name. I saw the confusion in your face earlier, and I had meant to clarify but couldn't in the moment. I ended up talking with my mother last evening and she informed me of her new hire."

Charlotte was relieved and a bit disappointed that the mystery behind Lord Wharton knowing her name was due to a simple phone conversation versus a more convoluted story. However, she was still a bit apprehensive about a few other occurrences thus far at Haddonford, like Frank Offley's ominous warning last night and Mrs. Offley's unwillingness to talk about the past, but perhaps only simple answers were needed.

"Richard, darling, I thought I would find you here." Lady Isabelle entered the room, her cheerful demeanor fading when she noticed Charlotte's presence. She smoothly took a seat beside Lord Wharton, crossing her legs in a perfunctory manner.

"Yes. Waiting for Mother to arrive," Lord Wharton said, gesturing with his glass toward Lady Isabelle. "Care for a drink, dear?"

"No, thank you. You know I don't drink spirits," Lady Isabelle replied with an air of offense, her tone indicating her displeasure with his offer. Then, turning her attention to Charlotte, she continued, "And Charlotte, now that we're all here together, why don't you tell us a bit about yourself?"

Charlotte couldn't help but feel that Lady Isabelle could use a drink to take the edge off, but she held her tongue. Lady Isabelle's sudden interest in getting to know her caught Charlotte off guard, and she wished she could take a sip of that drink herself.

"I'm not sure where to start," Charlotte replied nervously.

"Start with telling us what brought you here," Lady Isabelle commanded, her tone leaving Charlotte unsettled.

Suppressing her true feelings, Charlotte carefully replied, "Fortunately, I came across an advertisement in the morning paper yesterday for this position and decided to come here for an interview."

"Well, well, well, yesterday! My, so much to learn. And mind you, Lady Beatrice has very high expectations. You best believe it will be impossible to meet her standards," Lady Isabelle remarked, her words laced with a hint of condescension. "Can you remind me what Lady Beatrice called the position? What was it, caregiver or . . ."

"That's enough, Isabelle," Lord Wharton interjected, cutting her off before she could finish the sentence.

Lady Isabelle shrugged her shoulders in response. An awkward silence enveloped the room for a few minutes until Lady Beatrice and Lord Carrington returned.

"This can't be happening. First Henry, and now you two!" Lady Beatrice exclaimed, her disbelief evident as she momentarily stood frozen.

After gathering herself, she continued, "Please do not misunderstand. I am delighted that you are here. In fact, just about an hour ago, I mentioned to Henry how much I wished I could see you,

Richard, more often. It's quite coincidental that all my visitors have arrived earlier than expected and without prior notice. Perhaps I've been too generous with my invitations for extended stays."

"Those were my exact words earlier today!" Lord Carrington laughed, taking the liberty of using Lady Beatrice's silver bell to summon Margaret for some refreshments.

Once everyone had been served, Margaret turned to Charlotte and conveyed a message, "The dressmaker called to inform me that he will have to cancel your appointment today. He apologizes and hopes to come by tomorrow instead."

"Very amusing how the only person expected today is no longer coming," Lady Beatrice remarked, sipping her coffee. "Richard, dear, are you still staying through next week?"

"Absolutely, and . . ."

"And we would love to have a discussion with you about our wedding in the spring," Lady Isabelle eagerly interjected.

"Let's have dinner, shall we?" Lady Beatrice redirected the conversation, leading the party to the formal dining room for a delightful meal prepared by Rachel Offley. However, to Lady Isabelle's dismay, any talk of bridal planning was noticeably absent from the evening's discussion.

Chapter Six

The last thing Charlotte could remember was checking her window to ensure it was locked before flopping onto her comfortable mattress for a restful sleep. After a whirlwind of a first day, Charlotte almost convinced herself that the scream that pierced the night was merely part of a dream. However, when the second scream echoed through the halls, she knew it signaled a much more serious situation than any dream could create. By the time the third shriek filled the air, Charlotte had hastily grabbed her robe and slippers and rushed into the hallway, realizing she had forgotten to lock her bedroom door before falling asleep.

Down the hall, Lady Beatrice's frail figure hovered in front of Lady Isabelle's bedroom. Wrapped in a long ivory shawl, her normally prim and tidy hair was disheveled, evidence that the commotion had interrupted her otherwise peaceful sleep. As Charlotte approached, she noticed Lady Beatrice clutching a bronze candlestick with trembling hands, ready to use it as a weapon if necessary.

"Why isn't anyone coming?" Lady Isabelle screamed in frustration, flinging her door open. The sound of fast footsteps in the stairwell revealed Lord Wharton and Lord Carrington rushing to investigate the commotion. Both men, still dressed in their suits, suggested that neither of them had retired to bed yet. Charlotte couldn't help but wonder about the time, puzzled by what might be keeping them awake at this hour.

Lord Wharton nestled himself beside Isabelle, seeking to comfort her in this distressing moment. "What seems to be the matter, Isabelle?" he asked, attempting to make up for his delayed arrival.

"Urgh, does no one understand urgency? There was someone in my room! I saw them near the window," Lady Isabelle replied pointing to where the supposed intruder had been. Intrigued, the others, including Charlotte, cautiously peeked into the room to investigate.

"I feel suffocated," Lady Isabelle pushed her way out into the hallway.

Taking charge, Lord Carrington began searching the bedroom for any signs of the intruder. As he moved the curtains aside, Charlotte noticed the radiant yellow moon and the twinkling stars adorning the night sky, scattered like pearls from a broken necklace.

"Now, Isabelle, not to sound skeptical, but are you certain you didn't mistake the man in this painting by the window for an actual intruder?" Lord Carrington asked, pointing at the regal figure depicted in the artwork.

"This is outrageous! I know what I saw, and I am not delusional enough to mistake paintings for reality!" Lady Isabelle retorted, storming back into the room.

Lord Wharton moved to her side and examined the window's lock and hinges closely.

"Did you make sure to lock your window before retiring last night?" he inquired, effortlessly opening the window with a jiggle.

"Preposterous! This room is on the second floor. The notion of an intruder seems far-fetched. I admit, I didn't take the time to ensure it was locked. It seems utterly absurd!" Lady Isabelle responded, her voice laced with incredulity.

"Well, considering the trellis and gutter right outside your room, being on the second floor doesn't entirely exempt you from standard safety measures, my dear," Lord Wharton explained calmly.

Lady Isabelle took a seat on her bed, rubbing her temples in frustration. "I couldn't care less whether or not I checked the lock. What I want is a bit more concern for my well-being and some action taken against these midnight intruders!"

"Could you recount your evening for us?" Lord Carrington asked, concern evident in his voice.

Lady Isabelle sniffed before responding. "After dinner, I decided to open my window to enjoy the tranquility of the night. The countryside is quite pleasant compared to the bustling scene of my London flat. Anyway, after savoring the fresh air, I did close the window . . . although I don't think I locked it," she said slowly. "Come to think of it, it was already unlocked when I opened it. That's why I left it unlocked in the first place."

Lord Carrington pressed further, "Did you hear anything or recall any circumstances leading up to the presence of the intruder?"

"I lay in bed for some time, flipping through a magazine until I started to feel drowsy. I'm not sure what time I turned off my lamp, perhaps around half-past ten. But I distinctly remember hearing footsteps outside my door. I assumed it was one of you," Lady Isabelle said, glancing at Lady Beatrice and the others.

"I can assure you, it wasn't me. For once, I went to bed relatively early, probably due to the stress of all these unannounced visitors," Lady Beatrice spoke up, her voice trembling. She looked around and added, "I was asleep by half-past nine."

"Well, all I know is that I was fast asleep when I was abruptly awakened by a faint banging sound on the window. I was immediately startled and paralyzed with fear. An intruder, entering through my window in the dead of night, in such a secluded manor! Eventually, I managed to scream, but in my panic, I had covered my head and didn't see which way he went," Lady Isabelle recounted, still shaken by the experience.

"Did you notice any details about his appearance?" Lord Wharton pressed on, eager for more information.

With a hint of annoyance, Lady Isabelle turned off the lights and retorted sarcastically, "Do you think you can see anything in this dim light? And as I said before, I was genuinely scared and chose to hide."

She quickly turned the lights back on and hugged her robe closer to herself, emphasizing her discomfort. "I absolutely need to switch rooms."

"Let's make that happen. For now, let's all regroup in the Blue Room downstairs to calm down. You don't have to worry; Margaret will set up a new bedroom for you, and I'll be by your side throughout the night," Lord Wharton offered comfortingly, drawing Isabelle close to him.

Charlotte observed Lady Beatrice discretely rolling her eyes at the pair's display.

"Richard," Lady Beatrice signaled to him with a gesture. Although it was a struggle for Lord Wharton to disentangle himself from Lady Isabelle's hold, he managed and walked over to his mother, wearing an expression of worry. Meanwhile, Lord Carrington stepped in to assist Lady Isabelle in making her way downstairs, giving the mother and son a moment for a confidential chat.

"What's your take on all this?" he whispered to her, seeking her perspective.

"I'm not the one who encountered a supposed intruder in my bedroom," Lady Beatrice whispered back. "I'm not necessarily questioning her, but at the same time, it doesn't make sense. Why would there be a break-in on the second floor? I assume not all the windows are always locked, even on the first floor. Moreover, if you and Henry were awake, there would have been lights on, making thievery highly difficult and risky for the intruder."

"All of that is true, but sometimes the most cunning crimes occur right beneath our notice. Unfortunately for the intruder tonight, Isabelle was already in her bedroom, and she's not easily spooked," Lord Wharton remarked. "I have to acknowledge, our visitor is quite the audacious climber," he mused further.

Though her son's words clearly unsettled her, Lady Beatrice fought to maintain her composure. A ghostly pallor had taken over her complexion, hinting she was on the brink of collapse. Charlotte stepped closer, ready to provide support. However, Lady Beatrice, summoning her strength, steadied herself with a firm grip on the back of a nearby chair.

"Let's join the others downstairs. We need to find a more secure place to gather for now," Lord Wharton began, taking hold of his mother's arm and leading her out of the jungle-themed room.

At the foot of the main staircase, the trio was met by a flustered and worried Mrs. Offley, along with a stoically concerned Frank Offley.

"Oh, Lady Beatrice! My goodness! What a catastrophe! An intruder in such a fine establishment?" Rachel Offley exclaimed in distress.

"Samuel is conducting a thorough search of the grounds out-side, looking for anyone on the loose. I've started an internal sweep with Margaret, but we haven't found any leads on any suspicious individuals," Frank informed them.

"Oh, my stars, this is awful! It reminds me of my last place of work. No, no, no. I can't believe it," Mrs. Offley muttered nervously to herself as the group moved toward the Blue Room. "I need a moment to calm my nerves. Yes, I'll be right back with some com-forting food," she said, hurrying off to the kitchen.

In the Blue Room, the grandfather clock marked a quarter past four, leaving only two hours until the start of Charlotte's workday. As everyone gathered, she keenly watched their reactions. Lord Carrington, clearly troubled, attempted to maintain a composed appearance as he stood by the mantle, fidgeting with his pipe in a way that revealed his underlying anxiety. Lady Beatrice was in her preferred chair, her gaze fixed ahead, silent and immobile. Lord Wharton wandered near the expansive windows, lost in contemplation, stroking his chin thoughtfully. Meanwhile, Mrs. Offley found a spot on the sofa, mechanically consuming scones off a plate, her expression one of bewilderment. Lady Isabelle seemed less distressed and more determined, breaking the heavy silence in the room.

"I believe we should contact the police. We had a genuine break-in, and I am prepared to provide my statement. What if this happens again, and something worse occurs?" she proposed.

"We can do that, but how much can the police really assist us? Frank mentioned in the hallway that they've searched everywhere and found no signs of anyone on the grounds. I'm afraid that, given the remote landscape, the police might not be of much help," Lady Beatrice voiced her reservations.

"They can dust for fingerprints! They can station an officer here to monitor the grounds! They could question everyone to see if they noticed anything strange around the manor. What were you all doing anyway?" Lady Isabelle stared at Lord Wharton and Lord Carrington. "It appears you were still awake when the intruder entered my bedroom."

"Yes, dear, Lord Carrington and I were downstairs, finishing up a small chess tournament. Best out of three, and I must admit, the old man got the better of me this time!" Lord Wharton chuckled.

"Well, to be fair, I don't believe we were together during the time Isabelle mentioned someone was climbing into her bedroom. I, for one, can vouch that I was outside having a smoke. I know, I know, it's a hard habit to kick, especially on such a lovely night," Lord Carrington confessed, seemingly relieved to share his whereabouts truthfully.

"But I clearly heard someone's footsteps," Lady Isabelle insisted.

"Perhaps it was one of the staff members?" Charlotte suggested, searching for a simple explanation for the footsteps but remaining uncertain about the potential intruder on the second floor.

"That's a possibility, but I can't imagine any of them being upstairs that late in the evening," Lady Beatrice added.

"Not me for sure," said Mrs. Offley barely audible.

"Maybe my mind is playing tricks on me, but it almost felt as though the intruder lingered outside my room. Judging by the pattern of the footsteps, he walked towards my room and then headed back towards the stairs. I could have sworn it was one of you! I'm not crazy!" Lady Isabelle exclaimed, her frustration evident.

Charlotte's curiosity deepened with this additional detail. She had limited knowledge of the staff's habits, having been at the estate for only two nights. However, if Lady Beatrice was confident, they wouldn't be upstairs, it raised the possibility that someone within the group was lying.

"Are you certain that there really was an intruder, and it wasn't just part of your dream?" Lady Beatrice asked skeptically.

Her words pushed Lady Isabelle to the edge, prompting her to rise from her seat, ready to leave. Lord Wharton quickly intervened, rushing over to calm her down and ease the tension between the two women. Sensing the escalating anxiety, Mrs. Offley excused herself to find Frank, seeking a reprieve from the heightened atmosphere.

As the others engaged in conversation in pairs, Charlotte took the opportunity to gather her thoughts. She recalled the events of the previous night: Lord Wharton had been the first to leave the dinner table, retreating to the library to work. Lady Beatrice and Lady Isabelle departed a few minutes apart, followed by Lord Carrington. Charlotte assumed he was headed to his room, although it appears that she was wrong. The fact that the two men were playing chess at such an hour struck her as peculiar. Could there be more to their late-night rendezvous?

It also raised questions that Lady Isabelle's room was the focal point of the break-in, given the myriad of alternative access points available. This situation led to speculation about whether the objective was to scare or directly harm her, or if her room was chosen by chance, hinting at a more complex motive for the break-in. Charlotte recalled Frank Offley's cautionary advice about locking up on her very first evening, highlighting the importance of such safety measures. Despite this, she could not help but acknowledge her lapse in failing to lock her own bedroom, a detail that now seemed more relevant than ever.

Just then, Frank Offley appeared and approached Lady Beatrice, holding an envelope in his hand. "Madam, we found this in the hallway while we were completing our sweep," he explained, handing her the envelope before nodding curtly and exiting the room.

"Do we believe this is related to the intruder?" Lady Isabelle inquired, seeming to have set aside her recent disagreement with her future mother-in-law.

"Oh dear, I seem to have forgotten to open this earlier today. It looks like it arrived yesterday. Richard, it's too late for me to deal with this. Could you please open it and read it?" Lady Beatrice requested, relinquishing the task to her son.

Lord Wharton complied and began reading the contents of the letter. As he finished, he folded the paper in half and fell silent. Charlotte could sense something was amiss from the tense expression on his face and the pulsating vein above his temple.

"Well, what does it say?" Lady Beatrice inquired impatiently.

Charlotte exchanged a concerned glance with Lord Wharton before he finally spoke up. "We need to call the police," he said, his voice filled with urgency.

Chapter Seven

STATING SUCH AN OMINOUS SENTENCE FOLLOWING the arrival of a mysterious letter and the supposed presence of a second-story intruder naturally led to a flood of questions and frustrations from everyone in the room.

"Oh, so what I said earlier means nothing, but whatever is in this letter is somehow worse than a man in my bedroom!?" shouted Lady Isabelle.

"What does it say, Richard?" cried Lady Beatrice.

"Here's the phone!" exclaimed Lord Carrington, thrusting it into Lord Wharton's hands.

Amidst this commotion, Charlotte sat contemplating the unfolding events. Never in her years at the convent had she experienced such excitement as she had in the past fifty hours or so at Haddonford Manor.

"Will everyone calm down already? Let me read it out loud for all of you," Lord Wharton insisted.

Everything we do has consequences.

Even your actions will have their repercussions.

Lady Beatrice, who had just regained her composure, turned as pale as snow once again. Lord Carrington's nervous tremors had returned as well. Lady Isabelle seemed perplexed, perhaps wondering how the letter could be connected to her intruder.

In less than an hour, a short gentleman in a plaid jacket and a cap entered the room, followed by two policemen. His elongated face, featuring a pointed nose and brown eyes, reminded Charlotte of a hound following a trail. Introducing himself as Inspector Sinclair, he immediately requested a private conversation with Lord Wharton. Lady Beatrice glanced at the policemen standing in the doorway and shivered. Charlotte, sensing the tension, picked up a hand-knitted shawl and draped it over her. The clock now read half past six, and the sunrise was working its way up to start a new day.

"How long do you think it will take, Henry?" Lady Beatrice looked at Lord Carrington, who paced from one corner of the room to another.

"It might take some time," he responded.

"I hope not," Lady Isabelle sounded slightly annoyed. She crossed one leg over the other and impatiently tapped her fingers on the chair handle. "What does that letter mean anyway?" she asked.

Nobody replied. Lady Isabelle looked visibly unsettled as she thought back to the message, her brows furrowing in concern.

"Charlotte," Lady Beatrice addressed the young lady, "Do me a favor and check on Mrs. Offley and Margaret. I worry about those two. If Rachel hasn't driven Margaret crazy, she will soon, and I cannot afford to lose my maid. Also, I could use some coffee, so you might as well ask Rachel to set that up . . . and some tea, I suppose. Oh, and dear, do make sure to let me know what happens after you check on them."

Charlotte acknowledged the request and left the room. Quite frankly, she was pleased that Lady Beatrice sent her away. The monotony of the past hour had left her a bit bored, and this unexpected excursion presented the perfect opportunity to conduct some discreet investigations on her own. Her earlier attempts to extract information from Mrs. Offley had been confusing and fruitless, but Charlotte wasn't one to lose hope easily. As she pondered her next move, she decided that consoling the cook might be the key. Offering emotional support could open doors to discovering more about Mrs. Offley's history—perhaps something about her previous job.

In the kitchen, Mrs. Offley sat with Margaret, and if the maid weren't present, it would have seemed like she was delivering a monologue with the intense flow of words that escaped her mouth.

"You know, we need to get some guard dogs. Yes, Samuel can keep an eye on them, and we would all be protected. That's what we used on the farm growing up. Never a moment we felt unsafe."

Margaret, being a kind soul, didn't seem to hold much of an opinion on the matter. To her delight, the sight of Charlotte meant a possible escape from the cook's ramblings.

"Ah! Charlotte!" Mrs. Offley exclaimed. "You sweet child from the convent. Heavens me, nothing like this ever happened where you were raised?"

"No, I am lucky to say there were no such cases. The closest might have been when some raccoons discovered they could use one of the trees to reach a nook in the convent wall, and ultimately, they made their way into one of the bedrooms. Poor Sister Sarah! She was frightened half to death when her new roommates arrived."

Margaret chuckled at the story and made her exit, in search of a moment of fresh air.

"Oh dear, that does sound terrible," Mrs. Offley said. "All these disturbances have been robbing us of a good night's sleep. I'm utterly drained. I marvel at how Lady Beatrice manages to remain composed with everything that's been going on. Quite the flurry of events lately. Hmm, perhaps it's time for Lady Beatrice's coffee? I'll prepare it straight away. Today calls for an especially robust brew." With no further ado, Mrs. Offley resumed her morning tasks without pause.

Charlotte took the opportunity to "check on other members of the staff"—the excuse she stated to the cook as she left the kitchen—and explore Haddonford Manor to its fullest. There seemed to be more to the place than met the eye.

Charlotte walked down the hall to the front entrance, her mind racing with thoughts. "I can't imagine Frank and Margaret have truly checked every nook and cranny for an intruder. Besides, the police officers will be focusing on the East Wing, so I might as well seize this opportunity to do a bit of sleuthing on the west side of the manor." In the midst of reading a mystery, Charlotte felt a strong urge to play the role of a detective, an odd behavior she had developed as a child at the convent. Whenever loneliness crept in, she would immerse herself in the lives of the characters from the books she read.

Her footsteps echoed hauntingly in the long-abandoned and dimly lit corridors of the West Wing. According to Mrs. Offley, Lady Beatrice had ceased utilizing this section of the manor years prior, yet she had never provided a full explanation for this decision. One could surmise that the size of the estate became unnecessary and perhaps overwhelming for an elderly woman such as Lady Beatrice. However, the complete abandonment of a significant portion of her domicile hinted at underlying mysteries yet to be uncovered.

Intriguing peculiarities marked the West Wing; despite assertions that Margaret had supposedly ceased its upkeep, not a trace of dust or a single cobweb was to be seen. Moreover, the architectural layout and design of this section showed a striking resemblance to that of the East Wing, adding to the mystery of the manor's symmetrical yet forsaken halves. As Charlotte continued her exploration, she stumbled upon a room that bore a striking resemblance to the Blue Room, except for its red-themed walls and furniture. The air within carried a different energy, a departure from the rest of the neglected wing.

"There's something eerie and unsettling about this room," Charlotte thought, her fingers brushing against the surface of a red leather couch as she surveyed the Victorian and Rococo art pieces, each adorned with red motifs, on the walls. The layout's resemblance and the crimson color scheme evoked a strong sense of déjà vu. Yet, entwined with this recognition was an abrupt, spine-chilling sensation that eyes were upon her, observing her every move. Charlotte's heart raced as she whipped around, scouring the room for any sign of being watched. Her attention was captured by the intense look from a portrait of a young girl hanging on the left wall. The illusion crafted by the portrait's subject seemed to track Charlotte's every move, tightening the knot of anxiety in her stomach. Though the artwork appeared relatively modern, possibly created within the last century, Charlotte, lacking expertise in art, decided it was time to leave the West Wing. Driven by a sudden rush of fear, she quickly exited the room, making her way toward the nearest exit with a heightened sense of urgency. Swiftly traversing the corridor, Charlotte reached an expansive door with a formidable handle. As she forcefully swung it open, a surge of relief washed over her. The stables lay before her, and the crisp open air outside provided a sanctuary far more comforting than the abandoned expanses of Haddonford Manor's uninhabited wing.

The sun beamed high in the sky, indicating it was around noontime. Despite her growling stomach, Charlotte's determination to search the stables and possibly find Samuel or Frank propelled her forward. As she approached the building, her eyes fell upon a shovel and a pitchfork leaning against a stone wall, while neatly stacked empty feed baskets occupied the corner. The scent of clean straw tickled her nose, causing her to sneeze. In response, a horse nearby rubbed against a post and emitted a loud snort, as if sensing potential danger. Curious, Charlotte followed the sound and was surprised to discover that this immaculate and well-maintained stable housed only one brown stallion, suspiciously eyeing her from its stall.

"Hello, horse. Why are you all alone?" she spoke to the animal as if expecting a reply, extending her hand in an attempt to stroke its smooth skin.

The horse snorted and moved away.

"I won't harm you," Charlotte reassured, inching forward and trying once more. "I promise to be gentle."

The stallion observed her cautiously, unsure of her origins and the whereabouts of its usual caretakers.

"If you want to win Blazer's heart, give him a peppermint," a male voice startled Charlotte, and she quickly turned around to find Samuel at the entryway.

He rummaged through his deep pockets, producing a small handful of the horse's favorite treats. "He's a softy for these. Once, he followed me around the entire manor just because I had a few of them in my pocket," Samuel chuckled, handing Charlotte the candies and allowing her to feed the horse.

"There are so many stalls here, yet only one horse. Are there others elsewhere?" Charlotte inquired.

"Lady Beatrice keeps only Blazer. I think she may be waiting to retire the horses from the manor, you know," Samuel made a chopping motion at his neck, implying that she was waiting for the horse to pass away. Blazer nudged Samuel, seeking his attention, and the young man gently stroked the horse's mane.

"By the way, we haven't been properly introduced. I'm Charlotte," she said, extending her hand, which Samuel gladly shook. A friendly smile illuminated his face as he introduced himself.

"I'm Samuel, but you can call me Sam. Also, not to be nosy, but what brings you all the way over here? Lady Beatrice doesn't use the West Wing, and she has never paid attention to the stables, as far as I know."

Charlotte felt a rush of warmth to her cheeks, caught off guard by Samuel's questioning. She wished she had anticipated the inquiry and prepared a better response, but it was too late now. *Well, I might as well be honest,* she thought to herself.

"I decided to explore Haddonford while I had the chance to wander around," she confessed.

"Ah, yes, detective work must surely open up your schedule," Samuel quipped.

"Speaking of which, do you know anything about what's happening with the investigation? I must admit, I left the Blue Room a while ago and haven't checked back since. I got a bit lost in my explorations and stumbled upon a room where I felt like someone was watching me . . . Turns out it was just a painting . . . but it gave me quite a fright, so I made my way out of the building to find myself here."

"I did the exact same thing when I was first hired," he admitted. "I explored every room and corner of Haddonford, especially once I learned that Lady Beatrice only uses one wing. But trust me, Frank keeps a close eye on the West Wing and regularly checks it to ensure nothing out of the ordinary happens there. I don't think it's possible for an intruder to be here, especially given Lady Isabelle's description."

"So, you think she made it all up?" Charlotte asked, curious.

Samuel shrugged his shoulders. "I don't want to accuse anyone of anything, but Mr. Offley and I thoroughly checked the surroundings and found no signs of an intrusion. Maybe Lady Isabelle saw a shadow and thought someone was in her room. Or perhaps she experienced one of those half-awake, half-asleep dreams where things seem real but aren't."

Charlotte had considered those possibilities while reflecting on the events of the night. However, it seemed unlikely that Lady Isabelle would be so shaken and certain about an intruder if she had any inkling that it might have been a dream.

"You seem unconvinced," Samuel remarked, observing Charlotte's expression. She was not skilled at maintaining a poker face.

"Oh, I was just pondering what you said. It reminded me that I need to return to the Blue Room. I'd like to keep this job until we at least figure out what's happening here," she joked, deflecting Samuel's perceptive observation.

"Right then, cheers to that. If you need a shortcut, just head to the center of the building through the garden. You can enter through the French doors during daylight hours. I usually keep them unlocked, so I don't have to walk all the way around each time to enter the building."

Charlotte must have looked puzzled because Samuel added, "Actually, I'll just take you there. I could use a sandwich right about now."

Chapter Eight

As Samuel led Charlotte along the shortcut back to the East Wing her thoughts were consumed by regret. *"How foolish I was! I should have promptly returned to the Blue Room after checking on Mrs. Offley and Margaret. Only then, if Lady Beatrice still didn't require my assistance, could I have resumed my search of the grounds."*

Time perception had never been Charlotte's strong suit, despite her best intentions to remain mindful of the ever-ticking clock. Once as a ten-year-old, she had deviated from her path to the prayer room, lured by the temptation of finding a hidden book within the library's shelves. What she had anticipated as a brief detour turned into an hour-long escapade, resulting in missed prayer time and a stern rebuke from Sister Agatha. Ironically, that year, her sole birthday gift had been a secondhand wristwatch, a cherished possession she now wished she had never let go.

Charlotte's mind continued to spiral as she hurriedly made her way towards the Blue Room. The weight of potential consequences pressed upon her, envisioning the disapproval and possible dismissal that awaited her in Lady Beatrice's uptight demeanor. The prospect of seeking a new position elsewhere loomed before her, accompanied by doubts about her employability after being let go within only two days. Her thoughts raced, consumed by worry, until she was interrupted by the familiar voice of Lord Wharton.

"Oh, Charlotte, there you are," he calmly exclaimed as she rushed past the library. Startled by the sound of her name, Charlotte abruptly halted and turned to face him. He stood in the doorway, regarding her with his discerning gaze. A droplet of sweat trickled slowly down Charlotte's temple, and her breath came in ragged gasps.

Observing her flustered state, Lord Wharton couldn't help but smirk, finding amusement in the sight. "I see you're in quite a hurry," he remarked.

Apologizing instinctively, Charlotte asked, "Sir, am I in trouble?"

"Why would you be in trouble?" he chuckled. "Did you do something wrong? Mother did mention your tendency to rush around the estate." His words carried a trace of amusement as he enjoyed his playful jab at the young lady. "And if I'm not mistaken, you're hurrying back to the Blue Room where Mother is, since you've been away for quite some time. But don't worry, I've got you covered. I informed her that I had requested your assistance in searching my car for my sunglasses. It was quite amusing to observe how she dismissed the matter with minimal thought and proceeded to scold poor Lord Carrington. Their friendship has always been a source of entertainment and astonishment to me—entertaining because of their playful exchanges, and remarkable that he continues to visit despite her behavior."

With Lord Wharton's reassurance, Charlotte felt a wave of relief wash over her. The tension in her shoulders began to dissipate, and a grateful smile graced her lips. The unexpected support from him came at the right moment but Charlotte was still confused as to why he covered for her and how concerned was Lady Beatrice about her absence.

"Thank you for helping me out," Charlotte said sincerely. "Do you happen to have the sunglasses that I supposedly retrieved for you?"

"I rarely go anywhere without my sunglasses. You never know when the sun may be too bright or the remnants of a hangover too strong," he chuckled.

"Yes, well, I should make my way to the Blue Room and join Lady Beatrice. Cover or no cover, I mustn't shirk my duties," Charlotte said.

Lord Wharton leaned against the doorway, sipping from a snifter of brandy in his hand. "Mother is currently with Inspector Sinclair, recounting her side of the story. I just finished speaking with him myself," he revealed. "The possible intruder and the mysterious letter have cast a shadow of concern over our household. You see, I don't believe Isabelle was the intended target. While she may have made her fair share of enemies, from busboys to taxi drivers, I don't think she has done enough to warrant someone breaking into her room during her visit. No, it's quite possible that her bedroom served as an entry point for an outsider to maneuver their way through the house. I'm curious to see if the inspector arrives at the same conclusion I have," he mused.

Charlotte absorbed Lord Wharton's words. The safety of Lady Beatrice and the underlying motives behind the intrusion weighed heavily on her mind.

"What do you think the trespasser was searching for? And why target the second floor?" she pondered aloud. "I was in the West Wing less than an hour ago, and it seemed like there were plenty of secluded areas away from prying eyes if their intention was to commit theft."

Lord Wharton nodded, mirroring Charlotte's thoughts. "Exactly what I was contemplating! Why choose a more challenging route and risk being discovered? I can't help but wonder if their objective was to be as close to Mother's bedroom as possible. Additionally, we must consider the idea that the intruder was actually leaving rather than entering."

The notion of the trespasser exiting the manor hadn't crossed Charlotte's mind before, but she swiftly engaged her thinking, piecing together the puzzle. If the intruder intended to depart through the main entrance, he or she would have had to navigate past Lord Wharton and Lord Carrington, both of whom were awake and active on the first floor. Lord Carrington had mentioned briefly going outside for a smoke, which could have provided an opportunity for the intruder to slip into the hallway and seek refuge in the nearest available room, coincidentally being Lady Isabelle's.

Amused by Charlotte's quick mental processing, Lord Wharton smiled. "I must say, I thoroughly enjoy observing the gears turning in your mind. I shared a mere thought, and you've taken it and run with it. Pray tell, where did your musings lead you?" he inquired.

"I was actually contemplating what you just mentioned. The idea that someone could have been inside already and used Lady Isabelle's window as an exit from Haddonford hadn't crossed my mind. I still can't comprehend the intruder's initial purpose for being here."

Lord Wharton took a sip of his brandy. "Indeed, it's quite intriguing and coincidental that the trespasser's presence and the letter Mother received occurred on the same day. I can't shake the feeling that there's a connection between the two, but I'm at a loss as to what it could be."

Before he could delve further into his thoughts, a vibrant female voice cut through the air.

"Richard, there you are," Lady Isabelle entered the library, her demeanor initially coquettish but swiftly dropping when she noticed Charlotte's presence. "Oh, I hope I'm not interrupting anything of importance."

"No, my dear," Lord Wharton replied, "I invited Charlotte for a conversation while Mother is occupied with Inspector Sinclair."

"I see," Lady Isabelle responded with a hint of annoyance. "Well, I hope you're done because I require your assistance."

Recognizing her cue to exit the library and avoid getting caught in any potential nonsense between Lady Isabelle and

Lord Wharton, Charlotte quickly made her decision to go to her room. However, her plan was thwarted by the sudden appearance of Inspector Sinclair at the doorway, signaling for her to remain where she was.

"To save time, I would appreciate everyone staying in this room," Inspector Sinclair announced. "Please find a comfortable seat while my colleagues gather the others here for an important announcement." Despite the late hour the inspector appeared remarkably refreshed and alert.

Charlotte was left with no choice but to find a seat on the couch awaiting the forthcoming address. One by one, the remaining staff members, Lord Carrington and Lady Beatrice were guided into the library, adding to the gathering. Lord Carrington's usual composure seemed to have been replaced by restlessness, his eyes darting nervously around the room. Mrs. Offley, in her characteristic fashion, was fervently munching on yet another snack, while Frank stood in the corner, casting suspicious glances at the others.

Inspector Sinclair took command of the room, ensuring that all eyes were fixed on him before he began. "Let us commence with the facts," he stated. "Yesterday morning, Lady Beatrice received a suspicious letter—one that appears to have been typed on a typewriter." He paused, allowing the weight of his words to sink in.

Unbeknownst to Charlotte, Lord Wharton had silently approached her from behind, his voice teasingly whispering in her ear, "This detective is truly groundbreaking. I must have appeared as dull as a dodo if he had to emphasize that the letter was typed and not handwritten."

Inspector Sinclair cleared his throat, shooting a mildly annoyed glance in Lord Wharton's direction. "While this may seem like an obvious and mundane detail to some, those in the industry understand the significance," he continued, his voice brimming with authority.

"Well, enlighten me on the progress you've made in finding last night's intruder," Lady Isabelle interjected, her tone laced with defiance, seemingly provoked by Lord Wharton's playful banter with Charlotte.

"Our primary focus has been on the letter, as it appears to hold potential threats," the inspector responded, maintaining his composure despite the interruptions. "At this stage, I must consider everyone present as potential suspects until we can thoroughly eliminate and investigate external individuals . . ."

Lady Isabelle interrupted once more, her voice filled with incredulity. "Are you suggesting that one of us here wrote a letter threatening Lady Beatrice? I find this confusing! I woke up to a complete stranger in my bedroom—a terrifying experience that I wouldn't wish upon anyone," she stated, her gaze briefly lingering on Charlotte. "I feel like the victim here, not a suspect," she continued, looking up at Lord Wharton before turning her attention back to the inspector. "I know nothing about your expertise in situations like this, but I find your accusations utterly mind-boggling."

The inspector attempted to interject, but Lady Isabelle dismissed him with a wave of her hand. "You entered this room and began with 'Let's start with the facts.' Then you brought up the letter, which, by the way, was irrelevant until after I experienced the terror of a lurking criminal in the dead of night! Are you dismissing what happened to me?" Her voice reached its crescendo. "Are you implying that my ordeal this morning was unreal and therefore not factual?"

Lord Wharton approached Lady Isabelle, placing a comforting hand on her shoulder, trying to ease her agitation. "Isabelle, I don't believe Inspector Sinclair was drawing that conclusion. Rather, he is focusing on tangible facts and excluding leads that are more elusive, such as an intruder who vanished in an instant."

"Indeed, it is only fair to consider that everyone present has an equal opportunity to have written and delivered such an ominous note to Lady Beatrice. While it is possible that the letter was composed and left by someone from her past, it is also highly plausible that the culprit resides within the manor, existing in her present," the inspector explained.

Lady Isabelle snorted in response, and Charlotte braced herself for another outburst, but Lord Wharton's firm grip on Lady Isabelle's shoulder kept her in check. She shot a glare at Inspector Sinclair but remained silent.

Pointing toward the young officer of the law standing in the doorway, Inspector Sinclair continued, "Our sergeant made an interesting discovery today. He found a typewriter!"

"Congratulations to the sergeant," Lady Isabelle retorted, rolling her eyes. "I'm sure he'll receive an award for his remarkable find, and perhaps you'll earn a promotion for this breakthrough in the case. Every well-equipped household possesses a typewriter, so it wouldn't be unusual to find one here at Haddonford," she added sarcastically.

Inspector Sinclair tilted his head slightly and offered Lady Isabelle a mysterious smile. "Miss Reinford, are you aware of the existence of this typewriter?" he inquired, shifting his attention to Charlotte.

"No, I'm not," Charlotte responded sincerely. "All the correspondence I've had the privilege of witnessing has been done through handwritten letters. I haven't come across a typewriter in the Blue Room, where Lady Beatrice conducts her business."

The inspector then turned to Lady Isabelle and asked politely, "And what about you, Lady Isabelle?"

"I have no idea. Why are you asking me?" Lady Isabelle hissed.

"Because the typewriter was found in your room," the inspector revealed.

Lady Isabelle narrowed her eyes and pursed her lips, a clear sign of her suppressed anger. Charlotte could sense her strong urge to rise from her chair and slap the inspector across the face.

"Inspector Sinclair is not accusing you," Lord Wharton intervened calmly, addressing Lady Isabelle. "The letter arrived before both you and I came here. It is evident that you did not compose it, Isabelle, but it's possible that someone within this household did."

Lady Isabelle glanced up at Lord Wharton, completely ignoring the inspector. "And how do they know it's the right typewriter?" she questioned.

"We don't know yet," the inspector conceded. "But we will. We are taking it with us to the station for further examination."

Lady Isabelle appeared perplexed. "Where on Earth was it? Why don't I recall seeing any typewriter in my room?" she asked, seeking clarification.

"It was concealed inside a wooden box beneath the secretary desk," the inspector explained.

"You see!" Lady Isabelle exclaimed triumphantly. "I'm not an idiot. If it had been on the desk, I would have surely noticed it. Could it be that whoever was attempting to gain access to my room had an interest in the typewriter? If the letter was indeed written by someone among the staff, which I personally find preposterous, then disposing of the evidence that could lead to their exposure would have been necessary."

Lady Isabelle paused, deep in thought, before shaking her head dismissively. "No, this is ridiculous. If someone here wrote that letter, they would have found a simpler way to dispose of the typewriter than sneaking through the window in the middle of the night. Furthermore, I highly doubt Mrs. Offley has the ability to climb walls, and the same applies to . . . what's the name of the young lady who opened the door for us upon our arrival?" Lady Isabelle inquired, purposefully overlooking the fact that the maid was within earshot.

"Margaret," Lord Wharton promptly answered.

"Yes, Margaret and . . ." Lady Isabelle paused, struggling to recall a name.

"Samuel?" Lord Wharton suggested.

"Yes, those two."

Margaret huffed under her breath, seemingly resentful at being perceived as incapable of scaling walls. Samuel maintained his usual neutral expression, unaffected by the comments. Frank

Offley, who had remained quiet until now, decided to speak up, capturing everyone's attention. "In case any suspicions fall on me, officer, I served in the Great War and was known for my climbing skills. However, I can assure you that I am not involved."

"Thank you for sharing that information, sir," the inspector acknowledged, expressing his gratitude. "I will keep it in mind as I conduct background checks on each of you."

With those words, he granted everyone permission to resume their daily routines, except for a few individuals, including Charlotte, who still needed to be interviewed.

Lady Beatrice excused herself, expressing her intention to retire to her bedroom, and Lord Carrington kindly offered to escort her. She accepted the offer without protest, appearing tired and more fragile than usual. One by one, Mrs. Offley, Frank, Margaret, and Samuel exited the room. As Charlotte prepared to accompany Inspector Sinclair for questioning, Lady Isabelle halted everyone with a firm and assertive voice, leaving no doubt about her discontent.

"Wait, is that all? I have no intention of staying here any longer after what happened to me. This place is not safe!" Lady Isabelle exclaimed, passionately expressing her objection to remaining at Haddonford.

"Actually, miss," the inspector responded calmly, maintaining his composure. "It is necessary for everyone present to remain until further notice. Rest assured, I will assign one of my men to stay overnight, ensuring your safety."

CHAPTER NINE

PERHAPS IT WAS THE REASSURING PRESENCE of the policeman in the corridor, or the weariness that enveloped Charlotte, but she fell into a deep, peaceful sleep, awakening the next day fully revitalized. As she got ready and caught a fleeting look at herself in the mirror, Charlotte was enveloped by a sense of contentment. Her vibrant emerald eyes shone brightly against the refined olive dress she wore, a present from Lady Beatrice, while her dark brown curls elegantly cascaded over her shoulders.

At precisely 6:00 AM, Charlotte stepped into the corridor. Directly across from Lady Isabelle's room, a young policeman was slumped in a chair, his face showing clear signs of fatigue. Charlotte felt a wave of empathy surge through her, prompting her to consider a small act of kindness. She planned to fetch the officer a cup of tea, but her attention was diverted to Mrs. Offley, who was laboriously ascending the stairs with a tray laden with the aromatic Earl Grey. Each step she took was careful and measured, marked by deep breaths.

"I brewed you a cup of tea this morning," Mrs. Offley said.

The young policeman appeared visibly surprised, evidently unprepared for such a thoughtful gesture. His expression suggested reluctance, as if he was poised to decline the offer. Mrs. Offley's relentless persistence quickly overcame any lingering doubts he harbored, as she determinedly placed the tray firmly on his lap, effectively leaving him with no alternative but to accept the offering extended to him.

"Freshly made, please do enjoy," Mrs. Offley stated, her tone brooking no argument. "I bet you hadn't expected to spend the night here, love."

Gratefully, he admitted, "No, I did not." He took a sip of the warm tea and looked up, intending to return the tray to its owner. But Mrs. Offley ensured the tray remained with him.

"Tea is a balm for your mind and body," she proclaimed. "It strengthens against sickness, reduces stress, and can even enhance sleep, though you might not feel the need for that after staying up all night. Now, what's your name?"

"George," the young man said, his voice tinged with nervousness as his eyes moved between the tray and Mrs. Offley.

"George, my lad, please, do enjoy your drink," she instructed and began her descent down the stairs, now turning her attention to preparing a nourishing breakfast for the guests of Haddonford.

Meanwhile, the awakening manor was serenaded by the gentle swish of Margaret's dusting wand as she glided past, diligently attending to each delicate piece of furniture and the persistent ringing of the telephone piercing through the tranquility of the estate.

"Haddonford Manor, this is Frank speaking. How may I assist you?" Mr. Offley greeted someone on another end of the line with genuine attentiveness. Just as he finished his polite inquiry, the door handle turned, and Lady Beatrice emerged from her bedroom, her gaze oscillated between the young police officer still holding the tea tray and Charlotte. An unspoken request for clarification hung in the air.

With a gentle smile, Charlotte approached Lady Beatrice, offering a small bow. "Good morning, Lady Beatrice. I trust you had a restful night?"

"Charlotte, who is this police officer guarding my bedroom?"

"Lady Beatrice, there was a security concern that arose yesterday. It was decided that additional precautions should be taken to ensure your and Lady Isabelle's safety. The presence of the police officer was part of those measures."

"And why wasn't I notified?"

"Regrettably, I hadn't been able to exchange words with you since our last encounter the previous afternoon. By the time the inspector bade farewell to Haddonford and granted me permission to ascend the staircase, you had already retired for the night, closing your bedroom door."

A mixture of relief and annoyance washed over Lady Beatrice's face. "Next time, just knock on the door. I admit, I had a difficult night. If I had known there was someone watching over me, perhaps I could have found some solace and slept better."

"I apologize for any distress caused, Lady Beatrice," Charlotte said softly, her voice carrying a gentle assurance.

Lady Beatrice sighed, "What a nightmare. I hope it ends soon. I do not wish to relive another day like yesterday. Come in, Charlotte."

Seizing the opportunity, Charlotte accepted the tray from the young officer of the law, gingerly placing it near an ornate vase, awaiting Margaret's presence to reclaim it. Afterwards she ventured into Lady Beatrice's bedroom.

The soft pastel and creamy neutral colors of the room created a serene ambiance, allowing the carefully chosen furnishings and decorative accents to shine. The centerpiece was a four-poster bed made of rich mahogany, accompanied by bedside tables crafted from the finest wood. Crystal-cut table lamps cast a warm and gentle glow, enhancing the calm atmosphere of the room. Across from the bed, was a grand vanity table. Luxurious beauty products and golden brushes patiently awaited Lady Beatrice's daily routine, basking in the gentle glow of soft natural light that flowed through the large, draped windows. Thoughtfully arranged artwork adorned the walls, reflecting Lady Beatrice's refined taste and appreciation for the arts. A cozy Persian rug covered the floor, offering both warmth and a touch of exquisite texture. Charlotte's gaze shifted from the rug to a canvas above the bed. It depicted a young girl in a delicate white lace gown, holding a flower with a head tilted in a pose mirroring Lady Beatrice's current posture.

"Such a beautiful painting," Charlotte remarked, her eyes catching Lady Beatrice's reflection in the mirror. Unable to resist the observation, she continued, "I couldn't help but notice the striking resemblance. That's you, years ago."

"A beautiful painting, indeed," Lady Beatrice said, her tone resonating with sincerity.

"My father commissioned it for my fifth birthday. I recall despising the process of posing for it. The poor nanny had to chase me around this place, resorting to bribes of my favorite foods and activities just to coax me into sitting still for an hour. The smile captured in the portrait is far from genuine. Though I reluctantly agreed to pose, I never consented to wearing a smile. The artist had to improvise, for my father refused to pay for a painting of an angry child."

Charlotte's lips curved gently, her imagination painting vivid scenes of Lady Beatrice's mischievous escapades as a spirited five-year-old, darting through Haddonford's hallways with her nanny in pursuit.

"Did you spend your entire life here?" Charlotte inquired.

Lady Beatrice paused for a moment, "Most of it," she finally replied, her voice carrying a tinge of sadness. "This estate has been my home for decades, witnessing both the joys and sorrows that life has brought upon me."

Charlotte sensed the weight of unspoken stories hidden beneath Lady Beatrice's carefully chosen words. Her curiosity grew, fueled by a deep desire to understand the history that had shaped the woman before her. With a soft tone, Charlotte ventured further. "It must be quite remarkable to have a lifetime's worth of memories within these walls, Lady Beatrice. If these halls could speak, they would surely share tales of love, laughter, and perhaps even a touch of sorrow. Is there a particular memory that holds a special place in your heart? "

"Oh, there are many memories, " Lady Beatrice replied. "But patience, my dear Charlotte. The time will come when I shall reveal the secrets of my past to you. However, for now, let us focus on the present. Charlotte, my dear, have you noticed anything peculiar recently?"

Charlotte's brow furrowed slightly as she contemplated Lady Beatrice's question. "Peculiar in terms of people's behavior?" she asked for clarification.

"Yes," Lady Beatrice confirmed, her gaze focused intently on Charlotte.

"I must admit, Lady Beatrice, I am not well enough acquainted with the individuals here at Haddonford Manor to discern any notable changes in their behavior. Is there someone in particular you are inquiring about or a specific reason behind your question?"

Lady Beatrice paused, "Nothing of consequence, my dear," she finally replied evasively, leaving Charlotte confused.

Chapter Ten

When Charlotte entered the dining room, Lord Wharton was already seated at the head of the table, engrossed in the morning newspaper. Impeccably dressed in a bespoke black suit and a crisp white shirt with golden cufflinks glinting in the soft light, he looked up from his reading and greeted her with a warm smile. "Did you have a restful night?"

"Yes, unlike Lady Beatrice. I failed to inform her that George would be staying at Haddonford Manor," Charlotte admitted.

"Ah, you mean the young police officer assigned to guard the upstairs bedrooms?" Lord Wharton clarified.

"That's correct," Charlotte affirmed as she settled into her seat at the table, enjoying the plush cushion beneath her.

"Well, Charlotte, you didn't fail; you simply didn't have the opportunity. None of us did. Mother was already in bed and presumably asleep. Nonetheless, I'm glad to hear that you managed to rest. Do you usually read the newspaper?" Lord Wharton inquired.

"Not lately, but I occasionally do," Charlotte replied.

"You're not missing much unless you're interested in scandals and others' misfortunes," he said, folding the newspaper and casually placing it on the table. "The only article I found tolerable this morning was about the eighth wonder of the world."

"Have they found the amber room?" Charlotte asked with genuine curiosity.

Her knowledge about the amber room stemmed from conversations with one of the nuns whose family had immigrated to England from Russia shortly after the 1917 Revolution. Charlotte found the country's history fascinating and spent hours engrossed in Sister Olga's stories about the Hermitage, Peterhof, St. Isaac's Cathedral, and, of course, the amber room. Designed by the German baroque sculptor Andreas Schlüter and constructed by the Danish amber craftsman Gottfried Wolfram, the amber room had been considered the eighth wonder of the world. It was in Russian possession until it mysteriously vanished in 1943.

"They haven't found it, and I doubt they ever will. At this point, their best option would be to reconstruct it," Lord Wharton commented.

"Does the article offer any leads?" Charlotte asked.

"No leads, but it presents a peculiar proposition that the amber room is cursed."

"Intriguing. What is this curse based on?"

"According to the article, several people connected to the room have met untimely deaths," Lord Wharton explained.

Charlotte was taken aback. This was the first time she had heard about the curse. Walking over to the table, she picked up the newspaper and quickly scanned through the pages until she found the headline: "The Curse of the Vanishing Amber Room." Below was a headshot of a middle-aged man named Alfred Rohde. The article recounted the story of a museum director who led the dismantling process of the Amber Room in Königsberg in 1943. The room disappeared shortly after, and a few years later, Alfred Rohde and his wife mysteriously died.

"Do you believe in this curse?" Charlotte looked up at Lord Wharton, seeking his opinion.

"Of course not," he dismissed the notion.

"What curse are you discussing?" Lady Isabelle waltzed into the room. She was elegantly dressed in a flowing pale blue dress that accentuated her perfect figure. Delicate lacework embellished her sleeves, while a string of pearls encircled her neck, matching the shimmering earrings that dangled from her earlobes. Approaching Lord Wharton, she planted a peck on his cheek before diverting her attention to Charlotte.

"The curse of the Amber Room," Charlotte replied.

Lady Isabelle's eyes widened with mock excitement, "Ah, the Amber Room! You know, I heard a rumor that it was actually hidden in someone's basement all along. Can you imagine?" She glanced mischievously at Charlotte. "But who would willingly admit to hiding such a treasure? It must be a secret worth guarding with one's life. Oh, the power of having something that others dream to possess!"

Charlotte wasn't sure whether to believe Lady Isabelle or dismiss it as one of her playful jests. The idea of the Amber Room concealed in a basement seemed both absurd and captivating, leaving Charlotte torn between curiosity and skepticism. She wanted to continue the conversation but noted that Lady Isabelle had already redirected her focus solely onto her fiancé, completely oblivious to Charlotte's presence.

"Richard, if we have to stay here longer, could you speak to the Inspector and ensure that one of his police officers remains stationed here at all times? I felt much safer last night and would appreciate another peaceful night's sleep," Lady Isabelle requested.

"That would be lovely," Lady Beatrice supported the suggestion. Leaning on Lord Carrington's arm, she slowly entered the room, making her way to a plush upholstered chair at the head of the table. Charlotte found their relationship endearing. Despite Lady Beatrice's initial annoyance at Lord Carrington's early arrival and her resistance to his cheerful personality, she relied on his support and friendship. Unlike the past few days, Lady Beatrice seemed to genuinely enjoy his company this morning and appeared almost friendly towards Lord Carrington, whom Charlotte couldn't help but like.

"I believe we all deserve peace of mind," Lady Beatrice added.

"The best idea ever!" Lord Carrington enthusiastically exclaimed.

"A good night's rest works wonders for everyone! It's like a magical elixir that brings forth blossoms. The three of you look stunning today," Lord Carrington's compliment was directed at the three ladies present.

Lady Beatrice, oblivious to the previous night's police presence at Haddonford, dismissed Lord Carrington's words. Her own battle with sleep made her inclined to ignore his remark. Charlotte, appreciative of the compliment, smiled warmly in response. Meanwhile, Lady Isabelle's face twisted into an unwelcome grin, clearly displeased by the comparison drawn between her and the youthful companion of her future mother-in-law.

The table was set, and Margaret served coffee to Lady Beatrice.

Lord Carrington eagerly rubbed his hands together and exclaimed, "I can't wait to try Mrs. Offley's pastries!" Margaret handed him a cup of tea, and he raised it in a toast, "Cheers, Beatrice! To sunshine, friendship, and good food!" Taking a bite of the strawberry scone, he broke into a delighted smile. "Ambrosial, simply ambrosial!"

Lord Wharton and Lady Isabelle declined Margaret's offer of scones and tea, but Charlotte decided to join Lord Carrington in sampling Mrs. Offley's pastries. The cook's skills were excellent, and Charlotte found herself hungry.

"Did Rachel add sugar?" Lady Beatrice inquired as she reached for her coffee.

"Yes, ma'am, just the way you like it," Margaret replied.

"Last time it wasn't enough, and I'm afraid that after my complaint, she might have doubled the amount," Lady Beatrice contemplated, lifting the cup and pausing. "Scones are already sweet, and I try to limit my sugar intake. Perhaps I shouldn't consume both."

"Oh, that's nonsense, Beatrice," Lord Carrington interjected. "Sugar is good for you. Firstly, it provides an instant burst of energy, and secondly, it affects your mood and cognitive abilities. Just enjoy your coffee with the scone, and if you dislike the taste, let Mrs. Offley make you another cup with less sugar."

Lady Beatrice delicately tore off a small piece of the scone and sampled it, followed by a tiny sip of coffee. Almost instantly, she shook her head in disgust.

"Henry, if I want to enjoy this scone, I need another cup of coffee," she declared, handing her cup to Margaret. The maid promptly turned and hurried into the kitchen. The sound of her footsteps echoed down the hallway as Frank Offley entered the dining room. The sunlight illuminated his face, revealing deep wrinkles on his forehead and around his eyes. Short gray stubble covered his chin, indicating a neglected shave or a lack of time. He glanced at Lady Beatrice, seeking her permission to speak.

"Is everything all right?" Lady Beatrice asked, her voice tinged with anxiety.

"Inspector Sinclair called a few minutes ago. He wants everyone to stay put until he arrives, hopefully within the next hour or so. He will be collecting a writing sample from each of us," Frank informed her.

"Why a writing sample?" Lady Isabelle inquired. "And why does he need it from everyone? If this is about the letter, it was typed, not handwritten," she pointed out. "So why would he need a writing sample from everyone? Is Lady Beatrice now a suspect?"

"He may need to do it as part of the elimination process," Lord Carrington interjected, attempting to sound positive, though his appetite had clearly vanished. He set down his half-eaten scone on the saucer.

"What do you think, Richard?" Lady Isabelle turned to Lord Wharton.

"I believe it's prudent to adhere to the inspector's guidance," he suggested.

"This is all too much. I doubt my ability to cope," Lady Beatrice whispered. Her skin turned pallid, a bead of sweat emerging on her brow. Charlotte, observing closely, quickly recognized the symptoms of distress, feeling a surge of concern.

"Lady Beatrice, are you suggesting you find the inspector's request beyond your capacity?" Lady Isabelle asked, her voice filled with genuine confusion over the remark.

A sharp exclamation from Lady Beatrice shattered the room, as she attempted to stand, only to succumb to the chair's hold once more. Charlotte rushed to her aid with a supporting arm. Together, they navigated the room with careful steps. Despite Lady Beatrice's attempts to mask her suffering, the visible signs of her ordeal were undeniable.

Lady Isabelle, Lord Carrington, Lord Wharton, and Frank observed with deep concern. With each painstaking step, the extent of Lady Beatrice's struggle became evident. She endeavored to maintain her dignity, battling to keep her composure despite the mounting difficulty. Amidst this, Charlotte experienced a growing tension in her arm, nonetheless, her commitment to guiding Lady Beatrice to the safety and comfort of her bedroom allowed her to remain concentrated on their progress, pushing aside any personal discomfort.

Lord Carrington ventured to offer his aid, only to be met with Lady Beatrice's forbidding glance, halting him in his tracks. However, Lord Wharton, undaunted by his mother's stern expression, moved forward, extending his sturdy arm. After a moment of hesitation, Lady Beatrice consented to his support. Her dependence shifted, now leaning more on her son than on Charlotte. With each surge of pain, her grasp intensified, relaxing slightly as the agony ebbed. By the time they arrived at her bedroom, Lord Wharton was nearly cradling Lady Beatrice in his arms. Beads of perspiration dotted her ashen face, and she drew breath in shallow gasps as he gently laid her on the bed.

"She requires medical attention," Lord Wharton remarked to Charlotte. After bestowing a tender kiss on his mother's hand, he departed the room to arrange for a doctor's visit.

Chapter Eleven

The sunlight pierced through the lace curtains, casting a bright beam onto Lady Beatrice's pillow. She winced and squinted, unable to move her head to escape its intrusion. Sensing her discomfort, Charlotte swiftly drew the curtains closed, shielding her from the light.

Margaret entered the room carrying a small porcelain wash basin and a decanter.

Charlotte took a soft washcloth from Margaret's arm, saturating it with lukewarm water before delicately wiping Lady Beatrice's face.

"How is she?" Lord Wharton inquired, having been away for a few minutes to call the doctor and leave a message for the inspector, who was unavailable at the time.

"I'm afraid there has been no improvement," Charlotte responded with concern.

Lord Wharton pulled a chair closer to the bed, determined to remain by his mother's side until the doctor arrived.

"You may attend to other matters if necessary," he told Charlotte.

"I would rather stay," she replied, pouring more water onto the cloth, and gently wringing out the excess before placing it on Lady Beatrice's forehead.

"Is there a medical condition that Lady Beatrice has that I don't know about?" Charlotte asked in a hushed tone.

"Not to my knowledge. Mother has never experienced any significant health issues—only occasional migraines," Lord Wharton replied.

Although lacking medical expertise, Charlotte could discern that Lady Beatrice's condition was far from a mere stomach bug or indigestion caused by an undercooked scone. Her deterioration was rapid and alarming. The once-rosy hue of her face had turned pale, then almost green. A violent retch seized her frail body, causing her to convulse uncontrollably until she expelled the contents of her stomach into the waiting wash basin, held steady by Charlotte.

Seconds before the inspector's arrival, the doctor entered the room and instructed everyone, including Lord Wharton, to leave. The sole exception was Margaret, who brought in fresh linens and warm water.

Inspector Sinclair attempted to assert his police authority and enter the bedroom but was swiftly ejected. Frustrated, he paced the corridor.

"I've been away for less than 24 hours and look at this! What was the point of leaving you here?" he angrily exclaimed at George, who appeared bewildered by Lady Beatrice's sickness.

Charlotte felt sympathy for the young officer of the law. "It's not his fault," she said, defending George. "There's no way he could have prevented Lady Beatrice from . . ." Charlotte paused, hesitant to jump to conclusions, yet fairly certain that the doctor's diagnosis would confirm everyone's suspicions.

". . . from being poisoned?" Lord Wharton finished her sentence.

"Yes," Charlotte affirmed.

The inspector muttered something under his breath but refrained from contradicting the assumption. Leaning against the wall, he retrieved a small black notebook from his pocket and meticulously reviewed his written notes.

"I might as well clarify all the facts," he finally spoke up. "What was everyone doing when this occurred?"

Lord Wharton provided a detailed account of the morning, and the inspector fervently documented Lord Wharton's statements. Once finished, he closed the notebook. Since he still couldn't speak with the doctor or the patient, he proceeded downstairs to interview the guests and servants. George followed him, bidding Charlotte a quick, grateful farewell.

Alone with Lord Wharton in the hallway, Charlotte voiced her concerns. "Who would want to harm Lady Beatrice?"

"I have no idea."

"Do you think this incident is related to the mysterious letter she received?"

"Perhaps. The letter could have conveyed various meanings, and a warning to Mother was just one possibility."

"I'm worried about Lady Beatrice," Charlotte admitted.

"Mother is a strong woman and adept at concealing her pain. I'm surprised she didn't call for Frank and instead relied on us. Their relationship is unique and goes back decades. He followed her from Haddonford to Rochester after she got married and moved to my father's estate. He also remained by her side through her father's death and, a few years later, her husband's."

"What about Mrs. Offley?" Charlotte inquired.

"I don't recall when Frank and Rachel got married. Maybe around ten years ago? She moved to Haddonford shortly after. Rachel is a lovely woman and an exceptional cook."

"And Lord Carrington?"

"What about him?"

"How long have you known him?"

"My entire life. Just like Frank, he shares a special bond with my mother, and there's a history between them that they prefer not to discuss."

"A history?" Charlotte asked curiously.

"They were never a couple, but something has kept them connected all these years."

"Could it simply be a deep friendship?" Charlotte suggested.

"Perhaps. Lord Carrington's parents were socialites, well-known in their circles and good friends with Lord Haddonford. That's how Lord Carrington and Mother crossed paths. And now that we're on this topic," Lord Wharton said, "I'd like to ask you something. If it makes you uncomfortable, you don't have to respond."

Intrigued, Charlotte awaited his question.

"Have you ever tried to find your parents?"

She blinked, caught off guard by the direction of the conversation. Memories of the convent and the caring nuns who raised her held a special place in her heart. Charlotte never found it peculiar that she was the only child there. From as far back as she could remember, she received special treatment from each nun, all of whom held a deep affection for her, including Mother Superior, who recognized Charlotte's potential and knew she would eventually leave the convent walls. She spent countless hours imparting wisdom that Charlotte cherished.

"If you'd rather not discuss it, we can stop there," Lord Wharton offered.

"No, no, I can talk about it," Charlotte reassured him. "I grew up never questioning my circumstances. I thought my life was normal and as it should be. It was during my teenage years that I began to wonder about my past, but no one had any answers for me. I wanted to know who my parents were, if there was any note left behind—anything that could provide a clue. But there was nothing," Charlotte sighed.

"I don't believe that," Lord Wharton shook his head. "Someone was keeping the truth from you."

Surprise flickered in Charlotte's long lashes. "I don't understand," she murmured.

"What I don't understand is how they managed to keep you there all those years. There are laws that apply to everyone, including the nuns. No one can raise an abandoned child without reporting it to the police and going through proper adoption procedures. Someone at the convent knows more than she's willing to admit."

Speechless, Charlotte stared at Lord Wharton in utter shock.

"If you decide you want to find your parents, you should start with St. Helen," he stated firmly.

Before Charlotte could fully grasp the implications of Lord Wharton's words, the doctor emerged from the room, gesturing for them to come inside.

"Just as I suspected, arsenic poisoning. Your mother is fortunate that only a small amount entered her system. I've done everything I can, and she's improving. However, she'll need to be hospitalized for a few days under close supervision before she can fully recover."

"Arsenic?" Charlotte heard Inspector Sinclair's voice from behind. Like a tracking dog, he rushed upstairs and arrived just in time to hear the doctor's final assessment.

"How did it enter her system?" he inquired.

"I believe that's your job to find out," the doctor responded calmly. "I diagnose and care for patients, leaving everything else in your capable hands, Inspector."

Chapter Twelve

As the ambulance pulled up, Lord Carrington, Lady Isabelle, Frank Offley, and Samuel encircled the vehicle, their hearts heavy with the shocking revelation of arsenic poisoning.

Uncertain of how to react, Lord Carrington took a hesitant step toward the stretcher that Lady Beatrice was on.

"My sincerest apologies, Beatrice. I fear I have not fulfilled my role as your guardian," he expressed with concern. "This tragedy is profound, yet my relief is immeasurable knowing you're now safe. Before long, you'll return to Haddonford, challenging me as you always do."

A faint smile briefly graced Lady Beatrice's face, though her attention seemed to drift away. Charlotte, observing her expression, could sense that she was summoning the last of her strength to locate someone. Her gaze momentarily paused on Lady Isabelle, then Margaret and Samuel, before settling on Frank. As the male assistants placed the stretcher into the ambulance, Frank, engrossed in conversation with Inspector Sinclair, turned his head. Their eyes met for a fleeting moment before the vehicle's door closed shut, and the ambulance sped away.

"Is something troubling you?" Lord Wharton inquired.

"Yes," Charlotte admitted. "Something feels amiss, but I can't quite grasp what it is."

Charlotte prided herself on her ability to maintain focus and notice intricate details. Her mind functioned like a finely tuned camera, capturing snapshots of unfolding events—the actions, reactions, body language, and gestures of those around her. These mental images served as vital puzzle pieces, aiding her in finding solutions and navigating the complexities of her environment. This skill was the result of years of dedicated honing, nurtured by the mind games she engaged in with Mother Superior. One of their regular pastimes involved Charlotte carefully examining a selected room—a library, kitchen, or the beloved greenhouse of the nuns—before momentarily stepping away. Meanwhile, Mother Superior would subtly remove an object or rearrange items on a shelf. Within a strict time-limit of sixty seconds, Charlotte's task was to identify the missing or altered element. At first, she encountered difficulties with this challenge, but her perseverance and dedication led to steady improvement. Charlotte gradually honed her abilities to a remarkable degree, becoming adept at mentally capturing images and perceiving intricate details that others might easily overlook.

In a similar manner, when Lady Beatrice had conveyed a cryptic message to Frank a few minutes earlier, Charlotte may not have fully grasped its meaning. Nevertheless, she attentively observed their exchange, making a mental note of the interaction. Mother Superior had instilled in her the art of storing such mental images, awaiting the opportune moment to retrieve them and unlock their significance.

Despite her best efforts, Charlotte couldn't shake the persistent flutter of unease in her heart. It wasn't just the interaction between Lady Beatrice and Frank that troubled her; there was something more. She diligently tried to reconstruct the morning's events, piecing together the individuals, locations, and conversations, all while keeping a close eye on everyone around her. Inspector Sinclair and George stood on the gravel driveway, stealing glances at their watches. Collecting writing samples from those who hadn't provided them yet seemed like a minor task compared to uncovering the source of the poisoning and ensuring everyone's safety. Lord Carrington engaged in conversation with Lady Isabelle, while Margaret and Samuel listened attentively to Frank. Charlotte strained to decipher their words, but she sensed their significance, nonetheless.

"I've figured it out!" she exclaimed, gripping Lord Wharton's hand tightly. "We need to hurry."

"What is it, Charlotte, and where are we headed?" he asked concerned.

"To the kitchen! We must hurry before it's too late!"

Charlotte dashed forward with determination, prompting Lord Wharton to hasten his steps to match hers.

The kitchen door stood wide open, carrying a faint aroma of cinnamon in the air. Under different circumstances, Charlotte would have savored the scent, but now her stomach churned with unease. The cook, Mrs. Offley, was nowhere to be found.

"What are we searching for?" Lord Wharton asked.

"It's not 'what,' but 'who.' We need to find Mrs. Offley," Charlotte responded urgently.

"I only saw her this morning when she made tea for George. She was absent for the rest of the day and didn't come upstairs to check on Lady Beatrice. Furthermore, she was not present when the ambulance arrived to transport Lady Beatrice to the hospital, which is highly unusual."

"Rachel and Frank's bedroom is that way. We may find her there," Lord Wharton pointed to the right, taking the lead. In no time at all, they reached the heavy door at the end of the hallway, only to find it locked.

"Anyone got the key?" Inspector Sinclair's voice shattered the silence, making Charlotte jump.

He leaned against the wall, catching his breath—his knack for appearing out of thin air becoming an unsettling pattern.

"The key?" he repeated.

"Frank likely has it, I'm certain," Lord Wharton replied. "And maybe Margaret, though I doubt it."

George appeared behind the inspector, panting for breath. "I'm here, Sir," he announced.

"Excellent. Retrieve the key swiftly," the inspector commanded. "And inform everyone to remain in place. No one should approach this area!"

As the young officer of the law swiftly spun around and dashed off to carry out the orders, Inspector Sinclair crouched down to peer through the keyhole.

"No key, and I still can't see anything," he muttered irritably. "Now, would someone care to explain why we're attempting to break into this room?"

"Mrs. Offley came upstairs this morning," Charlotte began, pausing for a moment. She recalled George's apprehension about accepting a cup of tea while on duty and decided to omit the circumstances under which she had witnessed the cook's actions.

"I haven't seen her since. She didn't come to check on Lady Beatrice, which is unusual, and she wasn't outside with everyone else," Charlotte said.

George reappeared in the hallway, clutching the key in his hand. He handed it over to the inspector, who inserted it into the keyhole and turned it counterclockwise. With a satisfying click, the lock released, allowing the inspector to push open the door.

Inside the room, Mrs. Offley lay motionless on her neatly made bed, her eyes wide open, staring into an abyss of the unknown. A peculiar reddish hue colored her skin, a stark contrast to the life that had once pulsed through her veins. The inspector, with a solemn expression etched across his face, checked her pulse, and after a brief moment, he shook his head.

"We're too late," he declared, his gaze heavy with the weight of the unfortunate truth. "How did you know?" he inquired as he turned to Charlotte.

"I didn't . . . at first," Charlotte's voice quivered. "Mrs. Offley took great pride in her culinary creations, always striving for perfection. She would meticulously taste everything she cooked to ensure it was just right. And every dish I sampled from her was exquisite."

Memories of her first day at Haddonford flooded Charlotte's mind, vividly recalling the delectable supper the cook had served her.

"Lady Beatrice had coffee and a strawberry scone for breakfast," Inspector Sinclair consulted his pocket notebook.

"Yes," Charlotte confirmed. "But she only took a small sip of the coffee and barely touched her scone."

"Did anyone else consume scones or have coffee?" the inspector probed further.

"Only Lady Beatrice drinks coffee, and several of us enjoyed the scones," Charlotte replied thoughtfully.

"If it's the coffee, then we can deduce that Mrs. Offley brewed a fresh pot and taste-tested it before Margaret served it to Lady Beatrice," the inspector reasoned.

"That's it!" Charlotte exclaimed. The coffee was a bit too strong for Lady Beatrice's liking the last time she had it, and I recall her mentioning it to Mrs. Offley, who was a stickler for perfection. I believe she wanted to ensure it met Lady Beatrice's taste this time."

"And did it?" the inspector pressed for confirmation.

"No, it didn't. That's why Lady Beatrice didn't consume it. She began feeling ill almost immediately and requested to go to her room. It appears that Mrs. Offley also felt unwell and needed to rest, but we weren't there to assist her," Charlotte said, her voice filled with sorrow.

"Sir, you can't enter the room!" the young sergeant protested, attempting to block the entrance to the bedroom with his body. However, his efforts were futile against the determined Frank Offley.

"This is my bedroom, and I have the right to know what's happening." Frank's voice faltered as his eyes fell upon his lifeless wife. Overwhelmed with anguish, he lunged forward, only to be restrained by the combined strength of Lord Wharton, George, and Inspector Sinclair.

Frank's sobs permeated the atmosphere, his hands balled into fists so tight that his knuckles whitened. His eyes, brimming with despair and deep sorrow, cast a somber shadow throughout the room. Charlotte found the moment devastating, with tears cascading down her face, tracing moist paths along her chin and neck, soaking her dress. She was tormented by regrets, wishing she had discerned the warning signs earlier and averted the heartbreak somehow.

Chapter Thirteen

When Charlotte awoke the following morning, a severe headache tormented her. The haunting memories of yesterday's nightmare mingled with unsettling dreams that had plagued her before she succumbed to sleep well past midnight. Seeking relief from the throbbing pain, she reached out for a glass of water. Fragmented images of the past night flickered through her mind—an intense interview with the inspector, the submission of a writing sample, and the profound shock on Lord Carrington's face upon learning of Mrs. Offley's sudden demise. Beyond that point, all details dissolved into a hazy blur.

As Charlotte rubbed her temples in an attempt to ease the lingering ache, she knew she had to make her way to the hospital without delay—to inquire about Lady Beatrice's well-being and to seek solace in a change of surroundings. Every corner of Haddonford seemed to hold memories of Mrs. Offley—whether it was the spot at the top of the stairs where she had stood, tray of tea in hand, prepared for George, or the bustling kitchen where she had worked her culinary magic.

Seeking an escape, even if only for a few hours, became necessary. She dressed quickly in the quiet of her bedroom, the rustle of fabric and the soft click of buttons were the only sounds.

Afterward, Charlotte made her way to the library, hoping to find Lord Wharton there. As she opened the door, the scent of aged books and polished wood welcomed her.

As luck would have it, he was indeed there, seated at a massive oak table, deeply engrossed in writing something on a piece of paper. The soft scratch of his pen against the paper created a rhythmic melody in the room. As soon as Charlotte entered, the creak of the door barely audible, he lifted his head.

"I'm preparing to visit Mother. Would you like to accompany me?" Lord Wharton offered.

The warmth of his suggestion hung in the air, creating a brief, comforting pause. In response, Charlotte's eyes lit up with gratitude, her silent expression speaking volumes, surpassing any words she could have uttered. As Lord Wharton finished his sentence, he set aside his writing and rose from his leather chair, "Have you had anything to eat?" he inquired.

She shook her head, immediately feeling a sharp pain that shot from the back to the front of her head. The ground seemed to sway before her eyes, and she instinctively reached for the door to steady herself.

"I'm not hungry," she finally managed to say.

"Perhaps so, but we're still going to stop and grab something to eat before we see Mother," Lord Wharton asserted firmly. "I need your sharp brain to help me figure out the events of the recent week, and a well-nourished brain will undoubtedly serve us better."

A smile accompanied his words as he walked Charlotte to his slick conversable parked outside and extended a helping hand to assist her into the car.

The journey, a mere half-hour drive, passed swiftly with Lord Wharton's luxurious car effortlessly maneuvering along the country road. Its convertible top was down to allow the morning breeze to sweep through. The tranquil English countryside unfolded before Charlotte's eyes. Lush meadows stretched to the horizon, dappled with dew-kissed flowers and grazing livestock.

The breeze bore a delicate aroma of blossoming wildflowers and the earthly fragrances of the surroundings. It gradually worked its magic, dissipating Charlotte's headache. Although remnants of dizziness and mild nausea lingered, she found peace in the nature's comforting embrace.

Throughout the entire journey, Lord Wharton maintained a respectful silence, granting Charlotte the much-needed space. He navigated the car skillfully, reducing speed on turns, mindful of her well-being and ensuring a smooth and gentle ride that safeguarded Charlotte from further discomfort.

Arriving at their destination, Lord Wharton found a parking space directly in front of a quaint tea shop and turned off the car's engine. Inside, the tea shop welcomed them with its warm and cozy ambiance, adorned with elegant floral wallpaper. An elderly couple chatted quietly at a corner table, while at the center, a young mother and her daughter, barely five years old, shared a joyful moment. Their laughter filled the otherwise quiet tearoom, infusing the charming setting with a burst of life.

Lord Wharton allowed Charlotte to choose their seating, and she opted for a table by the window. Once they had settled in, a teenage waitress approached them. Dimples adorned her plump cheeks, and an eager desire to please radiated from her eyes.

"What would you like to eat and drink?" the waitress's melodious voice chimed like a bell, capturing their attention.

Lord Wharton looked to Charlotte, gesturing for her to order first. She contemplated for a moment before responding, "A cup of green tea, please. No milk and no sugar."

"Would you like to try our Victoria Sponge?" the young waitress asked. "My mother makes the best Victoria Sponge in all of England. She's an exceptional baker and also the owner of this place," she boasted with pride.

Charlotte wasn't particularly in the mood for something sweet, but she didn't want to disappoint the enthusiastic girl. She glanced at Lord Wharton, silently seeking his assistance.

"In that case, I'll have a slice," he interjected with a smile directed at the waitress, easing Charlotte's worry.

"Thank you, sir," the girl blushed, her cheeks marked with rosy color, captivated by his deep blue eyes.

"And a cup of tea for me as well," Lord Wharton added.

The girl nodded, still standing in place as if entranced by his handsome features.

"You'll have to forgive her," a woman in her late forties approached the table, gently nudging the waitress. "She's still learning."

Charlotte immediately noticed the striking resemblance between the two. The dimples on the woman's cheeks were a clear indication that she was, without a doubt, the girl's mother.

"Your daughter is absolutely delightful," Lord Wharton complimented. "She was just telling us how incredible of a pastry chef you are and how exceptional your Victoria Sponge is."

A smile illuminated the woman's face. "Well, I must admit, I have a bit of a reputation for it. But I'll let you be the judge of that," she hurried off to the counter to slice a generous portion of the sponge cake while her daughter attended to the tea.

"Are you feeling any better?" Lord Wharton turned his attention to Charlotte.

"Much better, thank you," Charlotte replied gratefully. She took a moment to gather her thoughts before continuing. "Lord Wharton, I'm perplexed by the writing sample we had to submit to Inspector Sinclair. Lady Isabelle pointed out that the letter was typed, not handwritten."

"The letter itself was typed, that's true, but the envelope wasn't," Lord Wharton concurred.

Charlotte contemplatively twirled a lock of her brown curls. "I'm guessing it didn't have a return address," she speculated.

"Correct. The inspector is tracing the stamp on the envelope to determine its origin, but it may not lead us anywhere. The letter was intentionally unsigned, suggesting that the sender didn't want to be identified."

"Do you think Mrs. Offley's death was an accident?" Charlotte asked. Yesterday marked her first encounter with a lifeless body, and it happened to be someone she knew and cared for deeply. Charlotte's heart ached as she vividly recalled the cook's round face with its rosy cheeks. She inclined her head ever so slightly, holding back the tears. Then, she closed her eyes, took a deep breath, and exhaled gently, attempting to regain composure.

Lord Wharton gently placed his hand over Charlotte's, offering a reassuring squeeze. She was surprised that she didn't withdraw her hand. Throughout her life, she had grown accustomed to strength and self-reliance. The nuns who cared for her had expressed support and affection in different ways, not through physical touch. Charlotte realized that she wasn't used to the touch of others, but, reluctantly, she found solace in the warmth of Lord Wharton's hand.

"I'm uncertain whether her death was an accident," he confessed. "Inspector Sinclair mentioned that he would update us as soon as he learns more. Once the body is released, I'll make the necessary arrangements for her funeral. My mother and Frank shouldn't have to worry about that. They need time to grieve."

"I'll assist in any way I can," Charlotte said sincerely.

The young waitress approached their table, her eyes fixated on Lord Wharton's hand resting over Charlotte's. "How's the Victoria Sponge?" she inquired.

"Ah, the sponge," he acknowledged and reached for a fork. Taking a small bite, he savored the flavor. "Delicious!"

The sparkle in the girl's eyes and the dimples on her cheeks indicated her satisfaction with his response.

Lord Wharton turned his attention back to Charlotte. "Are you ready?" he asked once she finished her tea. "We can either drive or walk to the hospital. It's just a block away."

"I prefer to walk," Charlotte replied, rising from her seat, and preparing to leave.

Lord Wharton settled their bill, and together they stepped out onto the street. The radiant sunbeams reflected off the windows of the old buildings, creating a picturesque morning scene. Birds chirped cheerfully atop the roof of a two-story structure with laced balconies and mosaic glass doors. For a brief moment, Charlotte felt a glimmer of happiness. However, her thoughts quickly shifted back to the tragedy of the previous day, and her beautiful green eyes welled up with tears.

"How about I ask you questions as we walk, and you provide the answers?" Lord Wharton suggested, attempting to distract Charlotte from her somber thoughts.

"What kind of questions?" she inquired.

He shrugged his shoulders. "I don't know . . . Questions about you?"

Charlotte nodded in agreement.

"Who's your favorite composer?"

"Chopin."

"And your favorite instrument?"

"A Stradivarius violin."

Lord Wharton regarded Charlotte with interest. "Why a Stradivarius?"

"Antonio Stradivari was a genius and his violins were of unparalleled quality. I had the opportunity to hear a Stradivarius once, and I fell in love with its heavenly sound."

"You amaze me, Charlotte," Lord Wharton commented, continuing with his line of questions. "Who's your favorite poet?"

"Charlotte Brontë."

"And your favorite artist?"

"I have many, but if I had to choose one, it would be Leonardo da Vinci."

"It's been said that da Vinci liked the color pink. What's your favorite color?"

Charlotte pondered for a moment. "I don't have one," she finally replied.

"If you could travel anywhere in the world, which country would you choose to visit first?"

"Russia," she responded without hesitation.

Lord Wharton paused and looked at her in surprise. "Why Russia?"

"I've always been captivated by Russian history. One of the nuns told me about the majestic beauty of St. Petersburg—the Hermitage, Peter and Paul Cathedral, and Saint Isaac's Cathedral. I hold great admiration for Catherine the Great. She stood as one of Europe's most enlightened monarchs and a prolific writer. Catherine embraced medical advancements, even becoming the first person in Russia to undergo smallpox inoculation. Her example inspired over two million people to follow in her footsteps."

"I hope I didn't bore you with my explanation," Charlotte said, a worried expression crossing her face.

"Not in the least," Lord Wharton assured her. "Your passion for Catherine the Great and Russia is contagious and ignites my desire to travel once more. Though, given my current circumstances, I find myself uncertain about the feasibility of it. I am among those who firmly believe that the company we keep holds greater significance than the destination itself. Even in the most ordinary of locations, an unforgettable experience awaits if one is accompanied by someone they genuinely delight in being with."

Charlotte looked at Lord Wharton, waiting for him to elaborate on his reference to "given my current circumstances." However, he swiftly changed the topic, announcing, "We've arrived. How about you wait here, and I'll see if we're allowed to pay a visit to Mother?"

Charlotte nodded in agreement, her gaze sweeping across her surroundings as Lord Wharton vanished behind the front door of a towering gray building complemented by meticulously maintained evergreen shrubs, standing tall along the perimeter. The busy hospital welcomed a constant stream of unfamiliar faces, creating a moderate buzz of activity. Yet among it all, Charlotte's attention was captured by two gentlemen in the distance, their silhouettes framed against the backdrop of the city street. There was a sense of familiarity about one of them that tugged at Charlotte's memory. A furrow formed on her brow as she took a few hesitant steps toward them. They were too far away to see their faces clearly or to hear the words. Charlotte could only observe their animated conversation, their gestures emphasizing a sense of urgency and importance in the exchange.

"Charlotte, where are you going?" Lord Wharton's voice called out.

She turned toward the sound, then looked back in the direction of the individuals who had caught her attention. But it was too late—they had already vanished.

"Did you see someone you know?" Lord Wharton inquired as Charlotte joined him in the brightly lit hospital foyer.

"I don't know. I thought I did, but I'm not certain," she replied.

"Who did this person resemble?" Lord Wharton probed.

"Mr. Offley."

"Hmm . . . It's possible that he came to see Mother. They have known each other for a long time, so he might have felt the need to visit her. We'll find out in a few minutes," Lord Wharton added. "The visitation hours are later this afternoon, but the doctor made an exception for us."

A young nurse led them to Lady Beatrice's room, which was guarded by a police officer. After a brief conversation between the officer and Lord Wharton, they were granted entry. Lady Beatrice opened her eyes as they walked in, her expression brightening upon seeing them. Charlotte immediately noted the signs of improvement—color had returned to Lady Beatrice's face, and her eyes sparkled with focus.

"I'm delighted to see you both," she said genuinely. "I don't like this place at all. The young nurse and the police officer outside the door don't count. They're nice, but they're not open to conversation, and I'm left here with my worries. How can anyone get better when it's just them and the white walls?" Lady Beatrice spoke in a single breath, then turned her head toward a beautiful bouquet on her bedside table. "By the way, thank you for the flowers, Richard."

"You're welcome, Mother," he leaned closer and planted a gentle kiss on her cheek. "I'm glad to see you doing well."

"You and me both," Lady Beatrice replied.

"Come, Charlotte, sit here with me," Lady Beatrice beckoned, tapping the blanket beside her. "I haven't had a chance to thank you properly, my child," she said softly. "It was quite an ordeal for all of us, and you handled it well. I hope I didn't bruise your poor hand by squeezing it too hard."

"No, you didn't," Charlotte assured her. "Is there anything I can do for you? Anything you want?"

Lady Beatrice didn't keep Charlotte waiting for an answer. "Take me home."

"Soon," Lord Wharton interjected. "You'll be home before you know it, Mother. The doctor said maybe another day or two. In the meantime, you need to rest."

"I can rest perfectly well at Haddonford Manor. By the way, the food here is tasteless. If I wanted to lose weight, I would have checked myself into this hospital. One look at what they serve, and you lose your appetite. It certainly makes me appreciate Rachel's cooking. By the way, tell Frank to look inside the top drawer of my writing desk. I made a list for him a few days ago, and some of the items need his immediate attention."

Charlotte's gaze shifted to Lord Wharton, discerning his rigid expression. It became clear that if the individual she identified outside was Frank, his presence in town did not pertain to Lady Beatrice. Unaware of Mrs. Offley's passing, Lady Beatrice remained in the dark, placing Lord Wharton at a crossroads. He was now tasked with deciding whether to disclose the somber news or continue to safeguard her from the truth for a few additional days.

"Mother, there's something I need to tell you, and I believe it's best coming from me," Lord Wharton finally spoke up.

Lady Beatrice froze in anticipation.

"It's about Rachel," Lord Wharton paused, his gaze filled with tenderness as he looked at his mother. "She passed away."

Lady Beatrice gasped, her hands trembling as she tried to loosen the collar of her hospital nightgown to allow herself to breathe.

"How? How did she die?" she asked, her voice quivering.

"Poisoned. She must have consumed something similar to what you had, but either her dose was higher, or we didn't reach her in time. When we realized something had happened, Rachel was already gone."

"Where did you find her?"

"Her bedroom. She must have felt sick after ingesting something and went there to lie down."

"Oh, dear Rachel," Lady Beatrice moaned. "What was it? Do you know?"

"We do not know for sure, but it could be the same poison that you consumed. The inspector will update us once he gets the results. His team collected pretty much everything they could find in the kitchen and took it to the police station."

"What a tragedy. How is Frank?" she asked, her voice filled with concern.

"Devastated."

Lady Beatrice covered her face with both hands, sinking into silence. Charlotte couldn't tell how much time passed before she looked up.

"You're right, Richard. I wouldn't want to hear this news from anyone else but you, and I need time to process it . . . alone," her voice was low yet determined.

Lord Wharton nodded in understanding, and together, he and Charlotte left the room. On their way out, he stopped by the front desk and asked the young nurse to keep an eye on his mother. The girl assured him that she would do her best.

"Did I do the right thing by telling her about Rachel?" he asked Charlotte as they walked back to his car.

"Yes," she replied firmly.

CHAPTER FOURTEEN

"WHERE HAVE YOU VANISHED TO?" LADY Isabelle declared theatrically, flinging the door wide for Lord Wharton and Charlotte. "It seems I'm the sole one available to greet you," she quipped, positioning herself as if she were the final doorman in existence following an imaginary doorman catastrophe. After a brief pause for dramatic effect, she warned, "Prepare for the gastronomic turmoil that awaits in the kitchen. Margaret endeavors to transform our pantry scavenging into a culinary feast. Yet, given the scant ingredients left by the police, I'm apprehensive that not even a goat would be enticed by the offerings! Bon appétit, or perhaps more fittingly, baa-n appétit?" A playful smile danced on Lady Isabelle's lips.

"I suppose we all have to embrace new responsibilities," Lord Wharton commented, acknowledging Lady Isabelle's newfound duty as the greeter of guests.

"Yes," Lady Isabelle sighed. "It's either this or the kitchen, and trust me, I'm more likely to burn the house down than make a decent meal. Besides, I don't think I can touch or eat any food here . . . at least for now. Speaking of food, Richard, I made reservations for us at The Ritz. Just the two of us tonight."

"I'd rather not tonight," Lord Wharton replied calmly, much to Lady Isabelle's dismay.

"I don't see why not. We've both been through a lot, and we deserve some time away from this madness. I'm not suggesting we pack up and flee the country; I'm simply asking for a few blissful hours where I can unwind and be myself again," Lady Isabelle persisted with determination. "You had your chance to escape this morning, and I'm not bitter about being left behind. I just want you to understand that I need my own space too, and . . ." Lady Isabelle moved closer to Lord Wharton, batting her eyelashes playfully, ". . . I really, really want to spend time with you."

Lord Wharton's jaw set firmly, and for a fleeting second, Charlotte believed she detected a blaze in his eyes before he mastered his emotions and stated, "Alright, Isabelle. But I must complete some work prior, and I seek no disturbances." He promptly made his way to the library, securing the door behind him. Lady Isabelle, with a gleeful smile, darted toward her room.

Charlotte decided it was time to check on Lord Carrington and update him on Lady Beatrice's condition. He genuinely cared for her and needed to hear the good news. Charlotte followed her instincts straight into the kitchen, where she discovered Lord Carrington perched on a tall stool, observing intently Margaret expertly peeling a potato.

"Delighted to see your return," Lord Carrington greeted Charlotte. "I was searching for you earlier this morning, not for anything urgent, but simply because I selfishly needed someone to talk to."

"I apologize for not being available, Lord Carrington," Charlotte replied. "Lord Wharton and I went to see Lady Beatrice, and I'm thrilled to report that she's recovering rapidly. She'll be back home in a day or two."

"What marvelous news!" Lord Carrington exclaimed, visibly relieved. "The unknown is simply unbearable, and there's been plenty of that lately. Have they discovered how the poison found its way into her system?"

"I'm afraid I don't have the answer to that. Lord Wharton mentioned that the inspector is pursuing several leads and will keep him informed of any developments. Hopefully, he'll unravel the mystery soon."

"I suppose we must maintain our patience and hold onto the hope that tomorrow will provide us with the answers we seek. However, as one grows older, the virtue of patience takes on a different meaning," Lord Carrington lamented. "Time isn't on your side once you cross sixty. Each year zooms by like a racecar on steroids. By the way, did you know that the British Grand Prix has a rich history dating back to 1926? It is widely regarded as the most prestigious motorsport event in the UK, attracting top drivers from around the world. Anyway, returning to the topic at hand, we often anticipate what tomorrow may bring, but it's important to remember that tomorrow is not guaranteed. This realization serves as a reminder to appreciate the present moment and make the most of each day. Margaret, are you absolutely certain that we should cube the potatoes for the lamb stew?" Lord Carrington asked, switching gears.

"Yes, sir," Margaret replied with confidence.

"And shouldn't we add some rosemary?" he continued, double-checking.

"Is there anything I can do to assist?" Charlotte interjected, glancing at Margaret as the maid reached for a skillet hanging by the stove.

"Maybe you could distract Lord Carrington?" Margaret suggested.

Charlotte nodded in agreement. "How about a game of chess, Lord Carrington?" she proposed.

"A game of chess?" the old gentleman echoed, as if confirming he heard correctly the first time. "Indeed. I haven't played chess in years. How did you know I'd be up for it?" he asked, intrigued.

"I took a guess," Charlotte admitted. "I'm sure there's a chess set tucked away somewhere in Haddonford. I just need to find it."

"There are several chess-sets here, including one with a folding board. Follow me," Lord Carrington declared, hopping off the stool with newfound enthusiasm. He led the way out of the kitchen, leaving Margaret to diligently tend to the stew.

"Did you know that priests were actually forbidden to play chess in the early 1100s?" Lord Carrington exclaimed, unable to contain his fascination.

"If Bishop Guy of Paris caught a priest engaging in a game of chess, he would have him excommunicated! But as they say, every cloud has a silver lining."

Charlotte's heart soared as she watched Lord Carrington become captivated by the topic. She was well aware of the story behind the silver lining but refrained from spoiling his excitement, allowing Lord Carrington to share his knowledge.

"And the silver lining in this case is that the first folding chess board was actually invented by one of those priests who had to conceal his passion for the game. He created a folding chess board that cleverly disguised itself as two stacked books. Isn't that remarkable?"

Charlotte agreed, her eyes sparkling as she observed the remarkable transformation in Lord Carrington's demeanor. His steps grew lighter, his eyes shimmered with newfound focus, and a youthful carefree spirit seemed to emanate from him. He guided her to a small table in one of the guest rooms, where a splendid chess set awaited them. Made from exquisite rosewood and dark walnut, it boasted a classic Staunton design. The intricately hand-carved pieces, especially the knights' faces, showcased meticulous attention to detail. The king's crown was adorned with a cross pattée, while the queen's bore a monde. Lord Carrington allowed Charlotte to choose the color, and she opted for white.

"Shall we begin?" he asked eagerly, rubbing his hands together.

"Absolutely. I'm ready," Charlotte replied and moved her pawn to D4.

"The pawn, a true underdog indeed," Lord Carrington commended as he moved his pawn to D5, directly opposite the white pawn. Charlotte surveyed the board, and after a moment of contemplation, she advanced her pawn to C4, exposing it to capture by Lord Carrington's black pawn on D5. Lord Carrington weighed his options and with a twinkle in his eye and a mischievous smile, he leaned back in his chair.

"Ah, the Queen's Gambit," he mused, savoring the suspense. "Excellent move, Charlotte. You're forcing me to make a critical decision right from the start. It could determine the outcome of this game. You must have played chess before," Lord Carrington commented, impressed.

"Yes," Charlotte confessed. "But I'm still a novice. Memorizing moves is one thing, but chess is so much more than that."

"You're absolutely right, my dear friend," Lord Carrington concurred, his eyes gleaming with insight. "Chess serves as a metaphor for life and the intricate dance of human relationships. Consider the pawn, for instance. With eight of them on each side, every pawn embodies the potential to fulfill a cherished dream—a true Cinderella story—where a lowly, hardworking individual can ascend to the heights of power as a queen," he emphasized, placing his finger gently on Charlotte's pawn on C4.

"But alas, not everyone will be fortunate. Some may succumb to adverse circumstances, while others will persevere but never quite reach the summit . . . just like this particular pawn here."

Charlotte anticipated that Lord Carrington would seize the gambit opportunity, yet he surprised her by retracting his finger from the pawn.

"If you wish to maintain relentless pressure on your opponent, the Queen's Gambit is an ideal move to commence the game," he explained. "By sacrificing a pawn, you gain strategic control. Regrettably, this mirrors a common pattern of human behavior. Throughout history, people have often sacrificed others to attain their desires—whether it be fame, fortune, or power. The annals of time are replete with such examples but forgive me for digressing."

Lord Carrington's words lingered in the air, resonating with the weight of experience and wisdom. With a deliberate move, he slid his pawn to E6, signaling his decision to decline the Queen's Gambit.

"I used to engage in countless chess battles with a brilliant player," Lord Carrington reminisced. "I dedicated endless hours to studying moves, practicing relentlessly, yet she effortlessly defeated me every single time. She had a penchant for initiating the Queen's Gambit, and I eventually learned that accepting it often led to my downfall. Declining it proved to be a safer path."

"Was it Lady Beatrice?" Charlotte asked.

A hint of a smile tugged at Lord Carrington's lips. "No, my dear. Lady Beatrice holds a deep disdain for chess. In her defense, she possesses valid reasons for such sentiments."

Although Charlotte's desire for further details lingered, she suppressed her inquisitiveness and refocused her attention on the game. Playing against Lord Carrington proved to be not easy. Charlotte could discern that his determination to win over an old friend had honed his chess skills. Every move he made was meticulously calculated, staying a few steps ahead of Charlotte's strategies.

"Checkmate!" Lord Carrington declared finally. "Thank you for a marvelous game, Charlotte. We must play again. You are a great opponent not to be missed."

"I still have a lot to learn, and there's a high chance that I might lose again," Charlotte said.

Lord Carrington shook his head and said, "Oh, my dear child, don't view it like that. Instead, think of every loss as a step closer to winning. You can't succeed without going through some failures. When we play chess next time, I'll explain my thoughts behind each move, so you can plan your strategies better."

"Deal," Charlotte agreed, eager to absorb Lord Carrington's wisdom.

Clearing the board, Lord Carrington left only a select few chess pieces in their positions, ready to embark on the next strategic encounter.

"I need to carefully consider this," he mused. "This scenario is identical to a past situation of ours. I believe I made a suboptimal move. I should have approached it differently."

Charlotte offered a reassuring smile and allowed Lord Carrington to contemplate the chess puzzle alone. Meanwhile, she decided to seek out Samuel. Since the passing of Mrs. Offley, she hadn't had a chance to speak with him and wanted to check on his well-being amidst the tragic events at Haddonford Manor. Moreover, she was eager to take him up on his offer to explore the West Wing. Beginning her search in the kitchen, she hoped that Margaret could provide some information on Samuel's whereabouts. She discovered the maid tiptoeing, her arm outstretched, attempting to retrieve an elusive item perched on the pantry shelf. With careful steps, Margaret hoped to extend her reach, but the precarious balancing act threatened to undermine her efforts.

"Nothing, absolutely nothing," Margaret lamented. The realization that the pantry shelves were barren cast a shadow over her culinary ambitions. Overwhelmed by a sense of defeat, Margaret sank onto a stool recently vacated by Lord Carrington.

"I don't understand how Mr. Offley manages to find the strength to carry on. Last night, I tossed and turned, unable to find a moment's peace, consumed by thoughts of Mrs. Offley."

Charlotte empathetically offered her perspective, "He may have experienced a sleepless night as well. It's difficult to know the thoughts and emotions of others. Some individuals prefer to conceal their pain and grieve privately, while others find peace in sharing their burdens. Mr. Offley might be one of those who copes with his pain in solitude."

"Perhaps," Margaret responded, "Mrs. Offley possessed a completely different personality. She was always warm and welcoming, never meeting a stranger. Being alone was unbearable for her, unlike Mr. Offley. He's always reserved and serious, whereas she was filled with joy. When I was first hired, I hardly had a chance to converse with him. He was constantly in and out of Haddonford

Manor, while Mrs. Offley rarely left this place. Who would want to harm her? She hardly interacted with anyone beyond Haddonford. Please don't misunderstand me," Margaret said, growing anxious. "Everyone here, including Mr. Offley, has treated me kindly. It's just that I feel uneasy around him. Nonetheless, I would choose my current circumstances over the orphanage where I grew up any day. My life was a complete nightmare before I arrived here. So, I follow instructions, refrain from asking too many questions, and thank the heavens for how fortunate I am to have encountered Lady Beatrice."

A surge of emotion coursed through Charlotte as she asked, "You're an orphan?"

"Yes, why do you ask?"

"Do you have any knowledge about your parents?" Charlotte inquired further.

"None at all. I was just a young child when I was left at the orphanage, and eventually, I ended up working there," Margaret replied.

"What about Samuel?" Charlotte probed.

"I have no idea. Why do you ask?"

"It's intriguing to me how we both share the circumstances of never knowing our birth parents and eventually finding ourselves working here," Charlotte remarked.

"Undeniably Lady Beatrice possesses a compassionate heart and is committed to helping those in great need," Margaret responded, offering her explanation. "I was candid with her about the challenges I faced in the orphanage and in my later life, and she hired me on the spot."

"Did she ask you for any references?"

"Yes, why do you ask?"

"It's just that she didn't ask me for any references," Charlotte replied thoughtfully.

"Perhaps she was in urgent need of hiring someone?" Margaret suggested.

Charlotte shrugged, uncertain of the exact reason.

Changing the topic, Charlotte asked Margaret, "Have you ever been to the West Wing? I'm quite curious about it. Mrs. Offley seemed to avoid discussing it."

"No, why do you ask?" Margaret responded.

Noticing Margaret's repeated "whys," Charlotte realized the need to provide a more thorough explanation. She didn't want to make the maid suspicious or anxious, considering the prevailing tension at Haddonford Manor.

"Inadvertently, I found myself wandering into the West Wing, and I couldn't help but notice how impeccably clean it was. I've observed you preparing rooms for the guests, and it seems as if you wield a magic wand, instantly transforming everything into a state of pristine purity. I assumed it was you who maintained the West Wing, making it appear as if it were still in use," Charlotte clarified.

"Thank you," Margaret beamed with a smile. "I do my best, but I have enough to take care of here. I don't clean the rooms in other areas. Lady Beatrice doesn't use that wing at all, so I don't go there. She hires a cleaning crew specifically for the West Wing from time to time," Margaret explained.

"That makes sense," Charlotte acknowledged.

Just then, Samuel entered the kitchen, carrying a large box. Placing it on the table in front of Margaret, he announced, "Vegetables, spices, and meat fresh from the market. I personally picked them, which wasn't easy. Trying to distinguish between a tenderloin and sirloin, Jersey Royal and King Edward potatoes, dill, and parsley—I had a crash course in culinary skills and farming tips. I think I did well," Samuel said proudly.

Margaret looked as if she was about to give him a big hug. "Aww, thank you! Now I can prepare a decent meal for everyone."

"Thank Frank. He deserves the credit. Despite the tragedy, he made sure everyone is taken care of. I simply followed his orders and accompanied him to town this morning to get groceries," Samuel explained.

"I'll be sure to thank him when I see him," Margaret replied, searching through the items, and finding the spice she was looking for. "I have everything I need now. Give me another hour or so and dinner will be served," she said excitedly.

As she headed out, Charlotte reminded Margaret, "Lady Isabelle and Lord Wharton will be dining out tonight."

CHAPTER FIFTEEN

"**I** SUPPOSE THERE'S NO BETTER TIME THAN now," Samuel declared upon learning of Charlotte's intention to explore the West Wing.

"To be honest, I'm not entirely certain of our purpose for going there but I am more than willing to accompany you. I've had my fair share of explorations, and I consider myself quite knowledgeable about that section of the manor," Samuel assured, taking the lead with Charlotte following closely behind. Instead of venturing outside, they walked through a series of interconnected ballrooms. Samuel's familiarity with the layout proved invaluable as he easily navigated them through various turns and dimly lit corridors, ultimately arriving at their destination: The West Wing of Haddonford Manor.

Eager to learn more about Charlotte's intentions, Samuel posed the question, "Which room would you like to see first?"

Charlotte's eyes fixed on a guest room that bore an uncanny resemblance to Lady Beatrice's beloved Blue Room. Luxurious furniture showcased a stunning blend of gold and burgundy, while majestic portraits adorned the walls in magnificent golden frames. Approaching a writing table, Charlotte gingerly lifted its top, only to discover its barren state, devoid of pens or notebooks. The adjacent side table sat similarly empty. Not a single trace hinted at recent or even prior use of the room. Impeccably maintained, the furniture and floors gleamed, devoid of even the tiniest speck of dust. The caretakers hired by Lady Beatrice had clearly executed their duties with exceptional precision. Straining her memory, Charlotte attempted to recall the elusive detail that had unsettled her during her previous visit to the West Wing. With determination, she meticulously surveyed the room's contents, her gaze sweeping over every object and corner.

"Any progress?" Samuel asked his voice filled with hope.

Charlotte's head shook slowly, "No, nothing yet."

Remember, there's an abundance of rooms within the West Wing. Shall we continue our exploration?" Samuel offered. "I'm more than willing to proceed, examining one room at a time, in the hope that something triggers your memory."

"I'm uncertain if there's a specific memory to trigger. It's more like a lingering feeling I experienced when I saw something . . . But what exactly did I see?" Charlotte pondered aloud, her voice filled with frustration.

"I wish I could be of more assistance," Samuel said, waiting patiently while Charlotte meticulously examined one of the paintings on the wall.

The artwork depicted a handsome man standing beside a chair, his hand gently resting on his wife's shoulder. A sweet little girl, wearing a lace cap and a white dress, sat on her mother's lap, her gaze fixed upon the painter, while the adoring looks of her parents were solely directed at her. Without a shred of doubt, Charlotte recognized the child as Lady Beatrice. A portrait of the same girl, only a few years older, adorned the countess's bedroom. However, it was the parents who captivated Charlotte's attention. Lady Beatrice had mentioned her father, but her mother's absence in her recollections struck her as peculiar. The lady depicted in the painting exuded exquisite grace, her beauty reminiscent of a delicate flower. The father's remarkable handsomeness seemed to pass down through the generations, as Lord Wharton inherited the striking features of his grandfather.

The room in which the family portrait was situated resembled any other room in Haddonford, perhaps even the very guest room Charlotte and Samuel currently occupied. Positioned to the right of Lady Beatrice stood a small table with a bouquet of red roses, while an identical table with a chessboard graced the left side of the father. Charlotte surmised that this arrangement had been accurately planned to showcase both parents' preferences. If her assumption held true and Lord Haddonford indeed had a fondness for chess, then why did Lady Beatrice despise the game?

Approaching the painting with genuine interest, Samuel asked, "Is this what you were searching for?"

Charlotte replied firmly, "No, this isn't it. But do you happen to know what became of her?"

"Do you mean Lady Margaret? Lady Beatrice rarely speaks about her. Frank might be the only person who can answer your question. He is the keeper of Lady Beatrice's secrets," Samuel revealed.

Charlotte locked her gaze with Samuel's, curiously attempting to discern whether he was serious or jesting.

"How do you know she has secrets?" she inquired.

"I don't have concrete knowledge, but there is an undeniable energy between them that defies explanation," Samuel elaborated.

Perplexed, Charlotte pressed further, asking, "What do you mean?"

"I believe they share a secret language of sorts. They can communicate without even uttering a word. Lady Beatrice looks at Frank, and he understands her desires," Samuel explained.

Charlotte couldn't help but agree with Samuel's assessment. She vividly remembered the intense gaze Lady Beatrice had directed at Frank when she was placed in the ambulance. Although she couldn't decipher its meaning, Frank evidently could.

"I guess Mr. Offley has learned to interpret Lady Beatrice's nonverbal cues, which is a common phenomenon among individuals who have coexisted for a substantial period of time," Charlotte said. "From what I gather, he has known Lady Beatrice longer than all of us combined."

This train of thought sparked another question in Charlotte's mind, leading her to ask Samuel, "By the way, are you an orphan?"

Samuel's eyes widened in surprise. "An orphan? Well, that's quite an unexpected inquiry."

Once again, Charlotte realized the importance of providing context for her questions. What seemed logical to her may not have been apparent to others.

"Allow me to explain the reason behind my question," Charlotte continued, eager to shed light on her thought process.

"Mrs. Offley mentioned that I was not the only candidate interviewed for the companion position. In fact, the job had been advertised multiple times before Lady Beatrice hired me on the spot. I felt fortunate and incredibly grateful for this opportunity, but I lacked references and prior experience. So, I wondered, why me? Recently, in a conversation with Margaret, I discovered that she, too, was an orphan, much like myself. The difference being that I was raised by nuns while she grew up in an orphanage."

"I understand now," Samuel acknowledged. "You asked if I was an orphan to test your hypothesis that Lady Beatrice tends to hire individuals who have experienced the loss or abandonment of their parents."

Charlotte nodded in confirmation.

"Well, I'm not an orphan," Samuel stated. "Both of my parents are still alive and well. They reside in Cheshire, and I actually plan to visit them during Christmas. Moreover, I had excellent references from my previous employers," he added with a touch of pride. "I had been doing odd jobs here and there until I crossed paths with Frank. He needed someone to take care of the stables, garden, and other miscellaneous tasks, particularly when he's not around."

Curiosity brimming within her, Charlotte inquired, "Do you happen to know why he frequently leaves Haddonford?"

"Isn't it evident? Someone must tend to the business matters. Frank is responsible for running Lady Beatrice's errands, and Mrs. Offley used to provide him with a to-do list that often included grocery shopping. Today was an exception. He specifically asked me to accompany him to the market and left me there temporarily while he attended to other matters. I fulfilled my part and waited until his return a few hours later. We then loaded everything into the car and drove back home."

Inquisitive, Charlotte pressed further, "Did he happen to mention where he went?"

Samuel smiled, a hint of amusement in his expression. "Why would he? I report to him, not the other way around. I assumed he was dealing with lawyers or banks. Perhaps he was purchasing something for Blazer or arranging for someone to come and fix the stable's roof. It started leaking, but fortunately, it's situated at the back, and the stallion remains unaffected."

Charlotte persisted, seeking further insight. "So, he didn't provide you with any information at all?"

Samuel's smile remained, but his response held a hint of mystery. "No, not a word. He was quiet the entire time, but that's typical of Frank. He's not a talkative person. I simply assumed he was occupied with matters concerning Lady Beatrice or the upkeep of Haddonford."

Charlotte pondered silently, acknowledging Samuel's explanation, yet her thoughts remained unspoken. Samuel's account confirmed that the person Charlotte had seen earlier in town was indeed Frank. However, the mystery of his presence near the hospital and the identity of the mysterious stranger persisted. It was evident that Frank Offley had more on his agenda than just grocery shopping.

"Shall we continue and explore one more room?" Samuel asked.

Charlotte noticed the encroaching darkness and considered the time. "Perhaps one more," she suggested, opening the door to an adjacent room. A cozy loveseat rested against one wall, accompanied by two tall chairs facing it, and a low table in the center. Next to the window stood a grand piano, its shiny surface illuminated by the fading light. Charlotte's eyes swept across the walls, eagerly searching for more family portraits, and her anticipation was rewarded. Right in front of her, a striking full-length portrait of Lord Haddonford caught Charlotte's attention. Draped in black attire, he exuded a commanding presence within the room. Intrigued, she drew closer to the painting, admiring the artist's skill in capturing Lord Haddonford's prominent features. He appeared no older than he did in the family portrait, yet there was a profound distinction. The man depicted before her undeniably resembled the figure in the previous painting, but his eyes held a subtle shift, a deep sadness absent in the familial depiction. Lost in contemplation, Charlotte pondered its significance when suddenly, a gust of wind forcefully swung open the nearby window. The curtains billowed, one of them swirling like a cloud, enveloping the grand piano, and toppling a crystal vase from its perch. The vase shattered into countless pieces, spilling water onto the keys, bench, and carpet. Red roses scattered across the floor.

Startled, Charlotte let out a scream and instinctively grabbed Samuel's hand, feeling his trembling just like her own. Both stood frozen in fear, their eyes fixed on the open window.

"What was that?" Charlotte whispered, her gaze locked on the window. "Wasn't it closed when we entered?"

"I don't remember," Samuel whispered back, his voice filled with uncertainty. "It could have been the wind."

"Of course, it was the wind, but what caused it?" Charlotte's voice remained hushed while her mind racing to find an explanation.

"A draft, perhaps?" Samuel offered.

"That's a possibility. It was unexpectedly strong and seemingly came from nowhere. It's plausible that someone opened a door across the hallway, and since the window in this room wasn't properly shut, the draft lifted the curtain, causing the vase to shatter," Charlotte hypothesized, her words barely above a whisper.

"There shouldn't be anyone here," Samuel stated, his tone lacking conviction. "I'll check," he declared before Charlotte could protest, swiftly pulling his hand away and venturing out of the room.

Charlotte remained pressed against the wall, fear gripping her, as she tried to regulate her breathing and focus on her surroundings. As the room gradually embraced darkness, suffusing everything in varying shades of gray, the remaining rays of the setting sun cast a final glow, illuminating the area. Charlotte's eyes were captivated by another painting directly in front of her. From her position, she couldn't help but notice the cute cheeks and adorable button nose portrayed in the artwork. However, one peculiar detail caught her attention—the painting was slightly off-center.

"No one is there," Samuel declared upon his return to the room. "I thoroughly checked everything—the doors and windows are securely shut."

A wave of relief washed over Charlotte, prompting her to exhale audibly.

"We must clean up this mess," she suggested, gesturing toward the shattered glass and water on the floor.

"I'll take care of it," Samuel offered. "It won't take long."

"Are you certain? I don't mind lending a hand, and I'm concerned about leaving you alone."

"I assure you, there's no one here," Samuel said. "It won't take me long to clean and attend to Blazer. It's past his feeding time, and he must be famished."

"Very well," Charlotte agreed. "Meanwhile, I'll check on Lord Carrington and Margaret.

"As she turned to leave the room, Samuel interjected, "Do you know how to find your way back?"

"Yes," she affirmed. "This time, I was actually paying attention and making mental notes while following you. I should be able to navigate back without any issues."

"That's great," Samuel replied.

"I suppose I'll see you soon," Charlotte said, her hand already reaching for the door handle.

"Wait, Charlotte," Samuel called out, halting her in her tracks. "Did you find what you were searching for?"

Charlotte hesitated for a moment, then replied, "Yes, I did."

A mixture of excitement and curiosity danced across Samuel's face. "What was it?"

"A clue," Charlotte responded.

"What? I'm completely lost," Samuel admitted.

"Have you ever worked on a jigsaw puzzle?" Charlotte inquired.

"Of course, countless times when I was a child," Samuel recalled.

"Then you probably remember that to piece together a puzzle, you start by assembling the border, sort the pieces by color, and pay attention to their shapes," Charlotte explained.

"I suppose so," Samuel acknowledged.

"Well, I have discovered a puzzle piece. Now I just need to find where to place it."

Charlotte noticed the effort Sam was exerting to comprehend her analogy.

"I'll explain everything in detail later," she promised, offering a reassuring smile, before swiftly departing the room. Samuel remained rooted in place, looking quite bewildered by her words.

CHAPTER SIXTEEN

LADY BEATRICE'S DETERMINATION TO ATTEND RACHEL Offley's funeral led to her early release from the hospital. She eloquently persuaded the medical staff that continuing her healing process amidst Haddonford's serene surroundings would contribute to a faster recovery. However, when she took on the task of personally handling the funeral arrangements, she encountered resistance from Lord Wharton, who insisted on taking charge. Despite her heartfelt pleas, she reluctantly acquiesced to her son's decision, understanding that his intentions were driven by love and concern.

In the days leading up to the funeral, Lady Beatrice sought solace in leisurely walks accompanied by Frank, her trusted companion. Meanwhile, Lord Carrington, respecting their need for privacy, devoted hours to unraveling intricate chess problems, finding both peace and distraction in the strategic intricacies of the game. In contrast, Lady Isabelle gracefully divided her time between showcasing remarkable piano skills and immersing herself in books while surrounded by the soothing outdoors. On the other hand, Lord Wharton retreated to the seclusion of the library but often emerged to handle funeral-related calls and coordinate with the police. With doors ajar and windows open, the seamless ambiance allowed Lord Wharton to be drawn into the harmonious world of Lady Isabelle's musical expertise—flawless renditions of challenging Chopin nocturnes and Beethoven sonatas and he simultaneously caught glimpses of her graceful figure as she relaxed outside the library window, engrossed in her reading.

Charlotte found herself in contemplation, uncertain whether Lady Isabelle genuinely enjoyed her musical performances and reading outdoors or if her pursuits were aimed at impressing Lord Wharton.

On the morning of the funeral, the weather was slightly cool, yet sunny. Charlotte felt a sense of apprehension and worry, particularly for the delicate Lady Beatrice, who appeared fragile in her black dress and hat. The funeral service took place at a small cemetery adjacent to a Catholic church, a location familiar to both Mrs. Offley and Frank as regular attendees.

"Rachel loved it here," Lady Beatrice remarked, her voice carrying a mixture of fondness and melancholy. "And now, here among the serene beauty of this place, she will find eternal peace. It is a truly fitting final resting place for her."

Charlotte fought back tears. The weight of their shared loss hung in the air, mingling with the quiet whispers of the wind rustling through the surrounding trees. It was as if the very essence of the place embraced Rachel Offley's spirit, providing comfort in her eternal slumber.

The funeral proceeded as Frank had requested, a private affair with only a select few close friends from the church in attendance. As the priest concluded the sermon, Frank stepped forward, gently placing a bouquet of vibrant red roses on his beloved wife's coffin. Next to her loyal chauffeur, Lady Beatrice clutched a handkerchief, wiping away the tears that welled in her eyes. Lord Carrington, Samuel, and Margaret observed the methodical movements of the shovels with somber gazes, while Inspector Sinclair and George stood at a respectful distance, keeping an eye on everyone present.

Charlotte assumed they were not just here to pay respects but to find answers to Mrs. Offley's demise. As her gaze lingered on the inspector, he turned his head, and their eyes met. He nodded a quick hello, and Charlotte reciprocated with a brief nod, then continued to sweep across the cemetery, searching for Lady Isabelle— the only person who seemed to be missing from the picture. Within seconds, Charlotte's eyes landed on a peculiar sight: Lady Isabelle marching toward Mrs. Offley's grave with determined strides. Charlotte couldn't fathom how long she had been away or what she was up to. Little did she know, Lady Isabelle's path to the grave would be anything but smooth.

In a twist of comedic misfortune, one of Lady Isabelle's high heels became wedged in a crack between the stones of the sidewalk. Time seemed to slow down as she teetered precariously, threatening to take a tumble. However, with a valiant effort and a series of awkward contortions, she managed to free her shoe and regain her balance.

Yet, Lady Isabelle's misadventures didn't end there. In her backward stumble, she unintentionally collided with a lady standing in the grass nearby. The startled woman let out a surprised yelp, caught off guard by the unexpected encounter. Lady Isabelle's face instantly transformed into an apologetic expression as she quickly approached the startled stranger, offering sincere words of regret, hastily readjusting her disheveled skirt, then swiftly rejoined the gathering by the graveside.

As Charlotte continued to observe the mysterious lady in black, she couldn't help but be intrigued. Her age was difficult to guess, thanks to the neatly arranged bun and the black veil that concealed her face. Throughout the funeral proceedings, she maintained a noticeable distance from everyone, including Frank, showing no inclination for conversation or socialization. As the ceremony neared its end, the woman hurriedly departed, sparking Charlotte's curiosity even further.

"Is there something troubling you?" Lord Wharton inquired,

his piercing blue eyes attentively studying her.

"Do you happen to have a list of the attendees for the funeral?" Charlotte responded, her reply taking the form of a question.

"Yes, I do. Are you attempting to identify the mysterious lady dressed in black?" Lord Wharton replied.

"So, you noticed her too?" Charlotte acknowledged.

"I saw you watching her," he admitted.

"Do you know her?" Charlotte asked.

"I don't believe so," Lord Wharton said, his memory searching for any connections.

"But you have the list, don't you?" Charlotte pressed.

"I don't have it with me at the moment."

"Let's check the registry then. Perhaps her name is there," Charlotte suggested, determined to unveil the lady's identity.

She walked briskly toward the church, and Lord Wharton was left with no other option but to follow her. As they entered through the ornate doors, a hushed silence filled the space. Charlotte's eyes were immediately drawn to the altar, which stood as the focal point of the sanctuary. Adorned with intricate carvings, gilded accents, and flickering candlelight, the altar served as the sacred space where the Eucharist was celebrated. The architecture of the church show-cased a blend of traditional and Gothic elements. High vaulted ceilings soared above, creating a sense of spaciousness. Stained glass windows depicted scenes from biblical narratives and the lives of saints, allowing streams of colorful light to filter into the interior. The richly polished wood of the pews added a touch of warmth and elegance to the space. To the left of the entrance, Charlotte's eyes fell upon the guest book. Rachel's name, elegantly inscribed in gold letters, embellished the cover. Charlotte carefully opened the registry and traced her finger down the list. Some guests had simply signed their names, while others had included their relationship to Rachel, identifying themselves as friends.

"Do you recognize any of these names?" Charlotte inquired, hoping for a breakthrough.

Lord Wharton meticulously scanned the list. "No, her name does not seem to be among them," he replied.

"I was hoping luck would be on our side," Charlotte sighed. "It seems we may never know who she was. Unless . . ." Her voice trailed off as she delved into deep contemplation.

"Unless we speak to everyone who attended the funeral," she continued. "Surely, someone can shed light on her identity and purpose for being here."

"And what if no one can provide the answers?" Lord Wharton questioned, skepticism apparent in his tone.

"We will find her," Charlotte asserted, maintaining optimism. "We must think positively because positive thoughts attract positive outcomes. It may contradict Coulomb's law, but it works."

"In that case," Lord Wharton conceded, "I will let you take the lead on this part of the investigation."

CHAPTER SEVENTEEN

After the conclusion of the funeral, the cemetery still teemed with guests who lingered, patiently waiting in line to pay their last respects to Frank before bidding farewell. Amidst the crowd, Charlotte's attention was drawn to the sight of the priest engaged in a conversation with an elderly parishioner. The woman's sorrowful expression suggested a deep connection to Mrs. Offley, leading Charlotte to believe she must have been one of her close friends. She distinctly recalled the woman standing by the coffin during the service and witnessing the poignant embrace she shared with Frank afterward.

"Richard, I was searching high and low for you," Lady Isabelle exclaimed, appearing in front of them with an air of urgency. "Where were you?"

Lord Wharton, maintaining his composed demeanor, responded, "I was checking the funeral registry, my dear Isabelle."

Lady Isabelle leaned in closer. "Why would you do that? Did something extraordinary happen? Do tell!"

"It's not a grave matter, my dear," Lord Wharton reassured, "Just a faint glimmer of a lead in the investigation into Rachel's tragic demise."

Lady Isabelle glanced towards Inspector Sinclair, who stood

watchfully observing the distant crowd. "Oh, well, isn't that his responsibility?" she retorted, her frustration evident in her voice. Continuing in a sarcastic tone, she added, "While you were engrossed in your detective work, I, quite brilliantly, managed to ruin my new shoes while foolishly chasing after a mere apparition. Today has proven to be a remarkably eventful day, to say the least."

Intrigued, Lord Wharton displayed genuine interest in her story.

"What happened?" he asked.

Lady Isabelle, slightly surprised by his sincere interest in her story, proceeded.

"You see, as I was strolling through the cemetery, a young lady approached me and handed me a folded piece of paper. At first, I thought it was a message of great significance, something related to the investigation. But as I unfolded it, all I found was a cryptic note that read, 'I'm here to pick you up, but please take your time.' Naturally, before I could inquire further or understand its meaning, the mysterious messenger vanished into thin air," Lady Isabelle sighed. "It was quite perplexing, to say the least. I'm not sure if it was a prank or if there's something more to it. But amidst the chaos of the day, I couldn't help but chase after that elusive ghostly messenger, leading to the unfortunate demise of my brand-new pair of shoes."

"Do you still have the note?" Lord Wharton asked.

Lady Isabelle sighed again, a touch of regret in her voice. "No, since I wasn't expecting a chauffeur or any form of pick-up after the funeral, I deemed it a mistake and tossed it aside. Oh, if only I had known what was to come! As I made my way back, disaster struck. My heel got ensnared in a treacherous sidewalk crack!" Lady Isabelle exclaimed, gesturing dramatically towards her damaged shoes.

"I shall gladly purchase you another pair," Lord Wharton offered a practical solution. "Now, can you recollect any distinctive details about the young lady who delivered the note?"

Lady Isabelle pondered for a moment. "Ah, indeed! She was young, perhaps in her early twenties, with chestnut hair and brown eyes. Although, it is only fair to mention that she seemed slightly shorter than me, but that is considering I am donning high heels today. Additionally, she possessed a certain *je ne sais quoi*, an elusive foreign accent that I couldn't quite pinpoint. Regrettably, that is all I can recall at present."

Lord Wharton nodded, finding the information helpful. "Most likely, the note was intended for someone else named Isabelle, possibly a parishioner attending the service."

"Well, I do hope that the intended recipient of that message eventually received it. Since the note was never delivered to the correct addressee, they might still be awaiting a ride," Lady Isabelle commented. Shifting gears to their present circumstances, she continued in a composed manner, "Speaking of our ongoing affairs, do you think we are nearing the conclusion of our business here?"

"Almost, my dear. However, I think it would be best if you were to ride back with my mother. I'm certain she wouldn't mind the company," Lord Wharton replied.

Lady Isabelle arched an elegant eyebrow, considering the proposition. Riding back with Lady Beatrice had not been her original plan, but she decided to go along with it.

Lord Wharton observed his fiancée as she gracefully entered the black Rolls Royce, then shifted his attention to the priest, who had just wrapped up a conversation with another parishioner.

"Father Sullivan? I hope you don't mind, but I would like to have a brief conversation with you, and I would appreciate Miss Reinford's presence as well," Lord Wharton addressed the priest politely.

"Certainly, Lord Wharton. How may I be of assistance?" the priest responded. Tall and distinguished, Father Benedict Sullivan carried himself with a serene demeanor that reflected his years of devotion to his faith. His salt-and-pepper hair added an air of wisdom to his countenance, while his warm brown eyes sparkled with a gentle compassion that drew people to him.

"Father, as you are well aware, Rachel's untimely passing has unfolded amidst suspicious circumstances, prompting an ongoing investigation. While the authorities are diligently pursuing their inquiries, Miss Reinford and I," Lord Wharton inclined his head subtly in Charlotte's direction, "We have also begun our own investigation and would like to pose a few questions, if you don't mind."

The priest nodded empathetically. "Of course, I'm here to assist in any way I can."

"Have you come across anyone named Isabelle among the staff here?" Lord Wharton asked.

"I'm not familiar with anyone by that name. I know my parishioners quite well, and there is no Isabelle among them," the priest responded, shaking his head. "But if you could provide me with more details, perhaps I can assist you further."

Lord Wharton paused, considering his next question. "Let's forget about Isabelle for a moment. Do any of your parishioners have distinctive accents?" he finally inquired.

A soft chuckle escaped the priest's lips. "Well, we all have accents of our own, in a sense."

"I agree. And I feel the need to clarify myself. We are searching for a young lady with brown hair and brown eyes. She delivered a note to Lady Isabelle, and we believe the note was intended for a different person, possibly named Isabelle. We would like to speak with the messenger about both the note and the person who gave it to her," Lord Wharton explained.

The priest's eyes brightened with recognition. "Ah, you might be referring to Marisa. She volunteers here and is always willing to lend a hand with various tasks. She moved here from Poland."

"How can we locate her?" Lord Wharton asked.

"She might still be here. Please, follow me," the priest replied, gesturing for Lord Wharton and Charlotte to accompany him.

Tucked away behind the church, the back area revealed itself as a tranquil extension of the hallowed grounds. In one corner, a quaint garden flourished, its flowers exuding sweet fragrances. Benches, thoughtfully situated under the soothing shelter of trees, provided a peaceful haven for rest and reflection. At the center of the yard, a petite fountain stood, its soft water flow weaving a harmonious tapestry of soothing sounds. Near the fountain, a young woman in gardening gloves was meticulously pruning roses, and arranging them on a bench.

"Marisa," the priest called, drawing her attention. Her face lit up with a warm, welcoming smile as she looked up. "I've brought some guests who need your help," the priest explained.

Marisa gently set down her gloves beside the roses on the bench. She was slight in stature, her smooth brown hair elegantly pinned back, and her almond eyes sparkled with a curious innocence. There was an ethereal purity about her, reminiscent of a child exploring the world with uncontained wonder.

"I will do my best to assist," Marisa replied softly, her voice carrying a gentle Polish accent.

"We are searching for the person who delivered a note to Lady Isabelle," Lord Wharton explained.

"That would be me," Marisa confirmed. "Did something happen?" a genuine worry laced her voice.

"No, nothing happened," Lord Wharton reassured her. "We believe that the note was given to Lady Isabelle by mistake."

"Oh no! I'm so sorry! It was not intentional, I promise."

"We know that," Lord Wharton said gently. "Can you provide us with any information about the person who handed you the note?" he inquired further.

"I will try," Marisa said. "He approached me outside the church and instructed me to give the note to the lady named Isabelle."

"Did he say anything else?" Lord Wharton probed.

"Yes, he mentioned that she was at the funeral. Since I didn't think to ask him for a description, I inquired around, and one person pointed towards the beautiful lady who had arrived with you and Mr. Offley. I waited for the right moment and handed her the note. I am very sorry for messing things up. I feel bad, knowing that I failed the man who sought my help. He seemed like a genuinely kind person. I hope I didn't cause him any trouble."

"It was a simple error, Marisa," Father Sullivan said softly. "No harm done."

"You never know." Marisa shook her head. "The man was simply trying to fulfill his duties, and I unintentionally disrupted everything."

"What do you mean by 'fulfilling his duties'?" Lord Wharton inquired, intrigued by Marisa's remarks.

"He was wearing a uniform and a hat. I saw him standing near a car parked in front of the church. At first, I thought he might be a friend or relative of Mr. Offley. Then, he left and didn't stay for the funeral. I got occupied with my tasks and didn't pay much attention. He returned later and handed me the note. I thought he might be working for someone, perhaps even the lady who was meant to receive the note. Will I face consequences for messing things up?" Marisa asked, visibly upset.

"No, of course not. I appreciate your honesty and cooperation, Marisa. You have been immensely helpful," Lord Wharton assured her.

Marisa shyly smiled and blushed in response.

As Lord Wharton and Charlotte walked towards his car, he voiced his concerns. "I must speak with Inspector Sinclair or George tomorrow. Tracking down a mysterious lady in black is like finding a needle in a haystack. Without their assistance, it may prove to be an impossible task."

"What can they do to help us?"

"They have access to resources that could expedite the process of locating a stranger in a big city. Presumably, the lady in black took a taxi to attend the funeral. Both the inspector and George would be better equipped to track down the cab driver who was on duty compared to you and me," Lord Wharton explained.

Charlotte nodded in understanding, raising a valid point. "However, they might not be willing to extend a personal favor for us."

A smile crept across Lord Wharton's face as he responded, "That's true, but remember the power of positive thinking? Didn't you say that if we maintain an optimistic mindset, the desired outcome becomes more likely."

Charlotte's voice trailed off as she contemplated her own words, quietly murmuring, "Yes, something along those lines, I suppose . . ."

Chapter Eighteen

Inspector Sinclair's scheduled visit to Haddonford Manor the next morning stirred a current of expectancy throughout the estate. He had summoned everyone, including staff members Margaret and Samuel, to gather in the Blue Room by five in the evening, promising to unveil the outcomes of his investigation. This announcement left the manor's residents in a state of heightened suspense, bracing for potentially startling disclosures.

Amidst her usual duties and the extra load of her culinary role, Margaret found herself swamped. In a moment of over-whelmed distraction, she accidentally shattered several dishes while preparing meals, the clatter of broken porcelain amplifying the kitchen's already tense atmosphere. Lord Carrington, visibly agitated, roamed the manor's halls and chambers, his anxious behavior increasingly irking Lady Beatrice. Seeking solace from the looming, uneasy discussion, she attempted to immerse herself in reading, but the mental strain soon manifested as a debilitating headache. Acknowledging her need for respite, Lady Beatrice withdrew to her quarters, yearning for a haven from the escalating strain. Outside, Frank engaged in the meticulous task of buffing Lady Beatrice's sleek black Rolls

Royce, finding comfort in the methodical, familiar activity; while Samuel devoted his attention to caring for Blazer, Lady Beatrice's esteemed stallion.

Charlotte was eager to learn about the advancements in Mrs. Offley's case. At the same time, she sought an opportunity to converse with Lord Wharton, who had been absent throughout the day. He returned to Haddonford Manor just before Inspector Sinclair's arrival. Peering through the window, Charlotte noticed Lord Wharton parking his convertible. Eager for a brief exchange, she stepped into the hallway. However, her plans were thwarted when Lady Isabelle swiftly intercepted Lord Wharton. Upon seeing her fiancé, Lady Isabelle grasped the sleeve of his elegant black suit and hurriedly led him into the library, closing the door behind them. With no alternative, Charlotte headed to the Blue Room, awaiting the inspector's entrance.

In a short span, the room filled with Haddonford Manor's residents, each silently settling into the plush sofas and chairs. Lord Wharton and Lady Isabelle entered last, just moments before Inspector Sinclair and his assistant George, who looked visibly weary, made their entrance.

Clearing his throat, the inspector addressed the gathering, "As you may well be aware, Haddonford Manor has been the site of several distressing events recently. We are actively working to uncover any links between these occurrences. My main focus is to determine who is responsible for Rachel Offley's demise. It is important to note that everyone here is under scrutiny."

He paused, scanning the room to observe the reactions. "My initial engagement with Haddonford was prompted by a mysterious letter received by Lady Beatrice. The letter was typewritten, leading us to inspect the typewriter found in Lady Isabelle's room. However, the typing did not match."

Lady Isabelle, mesmerized by the stunning engagement ring adorning her finger, raised her head with a solemn expression that seemed to say, "I told you so."

"Additionally," the inspector proceeded, "while the letter itself was typed, the sender manually inscribed Lady Beatrice's address on the envelope. We compared this handwriting against samples from everyone here but found no match. The envelope lacked a return address, yet we managed to trace its origin to a post office in London. This, regrettably, led us to a standstill. Rest assured, I am far from conceding. There are various leads I am pursuing, which I cannot reveal at this stage. It's crucial to consider that the perpetrator may very well be among us." He paused, allowing his words to sink in.

Lady Beatrice couldn't contain herself and let out a loud exclamation, immediately covering her mouth with her hands. Lord Carrington tugged at his shirt collar, seeking relief from its constricting grip, and took a deep, steadying breath. Lady Isabelle, attempting to mask her irritation, shifted her attention from the engagement ring to the sparkling diamond bracelet on her left wrist. Margaret and Samuel wore expressions of terror, while Frank's true emotions remained ambiguous, his face a blank canvas hiding any reaction to the outrageous accusation that someone at Haddonford Manor could be responsible for his wife's untimely death.

The inspector proceeded, unfazed by the tense atmosphere, "An individual introduced poison into Lady Beatrice's sugar bowl. As far as we are aware, those assembled here were the sole occupants of Haddonford at the time."

"What about the intruder? Lady Isabelle claimed to have seen someone in her room on the eve of the tragedy," Lady Beatrice interjected reminding the inspector of this crucial detail.

"We are not dismissing the possibility of an intruder. However, until further notice, it is imperative that everyone remains within the confines of Haddonford Manor." With a respectful farewell salute, Inspector Sinclair concluded his statement and exited the room, followed closely by George.

Charlotte eagerly anticipated the chance to converse with Lord Wharton, keen to extract insights from his recent exchange with the police about the mysterious lady in black. Regrettably, the occupants of the Blue Room showed no inclination to disperse. The shadow of suspicion, cast by the inspector's insinuation implicating one among them in Rachel Offley's death, had effectively immobilized everyone there.

Internally, Charlotte wasn't taken aback by these allegations, yet she found herself grappling with pinpointing the main suspect. Each person appeared to harbor their own hidden secrets, and she was determined to unveil the concealed truths.

"Charlotte," Lord Wharton gestured, breaking the tense silence. "May I request your company in the library for a private dialogue?"

A deep sense of curiosity filled the room, yet no one ventured to question the nature of their secluded discussion. Lady Isabelle, seemingly aloof, continued to fiddle with her bracelet, her attention detached from the evolving conversation. Meanwhile, Charlotte, relieved by Lord Wharton's invitation, eagerly followed him into the library.

"For the time being, I chose to keep Inspector Sinclair out of our inquiries," Lord Wharton said once they were alone. "He has his own leads to pursue and introducing our findings might only complicate matters. Instead, I turned to George. I must commend him for his dedication to his profession and his commitment to upholding his reputation. He understands the importance of trust between colleagues, including the inspector. So, I approached George, ensuring he was comfortable with the request I had in mind, and thankfully, he was."

Charlotte leaned intently, eager for the details.

"George weighed the merits and drawbacks of my proposal with great care. However, I do believe that it was his personal encounter with Rachel on the morning of her untimely demise that profoundly impacted him, ultimately tipping the scales in our favor," Lord Wharton clarified. "He refrained from questioning our motives behind tracking down the cab driver. With just a handful of phone calls, he provided me with a name—Nicolas Frey.

Nonetheless, he reserved the right to inform Inspector Sinclair of my request if he deemed it necessary. It's important to bear in mind, though, that Nicolas might not be the individual we're looking for. Our uncertainties will only be resolved once we've had a chance to speak with him directly," he continued, outlining their next course of action.

"Did George inform you of Nicolas's whereabouts?" Charlotte inquired.

"Yes, he did. He suggested we avoid confronting Nicolas at work, given the sensitive nature of our inquiry. It seems more prudent to visit him at home, where the conversation can be more discreet and less pressured. It's likely he'll be more open and at ease there," Lord Wharton replied thoughtfully.

"That makes sense. So, when shall we go to see him?" Charlotte queried.

"That's up to you. What do you think?" he deferred to her judgment.

"How about tonight? Would that work?" Charlotte proposed, eager to move forward.

Lord Wharton glanced at the clock, noting that it was quarter past six.

"Tonight, is as good a time as any. We don't know Nicolas's schedule, and he may work mornings, evenings, or both. We'll discover the specifics once we reach his place."

"Wait," Charlotte interjected, her voice brimming with excitement. "Are we allowed to leave Haddonford? The inspector instructed everyone to remain here until further notice."

"I believe the inspector's intention was to restrict extended travel. However, brief trips to London and back shouldn't pose a problem. I'll personally take full responsibility if my interpretation of Inspector Sinclair's orders proves incorrect."

CHAPTER NINETEEN

Almost an hour later, they ascended the stairs of an aging apartment building. Nicolas's address indicated that he resided on the second floor. The building exhibited signs of neglect, with torn and peeling gray wallpaper lining the walls. The handrails were inadequately secured, leaning away from the steps, posing a risk to anyone daring enough to utilize them. The first floor was dimly lit, but a broken window on the second floor allowed the warm sunlight and fresh air to seep into the hallway. Nicolas's apartment door showcased a fresh coat of deep navy paint. Affixed to the door was a prominent number 21. Charlotte delicately ran her finger over the paint's surface, checking to see if it was still moist.

"I suppose the door wouldn't be closed if it wasn't dry," Lord Wharton commented with a hint of amusement.

"Indeed," Charlotte concurred with a smile as she raised her hand to deliver a knock.

The anticipation hung in the air as they waited, a seemingly eternal minute passing before the sound of approaching footsteps reached their ears. Finally, the door swung open, revealing a young girl, no more than ten years old. Vibrant red curls framed her face, accentuating her large green eyes and freckles that adorned her fair complexion.

"Are your mom or dad home?" Charlotte asked softly.

"My dad is asleep," the girl replied.

"And your mom?"

"Mom is at work."

"Is your dad's name Nicolas Frey?" Charlotte inquired.

"Yes," the girl confirmed, opening the door wider to invite Charlotte and Lord Wharton inside.

Uncertain of their next move, both hesitated. It would be awkward to wait inside if the father was asleep, but equally awkward to ask the young girl to wake him.

"I believe we may return at a different time," Charlotte suggested, and almost immediately, a male voice emanated from within the apartment.

"Ivy, who is it?"

"Two people are asking for you," the girl responded audibly, allowing her father to hear.

"How can I assist you folks?" a man in his thirties emerged from behind Ivy, clad in khaki pants and a rumpled, hastily buttoned-up long-sleeved shirt. His cropped, red hair mirrored his daughter's shade.

"We're looking for Nicolas Frey," Lord Wharton announced.

"That's me. What can I do for you? Is something wrong?" Nicolas inquired, stepping out of the apartment, and closing the door to shield his daughter from the conversation.

"Oh no, nothing's wrong," Charlotte reassured him. "We didn't mean to alarm you. We simply hope you can help us locate someone whom we believe you picked up from a funeral."

Nicolas let out a relieved sigh. "Phew! For a moment there, I thought there was an accident or something, and I was worried sick about my wife."

"I'm sincerely sorry," Charlotte responded with empathy. "That was not our intention. We are searching for a woman dressed in black who attended a funeral we were present at. She possesses information that could be of assistance to us."

Nicolas's eyes flickered between Charlotte and Lord Wharton, studying them intently. After a brief pause, he gave a nod and responded, "Can you give me a description of the woman? I'm just a regular cab driver, you know. I shuttle around loads of folks every day, and I don't usually pay much mind to who's sitting in the back, unless they're chatty or leave a lasting impression. I can't promise I'll recall the specific lady you're after, but I'll certainly give it my best shot."

"The woman we are searching for was present at the funeral of our dear friend. She was dressed entirely in black, as is customary for such occasions. Her figure was slender, and though she seemed to be youthful, it was difficult to tell her exact age as her face was veiled," Lord Wharton said. "We're unsure of how she arrived there, but we do know that she left supposedly in a cab."

Nicolas furrowed his brow, lost in deep contemplation as he absentmindedly rubbed the back of his head. Meanwhile, behind him, the door creaked open ever so slightly, revealing a curious green eye peering through the narrow gap.

"Ivy, you can come out now," Nicolas called out. In response, the red-haired girl emerged from her hiding place behind the door, stepping into view.

"I think I might have an idea of who you're talking about," Nicolas continued. "I got a call to pick up a lady from a funeral named Isabelle Mattingly. I parked the car and waited, but she never showed up. I was stuck, not knowing what to do. I couldn't just sit there all night, but I also didn't want to leave without trying to find her. So, I took a chance and wrote a note, which I handed to a lady who was tidying up the church pews. I asked her to track down Miss Isabelle, who was supposed to be at the funeral. She agreed to help, but I don't think she found her because when Miss Isabelle eventually appeared, she didn't mention the note or anything else. She simply hopped in the cab, and that was that."

Charlotte leaned in closer, her eyes intently studying Nicolas's face for clues. "Did she mention anything else, anything significant?" she asked, eager for more information.

Nicolas paused. "I can't recall her mentioning anything, to be honest," he finally replied. "It was a rather quiet ride. She seemed lost in her thoughts, and I respected that."

Charlotte and Lord Wharton exchanged glances, contemplating the information they had gathered. It appeared they were on the right track, yet there were still numerous unanswered questions.

"I see," Charlotte replied. "Did she give any indication about herself or the funeral she had just attended?"

Nicolas somberly shook his head. "No, like I said earlier, she stayed silent the whole time. Although I did notice in my rearview mirror that her veil was lifted, and she was in tears."

"And where did you drop her off?" Charlotte continued her inquiry.

"She asked to be taken to Selfridges on Oxford Street," Nicolas recalled. "Though she didn't seem in any state for shopping. She paid in cash, thanked me, and quickly left."

"What's Selfridges?" Ivy asked, joining the conversation.

Nicolas affectionately ruffled his daughter's hair, his expression softening.

"Selfridges is a grand, prestigious store in London, darling," he gently explained.

It was then that Lord Wharton interjected, reaching into his wallet to produce a generous amount of cash. "This is for Ivy," he declared, extending the bills towards Nicolas.

Nicolas initially hesitated, clearly taken aback by the gesture. "Oh, that's very kind of you, but—"

Lord Wharton interrupted gently, "You've been extremely helpful, Nicolas, and this is a token of our appreciation. I'm sure Ivy will enjoy a little treat from Selfridges," he said, handing over the money with a sincere smile.

Nicolas's face brightened with gratitude as he received the generous gift.

"It was my pleasure to assist. Do not hesitate to contact me if you need anything else," he offered sincerely.

"We appreciate your offer," Lord Wharton replied, as he and Charlotte made ready to depart, concluding their cordial visit with Nicolas and his daughter, Ivy, on a note of heartfelt thanks.

Chapter Twenty

"What's our next move?" Lord Wharton inquired, stealing a glance at Charlotte as they approached his convertible.

Charlotte, still a novice investigator and lacking experience in solving any murders, felt a rush of uncertainty flood over her at his question. She pondered the motivation behind his words. Was it his way of giving her more responsibility in this case, a sign of trust in her abilities? Or perhaps, it might be a selfish desire to escape the confines of his spoiled fiancée's company and spend some time with Charlotte in their shared pursuit of the truth behind Mrs. Offley's death.

As they both settled into the luxurious leather seats of the convertible Charlotte set aside the mystery of Lord Wharton's intentions and focused on his question.

"Maybe we should consult a phone book to track down Isabelle Mattingly?" she suggested carefully. "It's possible that she works at Selfridges. Otherwise, why would she specifically request the cab driver to drop her off there?"

Lord Wharton mulled over her words. "Perhaps she wanted to ensure that nobody at home would question her whereabouts or suspect that she had gone anywhere," he proposed, considering the possibilities.

"That's a valid point," Charlotte admitted, nodding in agreement. "However, it does raise a question. Given that she was dressed in black, wouldn't someone in her household find it peculiar for her to leave the house dressed as if she were attending a funeral?"

A playful smirk tugged at Lord Wharton's lips. "Well, that depends. Black can be a fashionable choice for many women. Besides, it's also plausible that she changed her outfit both before and after the funeral," he suggested, entertaining the idea.

Charlotte contemplated his reasoning and conceded, "You're right, that's definitely a possibility we shouldn't overlook. The cab driver did mention that Isabelle was visibly upset and even shed tears," Charlotte said. "This suggests a close connection to Mrs. Offley. Selfridges, being a busy place, can offer solace within the crowd. One can find a sense of anonymity amidst strangers, finding distraction from pain without attracting attention. Personally, I believe that in times of grief, it's comforting not to be alone if possible," Charlotte said sincerely, then added, "Do you have any knowledge of Mrs. Offley's relatives? Were there any individuals at the funeral who may have been connected to her in some way, perhaps a family member or a distant cousin?"

"I can't recall any relatives attending the funeral. I hate to admit it, but I don't know much about Rachel's past," Lord Wharton confessed. "There was never any mention of her parents, and I did not think to inquire. She relocated to Haddonford after marrying Frank. It was a small ceremony, attended by only three people."

"Let me guess, Lady Beatrice, Lord Carrington, and you?"

"You are close. I couldn't make it," Lord Wharton revealed. "I was abroad at the time and only found out about Rachel and Frank's wedding when I returned. I didn't even know Frank was seeing someone."

"That means you don't know how they met," Charlotte deduced.

"That's correct. Neither of them liked to discuss it."

Charlotte found it peculiar. "Isn't that strange?"

Lord Wharton raised an eyebrow, curious about her perspective. "Why do you find it strange?"

"It's often said that happily married couples relish recounting how they first met," Charlotte offered. "Sister Anna mentioned it to me, though I can't be certain of her expertise in such matters," she added in a softer tone. "Do you think it's possible there were problems in their marriage?"

Lord Wharton shook his head, dismissing any speculation. "No, they were genuinely happy together but preferred to keep their personal life private."

Charlotte's curiosity persisted. "Who was the third person at the wedding then?"

"Ah, that was my father."

"So, your father attended the wedding which means he knew Lord Carrington?"

"Yes, indeed," Lord Wharton confirmed. "Lord Carrington was an old friend of my mother's. When she got married, she introduced him to my father, and they remained close friends until my father's passing."

Charlotte inquired further, "When did he pass away?"

"About a year after Frank and Rachel's wedding," Lord Wharton replied somberly. "It was a heart attack. But getting back to the matter at hand, the woman we're looking for was clearly connected to Rachel. She maintained her distance, even from Frank. It suggests that she either didn't know him or didn't want him to know she was there. Either way, we need to find her and have a conversation."

"I wouldn't be surprised if she has a phone line. Almost everyone has one nowadays. Do you know where we can find a telephone directory?"

Lord Wharton pointed towards a bright red kiosk with a prominent crown emblem, representing the British government. "Over there."

Charlotte corrected him gently, "That's a phone booth, not a telephone directory."

Lord Wharton chuckled, "Yes, exactly. I need to make a phone call."

Charlotte trailed him to the red telephone booth, observing silently as he fished out a pen from his suit pocket and a business card from his wallet. Balancing the phone between his ear and shoulder, Lord Wharton skillfully wedged the card against the booth's glass pane, quickly jotting down notes. Despite the constriction of the booth and the awkward pose, his skillful handling was unmistakable. Moments later, he stepped out, a satisfied smile playing on his handsome face, signaling a successful call.

"Eureka!" he exclaimed triumphantly, extending the inscribed paper towards Charlotte.

Charlotte glanced at the neat writing on a card and couldn't hide her genuine surprise.

"I'm astonished to find just three Isabelle Mattingly listed in London. Considering it's quite a common name, we must be either incredibly fortunate or not every Isabelle Mattingly is listed in the phone directory. By the way, may I inquire whom you contacted to obtain this information?" she asked.

Lord Wharton smiled, "Margaret."

"Margaret?"

"Who else? I called Haddonford, and she was the one who answered the phone. Frank must have been out running errands for Mother or occupied with tasks around the Manor."

"I understand," Charlotte scrutinized the addresses listed on the card in her hand. "Are any of these addresses within walking distance of Selfridges?"

Lord Wharton shook his head. "Not at all, which suggests that our starting point tomorrow won't necessarily be determined by proximity."

"Tomorrow?" Charlotte's disappointment was palpable upon realizing the time had slipped away. The day had vanished swiftly, turning Inspector Sinclair's afternoon visit into a distant memory. It was too late for unexpected visits, both impolite and likely unproductive. Understanding the need for a positive first impression and giving people time to respond, Charlotte conceded that haste wouldn't align with their best interests, despite her eagerness to advance the investigation.

"You're right. It wouldn't be appropriate to show up on Isabelle's doorstep this late. But why did you call Margaret for the addresses if you knew we wouldn't be going anywhere today? We could have obtained information ourselves once we returned to Haddonford," Charlotte questioned.

Lord Wharton laughed and admitted, "That's true. I didn't check the time until after making the call. My timing was a bit off."

Chapter Twenty-One

IF CHARLOTTE HAD AT HER DISPOSAL magical abilities, she would have eagerly sped up the clock, desiring to bypass the languid pace of time. With each moment, her eagerness grew, making the wait seem interminable. Bound to a tight schedule, she recognized the unlikelihood of setting off with Lord Wharton any time before the latter part of the day.

However, her anticipation regarding the progress she and Lord Wharton were making was difficult to keep in check. Her mind frequently ventured to the trio of leads that might direct them to Isabelle, igniting a passion that relegated her customary estate duties to the background. Ignoring the risk that the Isabelles they had pinpointed might not be the one they were searching for, she entertained the thought that the elusive Isabelle could merely be visiting London, postponing any additional suppositions for the future. Determined not to be bogged down by early anxieties, Charlotte held the belief that dwelling on potential setbacks only serves to manifest those very concerns. Choosing to maintain a hopeful outlook, she remained assured that their thorough exploration would eventually lead them to Isabelle, unraveling her narrative in the process.

Charlotte mentally revisited the addresses, scrutinizing their potential. She found no compelling reason to prefer one over another—each seemed equally likely to guide them to the correct Isabelle. After thoughtful deliberation, she resolved to suggest the first address on the list: 102 Marsham Street in Westminster. Lord Wharton had no objections to starting from the top.

The journey to central London was swift, and as the clock struck 4:00 p.m., Marsham Street unfolded before them—a bustling thoroughfare, alive with activity yet pleasantly devoid of overwhelming crowds. The architecture of the buildings that lined the street presented a uniformity, each structure bearing a striking resemblance to its neighbor. On the second and third floors, cozy residential quarters provided homes to the city's inhabitants, while at street level, an array of small local businesses flourished. Charlotte and Lord Wharton meandered past a pub as well as a charming lighting store that showcased delicate fixtures in its display window. Their leisurely stroll led them to their desired destination, where a sign above the entrance proudly declared the establishment as "Sunlight Laundromat."

"This seems to be the place," Lord Wharton remarked.

Charlotte took a deep breath, attempting to contain her excitement. Lord Wharton swung open the door, and they entered the building. The expansive foyer greeted them with pristine cleanliness, accompanied by the refreshing scent of freshly laundered linen and lavender. Ajar, a door revealed what appeared to be a small office space.

"May I assist you?" a woman in her thirties rose from her chair behind a narrow desk, approaching them. Her lustrous blond hair was elegantly gathered in a ponytail, framing her porcelain cheeks.

"We are in search of Isabelle Mattingly," Lord Wharton declared.

"That would be me," she replied.

"I am Lord Wharton, and this is Charlotte."

"I am well aware of who you are," she responded with a warm smile. "I have come across your photographs in numerous newspapers. There was one recently featuring your engagement to

Lady Isabelle. I immediately noticed the shared name between us. She is simply delightful! I also recall another picture of you playing polo and one from the airport, although I can't recall your destination."

"I had just returned from India," Lord Wharton disclosed.

"Yes, indeed," Isabelle concurred. "We keep newspapers and magazines here for our customers, so I often browse through the pictures when I have a moment of boredom. And let me tell you, reporters adore you, so you needn't worry about your image."

Isabelle edged closer to Lord Wharton. Her short skirt accentuated her curves, and her fitted top revealed her décolletage.

"Now, what brings you here? If you're seeking someone to launder your shirts, I'd be more than happy to personally handle them."

"Thank you for the proposition," Lord Wharton responded, "however, our presence here is driven by another purpose. The inquiry I'm about to pose might seem unusual."

"Believe me, I've long ceased to find anything strange," she interjected before he had the chance to ask. "You wouldn't want me to delve into my childhood memories. Nothing you inquire about will shock me."

"In that case, could you inform us if you attended a funeral recently?"

"How recent are we talking?"

"A few days ago."

"The last funeral I attended was in the autumn. It was one of our cherished customers, a kind old lady. She always remembered my birthday and would bring me a gift every year. In fact, she even left me a small sum of money, which took me by surprise. I used to be a laundry girl here for many years, and now I am the owner of this establishment," she said, radiating a sense of pride. "But I sense that's not the story you were hoping to hear."

"The story you've shared is truly admirable. You're doing an exceptional job here, and it's evident that your customers are highly satisfied with the quality of your service," Lord Wharton praised.

"I can't complain. I receive excellent reviews, and my customers are loyal, which provides me with job security. When you're single, you rely on none but yourself," Isabelle replied. "But why exactly are you looking for Isabelle Mattingly?"

"Miss Mattingly attended the funeral of our friend, and we believe she might have information that could help us find answers to some pressing questions," Lord Wharton explained.

"I don't mean to pry," Isabelle interjected, "but how could she possibly assist you?"

"Our friend's death occurred under suspicious circumstances, and we're seeking any information that might lead us to her killer," Lord Wharton clarified.

Isabelle gasped, her eyes widening. "Are you suggesting that the Isabelle you're searching for may know the identity of the killer?"

"We don't have that knowledge, but we hope she can provide insights into our friend's past," Lord Wharton responded.

Isabelle pondered the situation. "I see," she mused. "So, your friend had a connection you, as her friends, were unaware of, and now you seek to meet that friend in order to learn more about their relationship. But what if this Isabelle is not a friend at all?" She turned her gaze toward Lord Wharton. "Just a thought. I'm certain you know what you're doing."

"Nevertheless, we appreciate your perspective," Lord Wharton expressed sincerely. "And we're grateful for the time you've taken to speak with us."

With that, he bid Isabelle farewell and proceeded toward the front door, with Charlotte following closely behind him.

"Wait," Isabelle called out, halting their departure. "I might be able to assist you. Actually, I think I can help you," she corrected herself. "Do you have any details about your Isabelle? Her age, physical appearance?"

"We only caught a glimpse of her from a distance," Lord Wharton replied. "She appeared tall and slender. Unfortunately, a veil obscured her face."

Isabelle nodded understandingly. "I'm not sure how many Isabelles are on your list, but I can confirm that you can eliminate one of them. My father's sister is Isabelle Mattingly," she revealed. "I was named after her. She resides on Alloa Road. She's nearly eighty years old, rarely ventures out, and spends her time working on puzzles and reading. While she possesses keen eyesight and a sharp mind, I highly doubt she is the person you're searching for. Aunt Isabelle relies on a cane when she does go out and, sadly, her physical appearance resembles a walking question mark."

CHAPTER TWENTY-TWO

CHARLOTTE MARVELED AT THE VIBRANT CITYSCAPE while driving toward Camden Town. The lively streets, each brimming with unique character, captured her imagination. With every turn, she envisioned alternate lives, wondering what it would be like to call London home. The city's allure was undeniable, filling her with empowerment and enchantment.

"Do you wish you lived here?" Lord Wharton's question caught Charlotte off guard. She glanced at him. He was focused on the road, steering the car effortlessly with one hand, his left elbow resting casually on the side. The convertible's top was down, letting the late afternoon sun glint off his Rolex.

"I'm not sure," Charlotte mused. "Being here just feels . . . right."

"Like you belong," Lord Wharton chimed in.

"Is it foolish to think so?" she asked.

"Not at all," Lord Wharton replied sincerely. "You have a strong spirit. Everything I know about you suggests you're not one for a mundane suburban life unless it's part of a bigger plan."

As they took a corner, Lord Wharton slowed down, giving way for a construction truck to cross, carefully threading his way through the parked vehicles. Once the path was clear, he increased their pace, steering them onto a more expansive road.

"Do you believe in the transmission of thoughts, the power of emotions, or a sixth sense?" he asked.

"Yes, I do," Charlotte nodded.

"Then maybe there's more to your feelings about London," he suggested. "Perhaps connections from your past experiences or your parents. We've discussed this before," he continued. "There's a deeper story hidden in St. Helen, but it will unfold when you're ready. Your heart will guide you on this journey."

Parking the car, they stepped out onto a cobblestone street lined with charming houses in soft pastels and earthy tones. Boys played soccer nearby, their laughter mixing with the chatter of young mothers rocking their strollers.

"I believe this is the place," Lord Wharton said, pointing to a modest two-story building ahead.

The drawn curtains as well as neglected potted flowers stationed near the weathered front door did not look promising. Charlotte ran up the steps and pressed the doorbell. The moments that followed felt like an eternity as they stood in anticipation, their ears attuned to the slightest indication of life within the dwelling: a hint of a creaking floorboard, the shuffling of feet, or the faintest whisper of a voice.

"Are you looking for the new owners?" a boy with a soccer ball in his hands approached them.

"We are looking for Isabelle Mattingly. Isn't this her residence?" Charlotte asked.

"Are you asking if she lives here?" the boy clarified.

"Yes," Charlotte replied.

"Nope, she moved. A new family bought this house, but they haven't moved in yet," the boy explained.

A wave of disappointment washed over Charlotte, but she swiftly pushed it aside.

The boy placed the soccer ball on the ground and kicked it enthusiastically towards his friends, who cheered and quickly joined in, passing the ball between them with their feet.

"Do you happen to know her new address?" Charlotte asked.

"Of course!" the boy replied, masking his disappointment with Charlotte's question. "Everyone knows everything here. My mom always says we're like a big family, and family sticks together and supports each other," he said proudly.

"Your mom is absolutely right," Charlotte agreed warmly. "Could you please let us know the specific address where she moved?"

"Sure thing!" the boy pointed towards the houses at the end of the street. "You see that house with the hanging flowerpots on the first-floor windows? The ones with the yellow flowers? There's also a big bush near the front door. Mr. Mattingly trimmed it the other day."

Charlotte followed the direction of his finger and quickly located the house he described.

"That must be Mrs. Mattingly's new home," she confirmed with a sense of gratitude in her voice. "Your mom is very wise, and we truly appreciate your help."

The boy beamed with pride and skipped away to rejoin his teammates.

Charlotte and Lord Wharton continued their walk, heading in the direction of Isabelle's new residence. As they passed by young mothers pushing strollers, Charlotte couldn't help but notice their gaze lingering on the striking figure of Lord Wharton. He courteously acknowledged their presence with a nod of his head.

The houses at the end of the street appeared larger and more modern. Charlotte pondered the boy's remark about the tight-knit neighborhood where families supported one another, contemplating if this was one of the reasons Isabelle chose to stay in the area. However, she acknowledged that there could be numerous other factors influencing Isabelle's decision to purchase a home on the same street.

"Shall we?" Lord Wharton glanced at Charlotte, and upon her nod, he knocked on the door. Within moments, a woman in her mid-thirties opened it. She stood tall and slender, her chestnut hair elegantly pinned in a bun. Wearing a navy pencil skirt and a crisp white shirt, she exuded an air of poise. The instant Charlotte laid eyes on her, she knew with certainty that this was the same woman who had attended Mrs. Offley's funeral.

"May we have a word with you?" Charlotte asked politely.

"I'm not sure if I can be of assistance," the woman responded cautiously.

"A few days ago, you were present at the funeral of our friend, and we would like to ask you a couple of questions," Charlotte continued and almost immediately she noticed a flicker of panic cross the woman's face, but she quickly composed herself.

"I'm afraid you have mistaken me for someone else," she replied.

"Honey, who's at the door?" a baritone voice called from inside the house.

"No one. Wrong house," she replied, her tone hurried. "I'm sorry, I can't help you. I have to leave now." With that, she swiftly shut the door.

Surprised by her reaction Charlotte and Lord Wharton were left with no choice but to walk back to the car. The street had filled with people going about their evening activities. Several guys gathered around a gray truck, examining something under the hood. Two girls swung a rope in a circle, while their friends took turns jumping over it.

"What do you think she's afraid of?" Charlotte pondered aloud.

"Or rather, who is she afraid of?" Lord Wharton responded with a question of his own.

The sun was setting, casting a warm glow across the sky. Despite the cloudless appearance, the air felt muggy and hot, reminiscent of the calm before a thunderstorm. Lord Wharton undid the top button of his shirt and removed his tie, appearing more relaxed and oddly attractive. Charlotte forced herself to avert her gaze.

"She certainly didn't want her husband to know about our visit," Charlotte remarked, leaning against Lord Wharton's convertible. He stood so close that she caught a whiff of his cologne.

"If my assumptions about her husband are correct, then perhaps we'll have better luck speaking to her elsewhere," Lord Wharton suggested.

"Yes, but where?" Charlotte asked.

"We can try Selfridges later this week. I noticed the embroidered 'Selfridges' logo on her suit jacket hanging in the hallway when she opened the door."

Charlotte felt a wave of relief as she grasped the truth. Isabelle's employment at one of London's grandest and busiest department stores both worried and inspired her. The bustling atmosphere of such crowded places made them seem less intimidating, increasing the likelihood that Isabelle would be willing to share her story. However, the sheer size of Selfridges posed a challenge, making it difficult to locate her within the immense store.

"Hey!" a voice called out. Charlotte turned to see the same boy who had guided them to Isabelle Mattingly's new home standing a few feet away.

"Hey!" he repeated louder to ensure both Charlotte and Lord Wharton heard him. "Did you find Mrs. Mattingly?"

"Yes, we did, thanks to you," Lord Wharton acknowledged, turning toward the boy.

The boy flashed a satisfied grin.

"Mrs. Mattingly works at Selfridges, right?" Lord Wharton asked, and the boy nodded enthusiastically.

"Do you happen to know which department?"

"No," the boy replied, before darting off.

"Well, it was worth a try," Lord Wharton remarked, a hint of disappointment in his voice.

CHAPTER TWENTY-THREE

SINCE THE CONVERSATION WITH ISABELLE HAD to be postponed until the end of the week due to Lord Wharton's schedule, Charlotte decided to shift her focus to Haddonford Manor and its residents. Numerous unanswered questions lingered, urging Charlotte to clear her mind and approach her investigation more strategically.

Finding a spare moment, she locked her bedroom door and retrieved a pen and a leather-bound notebook from her writing desk. She swiftly began jotting down the names of everyone she had encountered since arriving at Haddonford Manor. Lady Beatrice claimed the first spot on the list, followed by Margaret, Frank, Lord Carrington, Lord Wharton, Lady Isabelle, and Samuel. Warm memories of Lord Carrington surfaced as she recalled her first meeting with him. Her friendship with Margaret and Samuel continued to strengthen, and she thought fondly of both. Although she hadn't interacted with Frank extensively, Charlotte sensed a kind and loyal heart beneath his seemingly unapproachable exterior. Lady Isabelle, on the other hand, evoked a mix of negative emotions that Charlotte tried to suppress. As for Lord Wharton, her feelings were a blend of complexity and growing fondness. Even now, she longed for his presence in the room as she went over the list of suspects.

"Suspects!" Charlotte examined the list of names, keenly aware of her scant knowledge regarding the history of each person listed. Before her lay eight individuals, each possibly harboring a secret dark enough to commit murder. With a pen twirling between her fingers, she pondered, then decisively added another name—George. A pang of guilt accompanied the action as she considered his role as night guard at Haddonford Manor, a position that might have afforded him the chance to interfere with the sugar bowl under the cover of darkness. Although Charlotte grappled with understanding why anyone would target Mrs. Offley, she opted to keep all names under scrutiny, making a singular exception for Lord Wharton. His actions had earned her confidence, leading her to exclude him as a suspect. With a firm motion, she struck his name from the list, solid in her judgment.

At first glance, the inhabitants of Haddonford Manor seemed unlikely candidates for murder, but who was Charlotte to claim expertise in human behavior? Her existence had been confined within the walls of St. Helen, sheltered from the outside world by Mother Superior and the nuns. Her understanding of humanity was derived solely from the pages of books, lacking the firsthand experiences that could have provided her with deeper insights. The books she had read conveyed that humans were complex beings, capable of both kindness and cruelty. If that were indeed the truth, then under certain circumstances, anyone within the confines of Haddonford Manor could have committed such a heinous act.

Disrupted by the echo of footsteps drawing nearer, Charlotte's focus splintered. An unidentified individual was traversing the corridor just outside her room, compelling her to sharpen her senses in an effort to trace the source of the noise. These footsteps methodically bypassed the sleeping quarters of Lady Beatrice and Lady Isabelle, moving toward the West Wing. In a rapid gesture, Charlotte stashed her journal in the deepest recess of her desk drawer and moved toward the door. Opening it slightly, she surveyed the hallway; it was empty, yet the diminishing sound of footsteps lingered in the air. Compelled by curiosity, Charlotte decided to follow the mysterious visitor, who seemed to glide with ease through the darkened corridors of Haddonford Manor, as if they were well acquainted with its secrets. The footsteps suddenly ceased, suggesting the stranger had stopped, perhaps sensing a follower. Charlotte held her breath, hiding her presence in the darkness, her heart thudding loudly against the silence. As seconds turned to minutes, her anxiety swelled, until the footsteps resumed, leaving a haunting quiet in their wake.

Charlotte quietly slipped off her shoes for silence and resumed her cautious advance. She navigated past several closed doors, drawing closer to a room that eerily mirrored Lady Beatrice's favorite Blue Room. Charlotte felt a chill creep down her spine as the silhouette by the window gradually came into focus, morphing into a ghostly form. It was as if the figure had sensed her presence, for it began to pivot slowly towards her. A surge of panic washed over Charlotte, so intense that it threatened to wrench a scream from her throat. Instinctively, her hand flew to her mouth, stifling the sound before it could escape. Her eyes, wide and filled with fear, remained locked onto those of the mysterious figure.

"What are you doing here?" he inquired in astonishment.

"I followed you," Charlotte confessed as she finally took hold of her emotions.

"I can see that, but why?" he asked.

"I didn't know it was you in the hallway. I heard footsteps and thought they belonged to . . ." Charlotte's words trailed off.

"The killer?" he interjected, seeking clarification.

"Yes," Charlotte affirmed. Her hand extended towards the wall and flickered the light switch. Brilliant beams of light emanated from two sparkling crystal candelabras.

Lord Carrington shielded his eyes with his right hand, momentarily overwhelmed by the sudden brightness. "Goodness, Charlotte, this is quite intense."

"Yes, but I prefer it to being left in the dark," she responded.

Lord Carrington offered a lighthearted quip, "Literally or figuratively?"

"Both," Charlotte replied, her voice tinged with a mix of seriousness and wry humor.

Lord Carrington fell silent. "You know you shouldn't be here," he finally uttered. "Following a stranger in the dark, alone, is not a prudent choice. You were fortunate it turned out to be me this time. However, luck may not always be on your side."

"Why are you here, Lord Carrington?" Charlotte inquired.

"First, let's find a seat," he suggested. "I need a moment to collect myself. I'm too old for this level of excitement."

"Of course," Charlotte agreed, offering her assistance as she guided him toward the couch.

Lord Carrington took a few minutes to rest before he continued. "I'm feeling better now. Where were we?"

"I had asked you why you were here," Charlotte reminded him.

"Ah, yes. You see, it's not advisable to leave me alone with my thoughts. The events of the past weeks took a toll on me. I'm sure you can sense it," he confessed. "While Beatrice has entrusted everything to the police, I grew tired of waiting. I decided to commence my own investigation."

"But why choose the West Wing?" Charlotte asked.

"Well, I have to start somewhere, and I chose to begin from the very beginning," Lord Carrington replied thoughtfully. "The West Wing used to hold a special place in my heart at Haddonford."

"What changed that?" Charlotte asked.

Lord Carrington's eyes flickered with a hint of sorrow. "Life and the unexpected turns it took," he responded melancholically.

A few minutes passed in silence before Lord Carrington raised his head, acknowledging Charlotte's presence with a weary smile on his face.

"Do you believe that the West Wing holds answers to Mrs. Offley's murder?" Charlotte asked.

"Rachel?" he exclaimed, surprised by her question.

"When you mentioned your own investigation, I assumed you were referring to Mrs. Offley's murder," she clarified.

Lord Carrington averted his gaze. "Rachel's death is undeniably tragic," he said. "I'm not sure if this will be of any help to the investigation, but I once caught Margaret sneaking out of Haddonford. She appeared hurried, and I had no knowledge of her destination. It wasn't her day off, that much I can say."

"Where did you see her?" Charlotte inquired.

"I happened to be near a window," Lord Carrington recalled, taking a moment to reflect. "It was after dinner, around 7:30 in the evening. I spotted her heading towards the stables, but she vanished from my sight shortly after. It was about a week ago or so. I initially dismissed it as insignificant, but now I believe it may be crucial to solving the case," Lord Carrington admitted.

Charlotte rose from the couch and moved closer to the window, her mind racing with possibilities. Parting the curtain slightly, she gazed outside. The stables stood to the right, and a gravel path encircled the beautiful brick structure that housed Lady Beatrice's stallion.

"Lord Carrington must have been standing at this very window when he spotted the maid," Charlotte thought to herself.

Bringing her attention back to the conversation, she asked, "How well do you know Margaret?"

"I'm afraid I hardly know her at all," Lord Carrington confessed. "Beatrice hired her. I met Margaret during one of my visits to Haddonford Manor. I don't interfere with Beatrice's decisions. She is the owner of this place, and I'm just an old friend who sometimes feels the weight of loneliness and seeks companionship. Without Beatrice, my life would have lost its meaning years ago. My advice to you, Charlotte, is to cherish the friendships you forge now, because someday, God forbid, they may be all you have left in life."

There was a genuine sadness in Lord Carrington's voice. "Richard is a remarkable young man. I've known him since the moment he took his first breath. On that day, I almost didn't make it. Beatrice sent Frank to fetch me as soon as she knew she was in labor. Frank drove like a madman, without a moment's rest, to ensure I arrived on time. Beatrice's father and husband were already there. When the doctor finally brought Richard out, wrapped in a soft blanket, I saw a glimmer of light in the dark tunnel I had been traversing for so long," Lord Carrington reminisced fondly. "Why am I sharing this with you, Charlotte?" He seemed momentarily puzzled before remembering. "Ah, yes, Richard. He is a friend I would cherish for life."

"Are you giving me advice?" Charlotte asked puzzled.

"Take it any way you want," Lord Carrington sighed.

Returning to the couch, Charlotte sat at the edge and carefully phrased her next question, "Was Lady Beatrice's mother present when Lord Wharton was born?"

Lord Carrington shook his head solemnly. "No, she had passed away years before."

"I've noticed only a few portraits of her around Haddonford Manor, mostly in the West Wing," Charlotte remarked.

"Indeed, that is correct," Lord Carrington confirmed. "Beatrice was very young when her mother died. I believe she was around three years old."

Curiosity burning within her, Charlotte pressed further. "How did she die?"

A shadow crossed Lord Carrington's face. "Some doors must remain closed, my friend. Do you recall the story of Pandora's box from Greek mythology? Pandora's curiosity led her to open a container entrusted to her husband, unleashing both physical and emotional suffering upon humanity. I am unwilling to tread that path. History has taught us a lesson that we all must heed," he concluded firmly.

While Charlotte vehemently disagreed with Lord Carrington's stance, she held herself back, recognizing that now was not the right moment to challenge him. Lord Carrington seemed guarded, and it was clear he was not yet ready to share the full truth.

CHAPTER TWENTY-FOUR

CHARLOTTE EXPERIENCED A SENSE OF GRATIFICATION upon learning that Lord Carrington's investigation had led him to the West Wing, just as it had led her. While she couldn't determine the precise correlation, she couldn't rid herself of the nagging notion that the wing held some connection, perhaps not directly to Mrs. Offley's murder, but to a secret guarded by Lady Beatrice and Lord Carrington. Uncertain whether Lord Wharton was privy to this information, Charlotte seized the chance to extract it from him while he was finally free to drive to Selfridges.

Charlotte was enchanted by the winding path. Each excursion through this landscape left her marveling at the countryside's beauty. The foliage on the trees transitioned, heralding the arrival of fall. A kaleidoscope of green melded with amber hues and intermittent bursts of scarlet. Fall was dear to her, awaited with eagerness for its magnificence each year, even as a subtle sorrow crept in with summer's farewell. Mindful of Charlotte's wish to savor the surroundings, Lord Wharton slowed their travel, adopting a more relaxed speed. With plenty of time before reaching the city, Charlotte relished the chance to unwind and absorb the breathtaking scenes from her seat.

"Haddonford Manor is a magnificent place," Charlotte commented. "Its surroundings are truly spectacular. You must consider yourself fortunate to have grown up here."

A smile formed on Lord Wharton's lips as he responded, "I suppose it would be more accurate to say that I am fortunate my mother resides here, allowing me to enjoy my visits."

"I believe you might have mentioned that before," she remarked. "When Lady Beatrice hired me, my mind was overwhelmed. Each day brought new faces and job responsibilities to grasp. Initially, it was quite challenging to keep up with the influx of information. However, I have reached a point where I can start piecing everything together. Still, there are a few gaps that remain."

"Ah, and what might those gaps be?" Lord Wharton inquired.

"One example would be the West Wing," Charlotte explained. "It appears to be unoccupied, yet Lord Carrington mentioned it used to be his favorite part of Haddonford."

"Did he now?" Lord Wharton's brow furrowed, displaying a hint of contemplation. "To the best of my recollection, Mother never utilized the West Wing. Perhaps Lord Carrington was referring to their younger days. They have known each other for what seems like an eternity. I'm not certain of the exact duration, but their acquaintance predates her marriage to my father."

"Do you happen to know anything about your grandmother?" Charlotte asked another question.

"Why are we discussing my grandmother?" Lord Wharton turned his head, locking eyes with Charlotte.

"I'm not entirely sure," Charlotte replied. "It's just that Lord Carrington refused to divulge any information about her."

"That's peculiar," Lord Wharton mused. "Strange that he would be reluctant to speak about someone he never knew. My grandmother passed away when my mother was only three years old."

"How did she die?" Charlotte inquired.

"I always believed it was due to health complications," Lord Wharton replied.

"I happened to come across her portrait in the West Wing," Charlotte confessed. "And just to clarify, I wasn't snooping around . . ."

"I know you weren't," Lord Wharton reassured her. "You need not explain yourself, Charlotte. When I was a child, I used to embark on exploratory adventures in the West Wing myself. Mother disapproved and assigned Frank to keep an eye on me. Nevertheless, I would still find ways to sneak out when Frank was occupied or during the silent hours of the night when everyone else was asleep," Lord Wharton chuckled. "It was the most exhilarating part of my visits to Haddonford."

"Did your mother reside there at the time?" Charlotte probed further.

"No, it was my grandfather who lived there. Mother moved back to Haddonford after his passing," Lord Wharton explained.

"I see," Charlotte remarked, realizing that Lord Wharton possessed limited knowledge about Haddonford's past. It appeared that Lady Beatrice, Lord Carrington, and perhaps Frank were the keyholders to the secrets concealed within the mysterious West Wing.

Around ten minutes to ten, Lord Wharton parked his car within a short walking distance of Selfridges. Both he and Charlotte found themselves uncertain about where to begin their search. Isabelle Mattingly could potentially be working anywhere within the vast confines of this renowned establishment.

The previous night, Charlotte had taken the initiative to acquaint herself with Selfridges, studying its history and familiarizing herself with the building's layout. Designed by the esteemed American architect Daniel Burnham, Selfridges had opened its doors in 1909. Each floor within the building boasted its distinct charm, catering to women, men, children, and household goods respectively. Locating Isabelle was almost an impossible task; however, Charlotte's determination remained firm, and she felt relieved to observe that Lord Wharton displayed no signs of surrendering.

As they stood at the street corner, surveying the size of the building, a glimmer of excitement danced in his eyes. It was evident that he relished the challenge that lay before them.

"Do you propose we divide the floors or work our way up together?" Charlotte asked, turning to Lord Wharton.

"Let's stay together. Having two pairs of eyes will be more advantageous. Moreover, if one of us locates Isabelle, they will have the task of finding the other among this labyrinthine space," he said extending his hand to Charlotte in preparation for traversing the bustling Oxford Street. Without hesitation, she accepted his gesture. There was a certain comfort in his sturdy presence and self-assured demeanor that Charlotte found herself appreciating.

The first few hours seemed to fly by as they navigated through the crowds, discreetly casting glances at every woman who appeared to be a store employee. The men's clothing and accessories section yielded no results; Isabelle Mattingly was either not working there or absent on that particular Thursday. The women's handbag and shoe departments were also checked off the list.

"You do realize that eventually we'll need to make a purchase here," Lord Wharton remarked. "Start thinking about what you need."

"Me?" Charlotte raised an eyebrow. "I don't need anything."

"Then what do you want?" he persisted.

"Nothing," Charlotte replied simply.

"Come on, Charlotte," Lord Wharton stopped and turned to face her. "Any other woman would give me a list of desired items. And you're telling me you don't want a single thing from Selfridges?"

"I truly don't," Charlotte insisted.

"Well, security might start getting suspicious. We've been wandering the store for hours without buying anything. We should at least make an investment, out of respect for this place," Lord Wharton chuckled.

"Fine, then you choose," Charlotte conceded.

Taking a deep breath, Lord Wharton once again clasped Charlotte's hand in his and led the way towards the jewelry display. Charlotte struggled to keep up, but holding hands prevented them from being separated by the stream of customers moving in the opposite direction. Making their way against the current was a challenging task, yet once they arrived at the dazzling array of diamond rings, necklaces, and earrings, they found themselves frozen in awe. It wasn't the precious gemstones that captured their attention, but rather the person behind the display. Isabelle stood there, clad in an elegant black suit with a white ruffled shirt that accentuated her slender figure. Bending down to examine the jewelry item a customer was pointing at, she retrieved a small key from a stretch band on her left wrist and unlocked the display case. With utmost care, she retrieved the desired piece and placed it on a small tray before the middle-aged gentleman, who scrutinized the intricate details of the marquise diamond ring. However, something about the ring failed to meet his expectations, leading him to return it to Isabelle. Stepping aside, he allowed Lord Wharton and Charlotte to take his place in front of the glass display case.

As Isabelle realized the identities of her next customers, her face turned pale. Trapped, she looked at them with a helpless expression, resembling a cornered animal.

"How may I assist you?" she managed to utter weakly, her voice blending with the hum of the crowd, making it difficult for Charlotte and Lord Wharton to discern her words.

"We would like to see a couple of diamond necklaces," Lord Wharton replied casually.

Isabelle's hands trembled as she laid out a few exquisite strands of the finest jewelry before him. Lord Wharton swiftly assessed each piece and selected one for Charlotte to examine—a stunning diamond solitaire pendant in platinum.

"What do you think about this one?" he inquired.

"It's beautiful," Charlotte responded. "But it must be quite expensive."

Lord Wharton smiled and stepped closer to Charlotte, gently placing the pendant on her graceful neck.

"Enjoy it, Charlotte," he said sincerely.

Blushing, she quickly averted her gaze.

"Miss Mattingly, we need to talk to you," Lord Wharton addressed Isabelle, his attention shifting. "Please believe me when I say that you might be the only person who can help us solve the murder of someone dear to us. We won't take up much of your time, and you won't have to answer any questions you're uncomfortable with."

Charlotte anxiously observed Isabelle's reaction, relieved to see her listening intently.

"I know you were close to Rachel; otherwise, you wouldn't have gone through the trouble of attending the funeral. Please, help us," Lord Wharton pleaded.

"My break is in about 20 minutes. There's a food hall on the ground floor that serves tea. I'll meet you there," Isabelle finally agreed.

Charlotte was flooded with mixed emotions upon receiving Lord Wharton's unexpected gift. The exquisite pendant was unlike anything she had ever owned, and she was thrilled, yet a whirlwind of questions swirled in her mind. How could she explain this lavish piece to Lady Isabelle, who was bound to notice it? Was accepting such a gift even a prudent decision? Charlotte wondered about Lord Wharton's intentions: Did he buy the pendant as a favor to Isabelle, to sell a high-value item from Selfridges, or was it simply an obligation to purchase something? Moreover, she questioned her interpretation of the moment their eyes met. Was she projecting her own feelings onto him, seeing a connection that might not exist? And crucially, what were her true feelings towards Lord Wharton? Amidst these reflections, Charlotte realized she was getting ahead of herself. She needed to concentrate on the present, especially with the impending conversation. Pushing confusing thoughts aside, she focused on the immediate priority: Isabelle had agreed to speak with them.

The food hall within the well-known Selfridges was unusually tranquil and notably sparse of patrons. Tables, elegantly draped in flawless white tablecloths and decorated with diminutive vases bursting with fresh flowers, were strategically dispersed throughout the space. Lord Wharton selected a table nestled in a secluded corner. This spot provided a comforting semblance of privacy, yet it maintained visibility, ensuring that they remained within sight of any newcomers venturing into the quaint, charming area designated for tea and pastries. It didn't take long for Isabelle to spot them.

"We appreciate you agreeing to meet with us, Miss Mattingly," Lord Wharton began.

"Please, call me Isabelle," she replied nervously, tucking her bangs behind her ear, and perching on the edge of the chair Lord Wharton pulled out for her.

"Isabelle," he smiled, attempting to put her at ease. "I want to assure you that this conversation will remain confidential among the three of us."

Tears welled up in Isabelle's eyes, and she nodded gratefully.

"How did you find out about Rachel's funeral?" he inquired.

"I saw it in the newspaper."

"Were you close to her?"

A tear rolled down Isabelle's cheek, and she delicately wiped it away with a snow-white handkerchief.

"Yes, we were very close . . . years ago."

"But not recently?"

"No, we went our separate ways after Rachel got married and moved out. But I always held fond memories of her. She was my only friend, and the only person who truly cared about me," Isabelle confessed.

"Why didn't you stay in touch then?" Lord Wharton inquired.

"It was a mutual decision, mostly mine. I wanted a fresh start and was terrified of anyone around me discovering the circumstances under which I met Rachel," Isabelle explained.

Lord Wharton's gaze remained fixed on Isabelle, waiting for her to continue.

"I felt guilty about it, but Rachel understood why I had to do it. My husband doesn't know about me attending the funeral or about my past, and I intend to keep it that way," she pleaded, looking up at Lord Wharton.

"Yes, of course. As I promised earlier, our meeting and everything you share with us will remain confidential," he reassured her. "Can you tell us how you met Rachel?"

Isabelle hesitated briefly before answering, "We met at Westling House."

Charlotte had never heard of this place and glanced at Lord Wharton, attempting to gauge his reaction, but his expression remained neutral as he focused on Isabelle.

"Rachel was the cook there, and a remarkable one at that. I had never taken much interest in food until I tasted her dishes," Isabelle reminisced.

Charlotte could empathize with that sentiment, recalling her first meal at Haddonford, which had been delectable and unforgettable.

"Over the years, Rachel and I became close friends. We would talk about everything—life, favorite recipes, places we hoped to visit one day," Isabelle continued. "But then she met her future husband and left. I missed her terribly, and we stayed in touch for a while, but eventually, I severed those ties."

"Why?" Lord Wharton probed.

"I left Westling House, found a job, and got married," Isabelle explained.

"But why keep Westling House a secret?" Lord Wharton pressed further.

"I didn't want anyone to know that I had been a patient there," Isabelle revealed.

Chapter Twenty-Five

"**W**HAT'S WESTLING HOUSE?" CHARLOTTE INQUIRED AS they found themselves alone.

"I'll show you," Lord Wharton replied mysteriously. "If you're up for it."

Charlotte pondered the proposition for a moment. Large stores filled with an array of items on display tended to overwhelm and overstimulate her. After the emotionally exhausting search for Isabelle at Selfridges, she felt completely drained. Nevertheless, her curiosity outweighed her exhaustion. She yearned to uncover the secrets of Westling House. With a nod of agreement, she followed Lord Wharton to his car.

Charlotte settled into the plush leather seat, deciding to embrace the journey. The convertible's top was down, and she relished the cool evening breeze gently tousling her hair. She closed her eyes, feeling her body relax, and the journey unfolded smoothly. Charlotte found herself drifting towards sleep but, determined to stay awake, she opened her eyes to observe the changing landscape. The clusters of houses gradually faded, replaced by isolated structures as residential areas vanished into the distance.

"If you'd like, you can take a nap," Lord Wharton offered, his voice calm and reassuring. "I'll wake you when we arrive."

Charlotte watched the sun dip below the horizon, its warm glow casting a golden hue over the landscape. The absence of residential homes added to the growing air of mystery.

"We should be there soon," Lord Wharton assured her, his tone confident.

As darkness enveloped them, the car's headlights pierced the night, illuminating only the road ahead. The periphery remained shrouded in shadows. Charlotte glanced in the side mirror, expecting to see other vehicles, but they were alone on this secluded stretch of road.

Feeling the significance of their journey, Charlotte sat up straighter in her seat, her anticipation growing. When they reached a fork in the road, Lord Wharton paused.

Let's head back to locate a marker," he proposed, maneuvering the vehicle into reverse.

"Have we gone off course?" Charlotte inquired, her tone laced with worry.

"Not precisely," Lord Wharton responded, "however, we must seek out a directional marker for our intended route." His gaze met hers. "Could you assist in keeping watch?"

Agreeing with a nod, Charlotte scanned the enveloping gloom. Suddenly, her eyes caught sight of something.

"Over there!" she declared, gesturing towards a timeworn post with barely discernible signs.

"Westling Hospital," the words barely legible on the eroded surface, suggested they veer left. Lord Wharton adjusted the gears, guiding them back to the divergence in their path. Opting for the less traveled, serpentine road on the left, they ventured further into unfamiliar territory.

"Is this path the right one?" Charlotte asked.

"This is new for me as well, yet the marker instructed a leftward direction," he assured. The roadway unfolded under a vault of ancient foliage, forming a natural tunnel. Overhead, branches intertwined like skeletal hands. A gentle gust rustled the leaves, their shadows dancing under the lunar glow. In the distance, an imposing bird sailed across the sky, wings widespread in silent flight.

"What creature is that?" Charlotte queried, mesmerized by its flight.

"It's an owl. The best time to spot them is either at dawn or dusk. We're in their territory, and this is when they're most active," Lord Wharton explained. "Would you like me to put the car's top up?"

"No, I'll be fine. Hopefully, we're almost there," Charlotte replied, mustering her courage.

"We are," Lord Wharton confirmed as he pulled into a grassy area.

Shielded by a dense barrier of tangled undergrowth, Charlotte and Lord Wharton remained hidden from the prying eyes of the imposing old mansion in the distance. Its Gothic-style architecture casted elongated shadows in the darkness. The façade was adorned with pointed arches and menacing gargoyles. The enlarged windows, while allowing for ample light, also acted as watchful eyes, observing the grounds with an air of silent vigilance. Charlotte's gaze shifted to the gargoyles, their grotesque forms adding an unsettling touch to the mansion's exterior. Though aware of their practical purpose as rainwater spouts, Charlotte couldn't help but acknowledge their secondary function—guardians that invoked fear in any unwelcome visitors.

"Why are we parked so far away? And what exactly is this place?" Charlotte whispered.

"I don't want to reveal our presence just yet," Lord Wharton explained in a hushed tone. "Westling House, also known as Westling Hospital, is a psychiatric facility specializing in the treatment of mental disorders such as depression, schizophrenia, and bipolar disorder."

Charlotte gasped; her eyes fixed on the hauntingly captivating building as she absorbed every detail.

"I can understand why Isabelle wanted to keep her time here a secret," she remarked with empathy. "She must have feared being ostracized if anyone found out."

"Yes, her job could have been jeopardized. Once people discover that you were a patient at a psychiatric facility, they often construct their own narratives, adding all sorts of twists and turns, turning you into an antagonist," Lord Wharton lamented. "Regrettably, they begin to believe the stories they've concocted in their minds, often depriving individuals like Isabelle the chance to share their own experiences."

"Isabelle must have despised being here," Charlotte whispered. "Wait, I realize I'm constructing my own narrative about this place," she said, shaking her head.

"Isabelle did mention that Rachel was her only friend, which suggests that she wasn't happy here. However, that doesn't necessarily imply mistreatment. It's possible that Westling Hospital appears different in the daylight," Lord Wharton suggested.

"I highly doubt it," Charlotte replied, studying the structure. "Why do you think the entire third floor is shrouded in darkness?"

"It could be designated office space," Lord Wharton offered.

"Do you think some of the staff actually live here?" Charlotte speculated.

"I have no clue, Charlotte. Your guess is as good as mine," Lord Wharton admitted.

"This place is quite far from London, making it difficult for employees to commute daily," Charlotte said. "I imagine at least some of them reside under the same roof as the patients."

"Perhaps, but why does it matter?" Lord Wharton inquired.

"I'm simply trying to understand the dynamics of this place," Charlotte explained. "If Rachel and Isabelle met here, then it's plausible that Rachel also encountered Frank in this setting."

"Possible, but we must remember that employees have time off. They could have met in town," Lord Wharton reasoned. "Isabelle only briefly mentioned Frank, and the way she spoke of him gave me the impression that she didn't know him well."

"I had the same impression," Charlotte agreed. "Even if Frank visited Westling Hospital regularly, Isabelle might not have crossed paths with him. Given the size of the building, which likely houses at least a hundred patients and employees, there could be someone here who held a grudge against Rachel and wanted her dead."

"Or someone with a vendetta against Frank and sought to harm him," Lord Wharton added. "Frank had two women in his life whom he deeply cared about—Mother and Rachel. Harming either of them would devastate him."

"We need to find a way to gain access to this place," Charlotte proposed.

Lord Wharton regarded her with curiosity.

"I don't mean breaking in," Charlotte clarified.

Lord Wharton stood mere feet away, his attractive gaze locked onto Charlotte.

"What I mean," she continued, slowly selecting each word as she formulated her plan aloud, "is that we should pay a visit to Westling Hospital and familiarize ourselves with its operations."

Lord Wharton moved closer to Charlotte, hanging onto her every word.

"You can't go there because someone will recognize you," Charlotte expressed her concern. "Your photos have been plastered across the front pages of newspapers and magazines, but no one knows me. I can pretend that I'm searching for a facility for my elderly father, who is battling severe depression after my mother's passing . . ." Charlotte paused, waiting for Lord Wharton's response.

He stood in silence, studying Charlotte's face.

"I'm impressed by your imagination and quick thinking," he finally remarked. "It's a solid plan that might actually work. However, before you decide to proceed, you need to consider an important detail. I won't be there to protect you if anything goes wrong."

"What could possibly happen to me?" Charlotte attempted to smile, but Lord Wharton's expression remained serious.

"Hopefully nothing, but you must promise me that you'll take every precaution while inside and call the police if anything feels amiss. Promise me?" Lord Wharton's tone was earnest.

"I promise," Charlotte affirmed with a nod. "You know, my appreciation for your generous present hasn't been fully articulated," she whispered, her fingers gently caressing the exquisite diamond necklace that lay upon her neckline.

"You don't need to thank me," Lord Wharton said.

A genuine smile spread across Charlotte's lips. "I want to, really. This gift is more than I could have ever imagined, and I'm truly grateful. The diamond is stunning."

"It does have a captivating allure, doesn't it?" Lord Wharton remarked, lightly touching the stone and admiring its exquisite beauty. "This diamond reflects who you are—a symbol of your inner radiance. Wear it with pride, Charlotte."

CHAPTER TWENTY-SIX

Westling Hospital and the events of the past week consumed Charlotte's thoughts throughout the night. Her mind raced from Rachel Offley to Isabelle Mattingly, from Haddonford Manor to Westling Hospital. What role does Haddonford Manor play in all this? Did Frank meet Rachel at Westling Hospital? Why was he there? Charlotte tossed and turned, unable to find solace in sleep as the clock ticked towards 5:30, signaling the start of a new day.

With a tired sigh, Charlotte rose from bed and splashed her face with cold water, hoping to shake off the remnants of a restless night. She dressed and prepared herself to meet Lady Beatrice in the Blue Room, but before that, she examined the agenda requiring Lady Beatrice's review. One bullet point stood out, piercing her heart with sorrow: hire a cook. Charlotte knew that finding someone to fill Mrs. Offley's shoes would be a challenging endeavor. The arrival of a new cook would only serve as a constant reminder of the absence left behind by Mrs. Offley. Charlotte herself missed her dearly, and she could only imagine the weight of this loss on others, particularly Frank.

"Good morning, dear," Lady Beatrice greeted Charlotte as she entered the room. She was seated on a sofa with a folded newspaper on her lap. "I noticed that Richard posted an advertisement in the daily," she remarked, referring to the paper.

"I know it was a challenging task for him, just as it was for me to make this decision. No one can ever replace Rachel in our hearts, but I must consider the well-being of others, including Margaret. If it were just you and me, Margaret could manage, but the ongoing investigation has placed an unbearable strain on the poor girl. She's doing her best, but the workload is simply too much for one person with all of us to attend to.

Richard often tells me that I worry excessively, but I can't help it. Speaking of Richard," Lady Beatrice's gaze momentarily fell upon the diamond pendant on Charlotte's neck, causing a pause. Charlotte braced herself for questions about the jewelry, but instead, Lady Beatrice continued.

"Richard keeps me in the dark regarding the investigation. I understand he's trying to protect me, and I appreciate his efforts. However, like him, I yearn for this case to be resolved and the person responsible for Rachel's death to be apprehended. I also wish to contribute and would be grateful if you could shed some light on the matter. I feel useless, unaware of what's happening. Tell me, Charlotte, is there anything I can do to assist in solving this heart-wrenching case?"

Caught in a nuanced situation, Charlotte wrestled with the complexity of balancing confidentiality and respect. If Lord Wharton had indeed chosen to limit his mother's involvement in the affairs, Charlotte recognized that divulging confidential information was beyond her prerogative. She deeply valued Lord Wharton's decisions and held Lady Beatrice in high regard, not only as her employer but also as a figure she sincerely admired and cared for. Faced with Lady Beatrice's inquiries, Charlotte knew she couldn't outright refuse but needed to navigate her response with significant delicacy.

"Lady Beatrice, your gracious support and the trust you've placed in me by allowing my participation alongside Lord Wharton in this investigation are truly appreciated," Charlotte expressed carefully. "While the police are conducting their investigation along established lines, we are exploring a slightly different angle."

Lady Beatrice leaned in; her eyes filled with curiosity. "Does this angle implicate anyone within Haddonford?" she inquired.

"No," Charlotte swiftly responded, noting Lady Beatrice's shoulders relaxing ever so slightly.

"I'm relieved to hear that," she admitted. "It troubled me greatly when the police insinuated that everyone within Haddonford could be a suspect. By the way, Inspector Sinclair inquired about you yesterday. I assured him that Haddonford is not a prison and that you are free to come and go as you please during your leisure time."

"I wonder why he was looking for me?" Charlotte pondered aloud.

"I'm not entirely sure," Lady Beatrice replied thoughtfully. "It may have something to do with a conversation he had with Lady Isabelle. But I could be wrong."

Since the beginning of the investigation, Lady Isabelle had not concealed her disdain for Charlotte or her unhappiness about staying in Haddonford. Although she never openly criticized Lady Beatrice's young companion, her actions were telling. For instance, when Charlotte spoke up about Margaret's overwhelming workload, Lady Isabelle had rolled her eyes dismissively and left the room abruptly. Another time, when Charlotte herself served tea in Margaret's place, Lady Isabelle had pointedly refused to drink it.

Sensing Charlotte's unease, Lady Beatrice offered comforting words. "My dear, don't let Lady Isabelle trouble you," she said, gently placing her hand on Charlotte's.

"People are a myriad of complexities. While some brighten your life, others may try to overshadow it. It's best not to dwell on those who only look for faults. Instead, cherish those who recognize and value your strengths. And remember, you have my permission to leave Haddonford during your working hours. It's the least I can do to honor Rachel's memory," Lady Beatrice added, her eyes reflecting a mix of kindness and determination.

Encouraged by her words, Charlotte immersed herself in her tasks for the day. She skillfully avoided any encounters with Lady Isabelle and barely had the opportunity to speak with Lord Carrington and Lord Wharton. Her only interactions involved sharing a conversation with Samuel in the garden, where he tended to the rose bushes, and Margaret in the kitchen, where she helped her with dinner preparations.

As much as Charlotte attempted to push the case from her mind, Isabelle Mattingly's assertion that Rachel was her sole friend persistently resurfaced. It made no sense that anyone would wish harm upon her. The cook's behavior had shown no indication of being troubled, leading Charlotte to ponder whether Mrs. Offley was truly the intended target.

Upon retiring to her bedroom, Charlotte retrieved a notebook from a locked drawer in the writing desk and meticulously transcribed the questions swirling in her mind:

Why did Frank specifically instruct Charlotte to lock her doors and windows at night?

Who authored the intercepted letter, and what did they mean by "Everything we do has consequences? Even your actions will have their repercussions"?

Was the killer targeting Mrs. Offley, or was someone else their intended victim?

What was Frank doing in London on the day following his wife's murder, and who was the person he conversed with when Charlotte spotted him?

How did Lady Beatrice's mother pass away?

What purpose did Lord Carrington have for being in the West Wing?

During her childhood, Mother Superior had taught Charlotte the importance of seeking answers directly from the source. This task was straightforward when the source was a book, but it proved more challenging with people. Charlotte's recent attempt to glean information from Lord Carrington had been met with a firm refusal to share any details. Now, she pondered whether Frank would respond similarly to her inquiries. The only way to find out was through a direct, honest conversation with him.

Since his wife's tragic passing, Frank had been reclusive, spending most evenings in the solitude of their shared bedroom, only leaving occasionally for errands in London on behalf of Lady Beatrice. Charlotte had been concerned about his wellbeing and had wanted to offer support, yet she struggled to find the right approach. She hoped their forthcoming conversation would not only provide answers to her questions but also show Frank her compassion. While they hadn't been particularly close, Charlotte felt a responsibility to reach out. Frank had suffered a great loss, and she believed in the power of a sympathetic presence.

As Charlotte descended the grand staircase, intending to speak with Frank, she caught sight of Margaret cautiously stepping out of the kitchen. Intrigued, Charlotte discreetly took cover behind a nearby column to watch Margaret's actions. The maid looked around carefully, seemingly ensuring she wasn't being watched. Satisfied with her secrecy, she quietly moved toward the main foyer. Charlotte observed with growing bewilderment as Margaret stealthily exited through the front door, leaving her perplexed by the maid's secretive conduct. With a heavy sigh, Charlotte realized that her conversation with Frank would have to wait.

The full moon cast an enchanting, almost magical glow over Haddonford Manor and its captivating gardens. This lunar radiance served as both an aid and a complication in Charlotte's clandestine mission. Its bright light provided her with clear visibility, enabling her to scrutinize the area around her. Yet, this illumination also made it challenging for Charlotte to stay hidden in the shadows.

Treading carefully, Charlotte followed Margaret from a distance. She moved silently across the open field, venturing into the forested area of Haddonford. The path, marked by flattened grass, showed signs of frequent use. Charlotte kept a watchful eye on Margaret, matching her pace while staying far enough to avoid detection. Each time Margaret looked back, Charlotte would quickly hide behind a tree, her heart racing with the thrill of the pursuit.

"I must be getting better at this, or maybe knowing the person I'm following makes it less scary," Charlotte mused. Yet, she quickly checked herself, realizing the flaw in her thinking. After all, she hardly knew Margaret. The mystery surrounding the maid's past made it impossible for Charlotte to dismiss her as a suspect.

Charlotte shivered, berating herself for not bringing a shawl to ward off the night's piercing cold. Each murmur and rustle of leaves, every concealed stir in the darkness, intensified her feeling of exposure, amplifying her escalating unease.

Maintaining sight of Margaret was a struggle; her form flickered and disappeared into the thick underbrush, accompanied by the eerie sounds of the night. A wave of panic overtook Charlotte, her heart pounding fiercely. She scanned the area frantically, seeking any indication of Margaret in the moonlit woods. As the path diverged to the right, it revealed no signs of the maid's passage.

"Perhaps she took the left through the thickets," Charlotte mused, pausing to listen intently for the faintest rustle in the undergrowth. However, only an unsettling quiet greeted her. Pushing through the dense foliage, Charlotte finally stepped into an open clearing. A vast field unfolded before her, leading to a village previously hidden by the forest's embrace.

The structure closest to the field's edge bore the resemblance of a pub. Charlotte's eyes fixated on a luminous sign: The Crown. A burst of laughter spilled out onto the dimly lit street as someone opened the pub's front door. Two men emerged, seeking a moment of a good joke and a smoke before departing on foot. One of the men walked with steady steps, while his companion required assistance to navigate his way home. His overweight figure swung from side to side, reminiscent of a pendulum. Charlotte stayed hidden, witnessing as the men slowly made their way down the street, eventually disappearing from view. Approaching the pub was risky; as a stranger, she would surely draw attention. Opting for discretion, Charlotte chose a window far from the entrance to observe the interior. To her surprise, the pub was quieter than she had expected, its patrons lost in their own lively exchanges. Unfortunately, the thick glass of the window muffled their conversations, making it hard for her to eavesdrop.

Her attention was drawn to a corner where Margaret was in deep conversation with a young man, possibly a bit older than her. From her hidden spot, Charlotte could only make out the young man's reddish, wavy hair and broad shoulders. Their seating arrangement, however, made it difficult for Charlotte to get a clear view of his face or to read his expressions.

Realizing she had collected enough information for the time being, Charlotte decided to end her surveillance. As she quietly retreated from the scene, she pondered over the new piece of the puzzle she had just uncovered. "Who is this young man, and what is his connection to Haddonford Manor?" she thought, making a mental note to add this question to her growing notebook of inquiries.

Chapter Twenty-Seven

"**W**HY DIDN'T YOU INFORM ME ABOUT your decision to follow Margaret?" Lord Wharton's brows furrowed as he and Charlotte walked towards the garage where his car was kept. Today marked their planned visit to Westling Hospital, with the pretext of finding a suitable treatment facility for Charlotte's elderly father, who was battling severe depression and anxiety following the unexpected loss of his wife.

"Charlotte, venturing alone into the woods at night is a dangerous proposition. If anything were to happen to you, none of us would be able to come to your aid. It's crucial that we adhere to common sense when playing the role of detectives. If you choose to pursue leads or chase someone in the dark, please ensure that I am aware of your intentions or, if I am unavailable, inform someone at Haddonford about your whereabouts," Lord Wharton explained firmly, looking her directly in the eyes.

"I understand," Charlotte nodded in agreement, acknowledging Lord Wharton's valid concerns. When she shared her observations from the pub, she didn't anticipate receiving praise for her bravery, but she also didn't expect to be lectured like a child. Lord Wharton's emphasis on communicating her intentions to someone else made sense, but the underlying issue remained—everyone at Haddonford Manor seemed to be harboring secrets, making it exceptionally challenging for Charlotte to confide in anyone other than him.

During the entire ride, Charlotte mentally prepared herself for what would be her first acting role since childhood. She cherished the memories of participating in various Christmas performances organized by the parishes surrounding St. Helen. Mother Superior had always insisted on Charlotte's presence during the rehearsals, giving her rare opportunities to interact with children her age. The laughter and camaraderie she shared with the young performers brought her immense joy, and she secretly longed for those moments to last forever. Year after year, Charlotte was invited back, thanks to her natural talent and Mother Superior's persistence. Those plays held a special place in her heart, and the memories still filled her with warmth. However, the upcoming performance at Westling Hospital stirred different emotions within her—a mixture of nervousness and guilt. Charlotte had never been one to deceive others, and now she was about to trick everyone into believing that she had a father suffering from anxiety and depression.

"If you feel uncomfortable with this plan, we can consider alternatives," Lord Wharton suggested, sensing Charlotte's unease.

"There is no other plan," Charlotte affirmed. "We must uncover the truth behind Mrs. Offley's murder. In situations like this, I'd rather seek forgiveness later than reveal my intentions beforehand. I can do this," she declared, her confidence serving as both self-encouragement and reassurance for Lord Wharton.

"Seek forgiveness? For what?" Lord Wharton looked puzzled.

"For lying," Charlotte confessed.

"So that's what's been bothering you? You're just playing a role. Think of it as a performance for a worthy cause. Our objective is to uncover the connection between this place and Haddonford, and to do that, we need to navigate the situation with tact and strategy."

"I'm trying, but it's different this time. When I performed on stage before, everyone knew it was acting. But now, no one will suspect that I'm playing a role. They will believe I'm telling the truth," Charlotte explained with concern.

Lord Wharton let out a weary sigh and replied, "That's precisely the essence of our plan, Charlotte. We want them to wholeheartedly believe you're speaking the truth. You've been secluded in the convent for way too long. The truth is people lie incessantly in their daily lives. On average, individuals can tell anywhere between 10 to 100 lies per day. Even when they conceal the truth, it's still a form of deception. Whether you like it or not, even your own Mother Superior hasn't been entirely forthcoming about your parents. I suspect she's aware of more than she's shared. So, you see, lying is an intrinsic part of human nature."

Charlotte grappled with the realization that Lord Wharton's assessment of human behavior held undeniable truth, even though she hesitated to accept it. Throughout her interactions with him, she couldn't recall a single instance where he had deceived her. Lord Wharton stood as the sole individual at Haddonford in whom she placed unyielding trust.

Curiosity sparked within her, and she posed a sincere question, "Have you ever lied?"

He took a thoughtful pause before responding, "Regrettably, yes. I have."

Observing his choice of words, Charlotte remarked, attempting to comprehend Lord Wharton's perspective, "When someone expresses 'regrettably' it often conveys remorse or accountability for their lies."

"In my case, the latter proposition holds true," he confessed.

"So, you don't feel remorse for your lies?" Charlotte inquired, seeking clarity.

"I'm not stating that. At the time, I believed I had no alternative. I recognize that individuals often employ such beliefs to rationalize their actions, and perhaps that applies to my situation. However, I must bear the consequences of my deceit . . . But for now, let us concentrate on resolving one issue at a time, Charlotte,"

Lord Wharton said, a radiant smile illuminating his handsome face. "Let's approach your visit to Westling Hospital in this manner: you're assisting a dear friend who has recently endured trauma and requires emotional healing. This individual possesses ample financial resources and is seeking a place for anxiety and possible depression treatment."

"Are you referring to a real person?" Charlotte asked, curious about the specifics.

"Yes," Lord Wharton nodded.

"Is it Lady Beatrice?" Charlotte speculated.

"Mother is a strong woman. I don't mean to diminish the impact of Rachel's loss on her, but she possesses resilience and has the ability to bounce back on her own. On the other hand, Lord Carrington is in need of help. I've observed a significant change in his behavior following Rachel's death, and I believe he would be an ideal candidate to spend a few days at Westling Hospital," Lord Wharton explained.

"Are we actually going to ask him to relocate here?" Charlotte inquired.

"Yes, just for a few days, and we will be transparent about our intentions," Lord Wharton confirmed.

"Do you think he will agree?" Charlotte wondered, considering Lord Carrington's response.

"I'm almost certain he will. Firstly, the stay at Westling Hospital will benefit his health, and secondly, he wants to find Rachel's killer as much as we do. He will go along with our plan. How do you feel now about the role you are about to undertake?" Lord Wharton inquired.

"Much better," Charlotte replied, feeling a renewed sense of confidence.

According to their agreement, Lord Wharton dropped Charlotte off at the corner of Abbey Road and Carlton Hill and waited for her to hail a cab. While his fancy convertible would have made for a glamorous entrance, arriving in a cab would help keep her visit to Westling Hospital inconspicuous.

As Charlotte approached her destination, she couldn't help but marvel at its transformed appearance in the warm sunlight. Meticulous care had been given to the maintenance of the lawns, where the grass was trimmed to perfection, and stately evergreen trees lined the gravel pathways with an air of elegance. The gray walls of the building were adorned with vibrant, verdant vines that gracefully climbed up to the second floor, adding a touch of natural beauty to the institutional façade.

Charlotte's eyes were drawn to the windows, noticing the subtle details that differentiated each floor. On the third floor, she observed the presence of metal bars securely installed from the outside. They appeared formidable, creating a sense of confinement. Meanwhile, on the first floor, some of the windows were left open, inviting the gentle breeze to permeate the interior, bringing freshness and a fleeting sense of freedom. An elderly gentleman sat on a bench, engrossed in a game of solitaire, paying no attention to Charlotte standing just a few steps away. A female nurse pushing an empty wheelchair cast a curious glance at Charlotte but said nothing, continuing with her duties.

"Welcome to Westling Hospital," a resonant, low-pitched voice rang through the air, uttering a warm welcome.

Charlotte's attention shifted upwards, and there stood a middle-aged woman, dressed in a perfectly tailored dark gray suit. The woman's sharp cheekbones were accentuated by her sleek, short haircut, giving her a distinguished appearance. Her eyes, framed by a pair of sophisticated glasses, bore a glint of keen observation, suggesting that nothing escaped her attention. The woman's poised stance and the confidence that emanated from her every move commanded respect, yet there was an underlying sense of restraint in her approach. It was as if she had mastered the art of maintaining professional boundaries while still acknowledging the human element. Every word she spoke and every gesture she made seemed purposeful, revealing her astute nature.

"I noticed you through my office window and thought I would personally extend a welcome. I'm Miss Hargrove, and I oversee this establishment. My staff is instructed to focus on their responsibilities. The safety and well-being of our patients is our top priority. With everyone here busy attending to their duties, it falls upon me to ensure that visitors receive a proper welcome," Miss Hargrove extended a hand in greeting.

"I'm Charlotte," Charlotte reciprocated the gesture.

"How about we go inside and have a conversation in my office?" Miss Hargrove suggested.

Charlotte glanced back and saw that the cab was still waiting. Lord Wharton had generously given the driver an advance tip to ensure that he wouldn't leave without her, regardless of the appointment's duration. Charlotte felt grateful for the reassurance of having an escape vehicle waiting outside, which helped alleviate her nervousness. She quickly ascended the steps and followed Miss Hargrove into the building. The wide vestibule was bathed in bright light, illuminated by a grand crystal chandelier hanging from the high ceiling. Miss Hargrove's office emanated an aura of sterility. The walls, curtains, and furniture all bore different shades of white, except for a few accents like a spiral-bound notebook, picture frames, and several chairs. While aesthetics seemed to hold little importance to Miss Hargrove, she took pride in maintaining a pristine and organized workspace. The office was minimally furnished, containing only the essential items for her daily affairs.

"Please have a seat," Miss Hargrove said, walking around her desk and settling into a chair. Charlotte followed suit, taking a seat in a similar chair across from her.

"What brings you here, Miss Reinford?" Miss Hargrove inquired.

"I have concerns about a friend," Charlotte replied. "Someone I know has been through a great deal, and I worry about his emotional well-being. I understand that people respond differently to stressful and traumatic events. Some find inner strength to cope, while others require support and guidance. I fear that my friend falls into the latter category. We have exhausted our own resources and are now seeking help from professionals experienced in handling delicate mental health situations. I've heard positive things about this place through word of mouth, so I decided to visit and assess it firsthand."

"Westling Hospital isn't suitable for everyone," Miss Hargrove responded in a cold tone.

"I am aware of that," Charlotte acknowledged. "That's precisely why I'm here. I was hoping to learn more about your hospital. Money won't be an issue," Charlotte continued. "It's the quality of services that Westling Hospital provides that interests me. My friend is grappling with depression and requires assistance in addressing trauma. However, if your hospital cannot offer the appropriate treatment, I will explore alternative facilities."

"I cannot offer any assurances without our doctor evaluating your friend," Miss Hargrove stated. "Most of our patients are referred to Westling Hospital by their own physicians. I assume you don't have a referral."

"No," Charlotte admitted, "I do not. But what about those who don't have a referral?"

"In rare cases, we do make exceptions," Miss Hargrove conceded.

"And what criteria do you consider when granting these exceptions?" Charlotte inquired.

"It depends on the individual circumstances," Miss Hargrove replied.

"I understand," Charlotte said. "Once again, money won't be an issue. In fact, I can assure you of a generous donation both upon my friend's admission and his discharge."

Miss Hargrove sat in silence, her fingers tapping on the edge of her desk.

"So, what would you like to know about Westling Hospital?" she finally asked.

"How do you assess a patient's eligibility for admission? What is the typical treatment duration? Are there designated visiting hours for patients? Could you describe the living conditions?" Charlotte inquired with curiosity.

"Without a proper diagnosis, it becomes challenging for me to provide specific answers to your questions," Miss Hargrove responded.

"Can you offer some general information then? I need to be able to reassure my friend's family. They are seeking answers. Sending a loved one to a facility like Westling Hospital is a difficult decision, even with your esteemed reputation. Nobody wants to publicly announce that their family member is receiving treatment at a psychiatric facility. If you could give me a general idea of what to expect, it would greatly satisfy them," Charlotte explained.

"If your friend, assuming it's a male based on your comments, is not a threat to himself or others, he will likely enjoy a considerable degree of freedom at our facility. This includes unrestricted visitation, opportunities for outdoor walks, and more. He will also have the option to discharge himself whenever he wishes," Miss Hargrove explained.

"What about patients who pose a danger to themselves or others?" Charlotte inquired.

"What do you mean?" Miss Hargrove's voice turned cold.

"Will my friend ever interact with patients who require stricter care than he does during his stay here?" Charlotte asked.

"Absolutely not," Miss Hargrove responded firmly. "As I mentioned earlier, the safety and well-being of our patients are our utmost priorities. Under no circumstances will their paths cross."

Charlotte couldn't help but contemplate the metal rods on the windows of the third floor and the impending conversation with Lord Carrington. If he agreed to spend a few days at Westling Hospital, Charlotte was determined to find a way to explore every floor of the building.

Miss Hargrove reached for a spiral-bound calendar on her desk, flipping through the pages.

"I have an opening next Monday at noon. Will that provide you with enough time to consult with the family and convince your friend to come in for an evaluation?" she asked, offering the available slot.

"Yes, that works perfectly," Charlotte responded, a sense of relief washing over her at the prospect of having a specific appointment time.

CHAPTER TWENTY-EIGHT

STANDING BY THE OPEN WINDOW IN her bedroom, Charlotte marveled at the breathtaking beauty of Haddonford Manor. The meadows and gardens before her resembled a magical fairyland, their vibrant colors shimmering in the gentle rays of the rising sun. As summer transitioned into autumn, the once vibrant hues mellowed into soothing shades of yellow and brown. The cloudless sky now wore a cooler blue, contrasting against the crispness of the fresh morning air. Charlotte took a deep breath, filling her lungs with the invigorating essence of the season then with a sigh, she closed the window to resume her daily duties.

Since the passing of Mrs. Offley, Lady Beatrice had chosen a path of partial seclusion, retreating to her bedroom until late afternoon and engaging in minimal conversation with others. It seemed she believed this was for the best, as her patience wore thin with everyone, including Lord Carrington. In one of their recent conversations, Lady Beatrice unintentionally expressed her frustration with what she described as his "needy behavior," unknowingly hurting Lord Carrington's feelings.

Consequently, he distanced himself from Lady Beatrice, relying more on Charlotte's kindness as his confidante and occasional chess partner. This newfound closeness with Lord Carrington gave

Charlotte hope that he might be more receptive to her audacious proposition of seeking assistance at Westling Hospital.

As anticipated, Lady Beatrice's bedroom door was closed, indicating her presence inside. The morning briefing would have to be postponed until lunch, but this delay didn't bother Charlotte. She had a long list of urgent tasks that required her attention. Descending the wide stairwell, Charlotte crossed the hall and entered the dining room. There, she found Lord Carrington, seated solitarily at the table, cradled a cup of tea, freshly steeped, in his hands. His gaze was drawn to the far window, where fluffy white clouds danced across the sky.

"Good morning," Charlotte greeted him, infusing the room with warmth.

"I hope it becomes one. A lonely cup of tea and some unsettling thoughts don't contribute to a good morning, but perhaps a mediocre one at best. How are you, Charlotte? Any progress in your investigation?"

"Some," Charlotte cautiously replied.

"Some is better than none," Lord Carrington remarked, taking a sip of his tea. "The thought of a murderer walking among us is chilling," he paused. "Imagine if the assailant had another in mind? Suppose Rachel was merely caught in the crossfire?"

Charlotte experienced a sense of déjà vu. This wasn't the first time Lord Carrington speculated on Mrs. Offley being an unintended casualty, suggesting the real target could be someone else.

"Do you believe the killer is male?" she inquired.

"I'm uncertain. It's hard for me to imagine that a woman would commit such a heinous crime, but I acknowledge that my perspective may be influenced by societal norms and the perception of women as delicate and gentle beings."

"And indeed, some certainly are," Charlotte affirmed, settling into a seat beside Lord Carrington.

"True," he agreed, "However, there are those who skillfully employ their intelligence or charm to deceive and manipulate others for personal gain. Moreover, some exhibit impulsive behaviors, resorting to threats or aggression to undermine the credibility of those around them," Lord Carrington took a sip of his tea. "Speaking of which . . . you missed quite a spectacle yesterday. Lady Isabelle was truly in her element. I was certain she would be arrested for verbally assaulting a law enforcement officer. Surprisingly, not only did she get away with her outrageous behavior, but she was allowed to leave Haddonford."

"I'm utterly bewildered. What happened exactly?" Charlotte inquired.

"Inspector Sinclair paid us a visit yesterday, for the second time this week. He only spoke with Frank and was about to leave when Lady Isabelle spotted him. I must say, she was already in a foul mood. She had been rude to everyone since breakfast, upon discovering that Lord Wharton was absent. Lady Isabelle proceeded to label Inspector Sinclair as an imbecile, adding a few colorful adjectives to embellish her description of his investigative abilities. She even recited her rights to depart Haddonford Manor at any time unless he possessed substantial evidence implicating her. In a final act, she handed him a card with her lawyer's contact information. Inspector Sinclair appeared defeated as he left in his car. I half-expected Lady Isabelle to pack her bags and leave, but she chose to stay. I must admit, I'm evidently not adept at assessing a woman's character, but it seems she revels in having control."

While Charlotte silently agreed with the observation, she refrained from commenting. Instead, she redirected the conversation, asking, "Does this mean that anyone at Haddonford can leave?"

"Yes, it seems so. Anyone is free to depart, but they must return promptly upon Inspector Sinclair's summons," Lord Carrington confirmed.

"That's good to know. In a way, Lady Isabelle did everyone a great favor," Charlotte remarked.

"I suppose," Lord Carrington reluctantly agreed, "although I don't think anyone here has intentions of leaving anytime soon."

"Lord Carrington," Charlotte began, edging her chair closer to his with deliberate care. "Might I impose upon you for a rather significant favor? Your assistance in the investigation could prove invaluable."

His response was immediate, laced with fervor. "Of course, Charlotte! How may I be of service?"

She took a measured breath before continuing, "I must ask you to consider . . . admitting yourself into Westling Hospital," she said, her eyes locked onto his for any flicker of reaction.

Surprise registered on his features first, followed by a dawning intrigue, then thoughtful consideration. A prolonged silence fell between them, during which Charlotte's anxiety crept upwards, fearing he might dismiss her request as ludicrous or take offense.

Yet, breaking the silence with a decisive nod, Lord Carrington declared, "I'll do it, under one condition—that my tenure at Westling remains concealed from Beatrice."

"Certainly," Charlotte agreed without hesitation.

"Then let Beatrice assume I'm in London visiting a friend, or better yet—she needn't know anything. She might not even register my absence for a few days," he mused, before his curiosity surfaced. "But tell me, why Westling Hospital? And why involve me?"

Charlotte was taken aback by his readiness to agree without demanding the particulars, which she had fully expected. "Lord Wharton and I suspect the hospital is linked to Mrs. Offley's untimely death," she disclosed. "Did you know Rachel Offley worked there before marrying Frank?"

Lord Carrington's nod was solemn. "Yes, and I'm aware of its nature as a psychiatric institution."

"And you're prepared to admit yourself there?" she pressed for confirmation.

"For as long as it takes," he declared, his voice carrying a determined edge.

Charlotte pondered his choice of words—"for as long as it takes." It hinted at a depth of involvement with Westling Hospital that he had yet to disclose, wrapping his intentions in layers of mystery.

"I've scheduled a preliminary assessment for you on Monday," she informed him, anticipating his cooperation.

"You know me well," he said, his smile conveying both agreement and a trace of shared conspiracy.

"I certainly hope so," Charlotte reflected silently as she squeezed his hand in gratitude.

CHAPTER TWENTY-NINE

Upon reaching the grand entrance of Westling Hospital, Lord Carrington's expression revealed profound admiration. "This establishment is nothing short of exquisitely mesmerizing," he commented, stepping out of the taxi with a sense of wonder.

Charlotte, closely tailing him, observed his enraptured state. "Is this the very first occasion of your visit here?" she inquired.

"Indeed, it marks my inaugural journey to this place," he acknowledged, his gaze absorbed by the complex's ornate and intricate craftsmanship. "Beatrice had occasionally alluded to it in our conversations, however, Rachel . . . she always demonstrated a noticeable reticence when it came to sharing her personal reflections or any particular experiences she had within these halls."

"Do you have any insight into her reluctance?" Charlotte asked.

He pondered for a moment, his face thoughtful. "Not really. Rachel chose to commit herself here, despite other possibilities. Yet, she guarded her reasons as if they were deeply personal secrets."

They made their way up the steps together, Lord Carrington moving deliberately, each step seeming to draw him deeper into contemplation about Rachel's silence.

Miss Hargrove awaited them at the entrance, exuding a warm

yet commanding presence. Dressed in a sharp navy suit and a complementary beige blouse, she epitomized the hospital's harmonious mix of mysterious charm and professionalism.

"Welcome to Westling Hospital," Miss Hargrove offered warmly. "I trust your trip was pleasant. Our somewhat secluded location often comes as a surprise to newcomers."

Lord Carrington replied with a light chuckle. "We entrusted our route to the expertise of our cab driver. Had he lost his way and taken us in circles, I doubt I would have noticed. This is, after all, my very first visit to such a unique establishment."

"I hope our facility meets your expectations," Miss Hargrove said, guiding them towards her office. "And let me express my sincere appreciation for your generous donation," she added, indicating a chair for Lord Carrington.

"The donation wasn't directly from me, but rather on my behalf," Lord Carrington clarified, sharing a glance with Charlotte.

It took Charlotte a moment to realize that it must have been Lord Wharton who had transferred a substantial sum of money to the hospital's account. After her previous visit to Westling Hospital, Charlotte had mentioned the possibility of a donation, which had evidently softened Miss Hargrove's demeanor and made her more inclined to accommodate Lord Carrington. While Charlotte hadn't expected Lord Wharton to act so swiftly, she was grateful for his intervention. Miss Hargrove radiated joy, making their visit all the more pleasant.

"We have been facing some financial struggles, and your donation came at the perfect time," Miss Hargrove expressed her gratitude.

"I'm glad to hear that. I understand that you provide treatment to anyone in need, regardless of their financial situation," Lord Carrington acknowledged.

"We do our best," Miss Hargrove replied.

"If my stay here leads to the results I'm seeking, I will double the initial donation upon my discharge."

"You won't be disappointed. If you'll excuse me for a moment, I'll call our psychiatrist, for the initial evaluation," Miss Hargrove picked up the receiver and within minutes, a slightly bald, medium-built man entered the room. Wearing a pristine white coat with a stethoscope draped around his neck, a pencil and glasses peeking out from his pocket, he introduced himself as Doctor Wayne Thomas and awaited the signal to begin the examination.

"This discussion is confidential," Miss Hargrove stated, her gaze shifting to Charlotte.

"Understood, I'll wait outside," Charlotte replied, excusing herself from the room.

Once in the hallway, Charlotte found herself in a space as immaculate and serene as Miss Hargrove's office. Her eyes were drawn to an imposing painting on the distant wall, depicting a hunting scene. At its heart was a young, strikingly beautiful woman, seated confidently on a spirited horse. Her riding attire, embellished with fine lace and silk, radiated aristocratic grace. The horse, with its glossy coat and powerful build, appeared almost ethereal, its eyes alight with vigor. The woman's grip on the reins was both gentle and assured, a symbol of her commanding presence and profound bond with the animal. In the backdrop, a group of hunters engaged in conversation, their horses ready and alert.

"She was our first patient here," a gentle, melodic voice interrupted Charlotte's observation.

Turning, she saw a young woman in her twenties, matching Charlotte in height, with straight brown hair that fell to her shoulders and deep blue eyes that captivated. Charlotte recognized her as the nurse she had seen earlier, maneuvering an empty wheelchair.

"What's her name?" Charlotte inquired, her gaze fixed on the painting.

"Lady Dianna," the young nurse replied. "The full story is unknown, but it's said that she had an undiagnosed mental disorder until her teenage years. Her father tried to keep it a secret, but eventually he realized she needed medical help. He hired the best doctors, but sadly, the treatment didn't succeed, and she took her own life. After her death, her father transformed this place into a hospital to aid others like her."

"What a tragic story," Charlotte remarked.

"This place holds many stories like that," the nurse acknowledged.

"I hope most of them have happier endings," Charlotte expressed.

"Many do, but not all. Science has progressed since Lady Dianna's untimely death. Our patients receive excellent care, and many are able to resume their normal lives after their time at Westling Hospital."

Seemingly attuned to Charlotte's thoughts, the young nurse interjected, "Although it's officially known as Westling Hospital, patients affectionately refer to it as Westling House."

"I see," Charlotte recalled that Miss Hargrove had used the term "Westling Hospital," while Isabelle Mattingly had referred to it as "Westling House."

Charlotte noticed that her newfound acquaintance didn't appear to be in a rush, so she decided to seize the opportunity and learn more about the hospital.

"One of my closest friends is currently being assessed by Doctor Thomas, and there's a possibility that he'll be admitted for a few weeks. I intend to visit him as often as I can, but I need reassurance that he'll be safe when I'm not around," Charlotte shared her concerns.

"The safety of your friend is our utmost priority," the nurse replied with confidence, her words and tone reminiscent of Miss Hargrove's authoritative and reassuring manner. "I promise that we will take excellent care of him. If you would like, I can personally keep an eye on your friend when you're not here. What is his name?"

"His name is Lord Carrington. I'm Charlotte, by the way," she introduced herself, extending her hand gracefully.

"Nice to meet you, Charlotte. I'm Emily Aldridge," the young nurse responded, shaking Charlotte's hand vigorously. "I work on the second floor, which is most likely where Lord Carrington will be staying."

"You seem quite confident about that," Charlotte remarked with a smile. "Who stays on the third floor?"

"The third floor is reserved for special cases, and a different team of nurses works there. You can easily identify them by their light teal coats," Emily explained.

Charlotte's curiosity grew stronger upon hearing about the third floor. "Have you ever been there?"

"No, my permissions don't extend to that region. Additionally, I've not undergone the essential training needed for tasks on the third floor. After a horrifying event took place, the hospital enhanced its security precautions. Consequently, encountering anyone on the third floor could provoke serious issues," the young nurse detailed prudently.

Intrigued by Emily's comments, Charlotte inquired, "Can you tell me more about what occurred during that horrifying event?"

Emily hesitated for a moment, then began to recount, "The incident predates my time here, so I can't vouch for the accuracy of the story. However, I can tell you that the entire hospital underwent significant restructuring as a result of it. I don't recall the name of the doctor who was present during that time, but it wasn't Doctor Thomas. Legend has it that he was a young and handsome physician, exceptionally skilled in his profession, and had achieved remarkable progress with numerous patients. However, one day, he mysteriously vanished," Emily shared but before she could conclude her story, an alarm abruptly blared throughout the hospital.

Charlotte looked around, trying to pinpoint the source of the loud noise. Emily reached out and touched Charlotte's shoulder attempting to get her attention. Her lips were moving, but it was difficult for Charlotte to comprehend the words. Finally, Emily raised her right hand and began to count down with her fingers: five, four, three, two, and one. Within seconds, silence descended upon the hospital.

"Sorry, I have to go," Emily hurriedly excused herself. "When the alarm goes off, it means one of the patients is missing."

"I thought you said that this place was safe," Charlotte voiced her concern.

"It's completely safe here. We have comprehensive security measures, like the one you just saw. If a patient from the second floor is out of sight of their caregiver, an alarm alerts the entire hospital staff," Emily assured Charlotte.

Charlotte, still puzzled, asked, "But aren't patients on the second floor allowed to move freely and leave whenever they wish?"

"It varies," Emily clarified. "Each patient has a unique situation and level of freedom."

Intrigued, Charlotte delved further. "And what about those on the third floor?"

"I don't know much about the third floor, and honestly, it's not within my purview to know," Emily replied sincerely. "I apologize for cutting our conversation short, but I really must go."

"Wait," Charlotte stopped her. "You didn't finish your story. What happened to the doctor?"

"Which doctor?" Emily asked, momentarily confused.

"The one you mentioned earlier, the young and skilled doctor," Charlotte clarified.

"Ah him, he was subjected to an assault by one of the patients and subsequently went missing," Emily imparted in haste and hurried towards the entrance.

As Charlotte observed the young nurse's swift departure down the corridor, a cloud of puzzlement descended upon her. The story Emily had shared with her anchored itself in her mind, sparking a relentless curiosity. Although an attack on a physician is indeed an unusual event within the confines of a psychiatric institution, it seemed an insufficient reason for a distinguished doctor to suddenly relinquish his role and opt for relocation. It became increasingly clear to Charlotte that further details of the situation were shrouded in secrecy, known perhaps to a select few, yet remained closely guarded and not freely shared.

CHAPTER THIRTY

A WEEK AT WESTLING HOSPITAL SEEMED TO work wonders for Lord Carrington's well-being. Charlotte couldn't pinpoint whether it was the effect of medication or the one-on-one sessions with Doctor Thomas, but with each visit, she observed a subtle transformation in Lord Carrington's demeanor. He appeared more at ease, attentive, and composed. He even made a few attempts at humor, eliciting smiles from Charlotte. It was a joy to witness him gradually returning to the person she had first encountered at Haddonford Manor a few months ago. However, the progress she hoped to make regarding the connection between Mrs. Offley's death and Westling Hospital was less promising.

During her visits, Charlotte made it a point to seek out Emily in order to gather more information about the case involving the young doctor. Unfortunately, the young nurse had limited knowledge of the incident, providing little assistance. Charlotte also attempted to engage Miss Hargrove in conversation, as she had been a nurse at the time of the event, but her efforts were met with indifference and avoidance. Miss Hargrove showed no willingness to spare even a minute of her time for Charlotte.

Yet, Charlotte did manage a small victory in her investigation by learning about the hospital's operational schedule. Westling

Hospital had two shifts: the day shift starting at 6:00 in the morning and the night shift commencing at 6:00 in the evening. A thirty-minute break occurred between shifts, during which nurses received patient updates and specific instructions from either Doctor Thomas or Miss Hargrove. These meetings were scheduled in a way that ensured patients were never left unattended. Charlotte also observed that nurses in light teal coats held separate meetings and used a different staircase, indicating that they likely had no interaction with the nurses on the second floor and possibly were unfamiliar with one another.

Furthermore, Charlotte made a startling discovery that the older hospital records were securely stored in a locked room just a few doors down from Miss Hargrove's office. Meanwhile, the most recent patient files were housed in Doctor Thomas's office on the second floor. Despite Charlotte's repeated efforts to engage in a private conversation with Doctor Thomas, various obstacles consistently stood in her way. Miss Hargrove, in particular, seemed to possess an uncanny ability to intervene, materializing out of thin air whenever Charlotte attempted to approach the psychiatrist and swiftly whisking him away before any meaningful exchange could take place. After facing numerous failed attempts, Charlotte decided it was time to revise her strategy. She pondered whether introducing a male presence into the equation might yield better results. Taking this into consideration, Charlotte devised a plan and extended a compelling invitation to Lord Wharton, proposing that he join her on the upcoming visit to Westling Hospital. She believed that his presence could potentially overcome the barriers she had encountered thus far and lead to more favorable outcomes.

"How do you know it's going to work?" Lord Wharton questioned Charlotte as they briskly walked towards the hospital in the rain, without umbrellas or raincoats.

"I don't know if it will work, but it's worth a try. It seems that Miss Hargrove doesn't like me," Charlotte replied.

"I can't imagine that. It doesn't take you long to win people over," Lord Wharton said.

"But she wouldn't even give me a chance," Charlotte lamented. "And maybe it's not about liking me but rather trusting me."

"And why do you think she will trust me?" Lord Wharton inquired.

"For one, you're wealthy," Charlotte said with a smile. "You're also smart, confident, handsome, and charming. She is a woman, after all, and hopefully, one of your fine qualities will win her over."

"What if she is like you? None of my so-called 'charms' affected you, or have they?" Lord Wharton chuckled.

Charlotte paused thoughtfully, weighing her words. "Could you please speak with Miss Hargrove about the event that necessitated the reorganization here?" she asked gently. "I'm particularly interested in the details, including the names of the involved doctor and patient."

Lord Wharton raised an eyebrow, "What draws you to this particular incident?"

With a noncommittal shrug, Charlotte responded, "It's wrapped in such secrecy. There seems to be limited information available, and I suspect Miss Hargrove might be the only remaining person who was actually there when it happened."

"When did you say it happened?" Lord Wharton inquired.

"At least twenty years ago," Charlotte replied.

He paused, deep in thought. "If my math is correct, Rachel was already working here at that time."

"That's what I thought," Charlotte nodded. "Could you please ensure that your conversation with Miss Hargrove lasts at least twenty minutes? And I would greatly appreciate it if you could keep her occupied even longer. Whatever it takes, please don't let her leave the office."

Curiosity sparked in Lord Wharton's eyes as he asked, "What are you planning to do?"

"I'm going to search old files," Charlotte replied.

"Don't you need a key?" he asked.

Charlotte flashed a mischievous smile. "I'm all set." With a flourish, she indicated her elegantly styled hair, where several hairpins were cleverly concealed.

Lord Wharton's expression was one of surprise. "How did you acquire such a unique skill? Surely it wasn't the nuns who taught you lockpicking with a hairpin?"

With a nod of pride, Charlotte replied, "Indeed, it was Sister Ann's doing. She was adamant that every lady should be equipped to defend herself and find ways out of perilous situations."

Raising an eyebrow in fascination, Lord Wharton commented, "That's quite extraordinary. I'm eager to discover more about your varied skills once we return to Haddonford. How long will you need? Half an hour?"

"Twenty minutes should suffice," Charlotte responded.

"Perfect, that's entirely manageable," he confirmed with a nod.

Chapter Thirty-One

As the rain intensified, Charlotte and Lord Wharton quickened their pace and reached the top step of the hospital entrance just as Miss Hargrove flung open the front door.

"Come in, come in," she invited them. "The weather is quite dreary today. I hope it clears up soon. Sunshine and fresh air have a tremendous impact on our mood. Here at Westling Hospital, we strive to help our guests develop a positive mindset. I don't like to use the word 'patients,'" she clarified. "It carries a negative connotation in my opinion. Anyway, we promote a positive mindset through our words and actions. We offer group sessions that allow our guests to share happy moments in their lives and teach them different perspectives. You often can't control what happens to you, but you can control how you react to it. You can choose to focus on the negative or find the positive, even in a difficult and stressful situation."

Charlotte observed Miss Hargrove with keen interest. While her monologue had some valid points, certain aspects didn't quite add up. Miss Hargrove referred to the individuals receiving treatment as "guests," yet she called the establishment "Westling Hospital" and not "Westling House." Charlotte attributed this inconsistency to Miss Hargrove's nervousness and eagerness to please an important guest, possibly a potential donor. After exchanging a few polite remarks, Charlotte excused herself, claiming she needed to visit Lord Carrington. However, instead of heading upstairs to his room, she turned a corner and waited discreetly.

As soon as she heard the door to Miss Hargrove's office close, Charlotte seized the opportunity and made her way towards the room housing the old hospital files. She was well aware that Doctor Thomas typically had a meeting with the nurses in his office at this time, which meant fewer people would be lingering on the first floor. The only uncertain variable was the unpredictable alarm that could go off if a patient went missing or was out of sight. Fortunately, the rain played in Charlotte's favor, compelling everyone at Westling Hospital to remain indoors. The front yard lay empty, and anyone daring enough to venture out would be easily spotted by the vigilant staff.

As expected, the door to the file room was locked. Charlotte swiftly withdrew a hairpin, allowing her luscious curls to cascade down her shoulders. She cautiously glanced around to ensure no one was observing her, then squatted down to align herself with the keyhole. Delicately inserting the hairpin, she attempted to turn it, but to no avail.

"What are you doing here?" a voice whispered in her ear.

Startled, Charlotte swiftly turned towards the person standing behind her and froze in astonishment.

"And what are you doing here?" she whispered back, striving to keep her voice low. "They're going to set off the alarm. Everyone is likely searching for you."

"No," Lord Carrington replied, flashing a sly smile. "They think I'm taking a mid-morning nap."

"But why are you here? Were you following me?" Charlotte questioned in a hushed tone.

"I wasn't following you," he pouted, his demeanor reminiscent of a sulking child. "I'm guessing we both had the same idea—to look at the files."

Charlotte was taken aback by Lord Carrington's unexpected presence, but she quickly regained her composure and endeavored to think clearly. Surprised as she was to find him attempting to break into the filing room, she realized that she had shared her plans to arrange Lord Wharton's visit to Westling Hospital with him earlier in the week. She had even provided him with the precise date and time of Lord Wharton's meeting with Miss Hargrove. However, she intentionally withheld her intention to stay behind and not partake in the conversation. The fact that Lord Carrington happened to be at the door precisely when Miss Hargrove was meeting with Lord Wharton could not be dismissed as mere coincidence.

"Lord Carrington, how did you plan on gaining access to the filing room?" Charlotte inquired, her suspicion evident in her tone.

"I intended to unlock it," he responded.

"What? Do you have a key?" Charlotte asked.

"I certainly do," Lord Carrington proudly declared. "I borrowed it."

"Borrowed or stole it?" Charlotte questioned, taking the key from Lord Carrington's hands, and using it to unlock the door.

"Does it really matter?" he shrugged nonchalantly. "We're in!"

"What were you hoping to find here?" Charlotte asked.

"In all honesty, I'm not entirely sure what I'm hoping to find," Lord Carrington admitted, his voice barely audible. "I took the key on a whim, driven by curiosity and a desire to uncover the secrets hidden within these files. But now that we're here, I don't know where to begin."

Charlotte understood Lord Carrington's dilemma. The sheer number of drawers filled with files was overwhelming, and they couldn't afford to spend years sifting through them all. She pondered for a moment, contemplating the best approach.

"Let's start twenty years ago," Charlotte suggested, trying to ease his apprehension.

"The incident!" Lord Carrington exclaimed, his eyes widening. "What exactly should I be searching for?"

Surprised by his knowledge, Charlotte probed further. "Wait, so you're aware of it too?"

"Ha! Everyone around here knows, but it's an unspoken secret," Lord Carrington replied with a knowing smile.

"That's precisely the issue. I need to uncover the names of the patients during that time," Charlotte explained, her gaze focused on the file labels.

After a moment of searching, she exclaimed, "Here it is—1939!" She gingerly opened the drawer, revealing a stack of weathered folders covered in dust. The musty scent of aged papers filled the air as she retrieved them.

"We need to be meticulous and return these files exactly as we found them," Charlotte reminded Lord Carrington, emphasizing the importance of maintaining order and avoiding any suspicion.

With a shared understanding, Lord Carrington took the top half of the files, while Charlotte held the rest. They positioned themselves near the window, utilizing the limited natural light to examine the documents. Charlotte couldn't help but observe Lord Carrington closely, hoping to discern his intentions. He seemed to be searching for something specific but remained elusive about his purpose.

With limited time at their disposal, Charlotte delved into the first file, swiftly scanning through the contents. Each document followed a similar pattern, detailing the patient's name, admission date, and a concise summary of their reasons for seeking treatment at Westling Hospital. Some files were thicker than others, hinting at the severity or duration of the patient's condition. Charlotte also noticed a consistent signature at the bottom of each file—a neat and legible script belonging to Doctor James Hurst. The doctor's distinctive 'H' caught her attention with its slightly rounded appearance, resembling a capital 'U' but unmistakably an 'H'.

Curiosity compelled Charlotte to explore further. She ventured to the adjacent drawer, labeled '1940', and pulled out a file. This time, the signature differed significantly. The letters were elongated and pointed, revealing a distinct style belonging to another doctor—Doctor Wayne Thomas.

As the urgency of their situation weighed upon her, Charlotte knew it was time to wrap up their investigation.

She glanced at Lord Carrington, "Our time is running short. Miss Hargrove's meeting should be nearing its end, and there's a chance she might come here," Charlotte cautioned. "We cannot risk being caught, and we must also consider the possibility of Doctor Thomas searching for his missing key."

Lord Carrington merely shrugged, seemingly unperturbed by the impending risks.

"Richard's charm will ensure Miss Hargrove remains occupied until he deems it time to leave."

Charlotte's gaze narrowed with concern. "Nevertheless, we must leave. Time is of the essence," she insisted. "Did you find what you were searching for?"

A flicker of disappointment crossed Lord Carrington's face as he handed Charlotte the files.

"No," he admitted, his tone tinged with frustration. "And you?"

"Yes," Charlotte nodded affirmatively.

Chapter Thirty-Two

CHARLOTTE INSISTED ON LORD CARRINGTON RETURNING the key immediately and joining her in the spacious guest room on the first floor. During one of her previous visits to the hospital, she had discovered a grand chess set resting on a square coffee table, nestled between two elegant Victorian chairs upholstered in burgundy velvet and adorned with a polished mahogany finish. This spot had become their exclusive meeting place, tucked away at the back of the room, ensuring their conversations remained private. The shared interest in chess between Charlotte and Lord Carrington worked in their favor, as they were the sole enthusiasts. They enjoyed the luxury of having the chess area to themselves without any interruptions.

Charlotte's anticipation grew until she finally laid eyes on Lord Carrington as he entered the room.

"Did you manage to return the key?" she anxiously inquired.

"Without any difficulty," he replied, sinking into a comfortable chair positioned across from Charlotte. "How about a game of chess?" he suggested.

Charlotte observed his relaxed posture and noticed a mischievous smile playing on his lips, causing her to feel suspicious.

"Not until I get some answers," she responded.

Lord Carrington leaned back, his demeanor calm. "How about we make it one question per move?" he proposed.

"Deal," Charlotte accepted the challenge. "I can't help but feel that you're keeping something from me."

"Would you like to play as white?" he asked.

"Black," Charlotte declared. "Who assisted you in obtaining the key?"

"Why do you think anyone helped me?" Lord Carrington adjusted the chess set, positioning the black pieces closer to Charlotte.

"Just a hunch," she replied.

"No one, and let's pause there for now. If you have other questions, I'll do my best to answer them. Just remember our agreement: one question per move," Lord Carrington reminded her.

Despite a slight hint of annoyance, Charlotte nodded. "Why are you at Westling Hospital?" she inquired.

"You know, my child, why I am here. You asked for my help, and I agreed," Lord Carrington responded, moving his white king's pawn to E4.

"What were you hoping to find in that room?" Charlotte placed her pawn on E5.

"Like you, I wanted to examine the files," Lord Carrington replied, moving his knight to F3.

Charlotte's central pawn was now under threat of capture, forcing her to decide whether to challenge the white pawn on E4 or support the black pawn on E5.

Lord Carrington had chosen to play the Italian Game, one of the oldest chess openings dating back to the 1600s. Charlotte noted that he could have opted for a more complex strategy, yet he deliberately selected one of the simplest and most basic openings. She assumed this choice was intended to prioritize their discussion over the intricacies of the game.

"Why are you interested in the old files?" Charlotte asked, moving her knight to C6.

"The incident that led to the restructuring of this place occurred during Rachel's employment here. Truthfully, I wasn't sure what I hoped to find in the old files, but I believed it was worth investigating," Lord Carrington replied, moving his bishop to C4.

"Why aren't you telling me everything?" Charlotte placed her bishop on C5.

Lord Carrington paused, locking eyes with Charlotte. "Everything has its time, my friend. Meanwhile, let me offer you advice. As René Descartes once said, 'de omnibus dubitandum'—doubt everything—and you will find your answers."

Charlotte hesitated, contemplating the quote. Was Lord Carrington trying to warn her about something, or was it a wise reminder to stay alert? Her thoughts were interrupted by Lord Wharton's entrance into the room, a broad smile adorning his handsome face.

"I thought I would find you two here," he greeted them warmly, pulling a chair closer to Charlotte. "How have you been?"

Lord Carrington chuckled, a lightness in his voice. "Marvelous," he replied. "I almost feel like my old self again."

"That's wonderful news," Lord Wharton expressed sincerely. "It appears that your time here may be drawing to a close."

Lord Wharton's statement caught Charlotte and Lord Carrington off guard, causing them to straighten up in their chairs and focus their attention on him. The unexpected revelation hung in the air, igniting a flood of questions, and stirring a mix of emotions within them.

"According to Miss Hargrove, Doctor Thomas believes that you may be ready to return to Haddonford," Lord Wharton relayed the information. "She didn't reveal any personal details out of respect for patient privacy. However, she did mention that you are making significant progress, and there's no reason for you to prolong your stay here."

"That's interesting," Lord Carrington murmured. "Neither of them mentioned anything to me. I hope they're not trying to hasten my departure."

Intrigued, Lord Wharton sought further clarification. "Why would they do that?"

Lord Carrington nonchalantly shrugged his shoulders, his expression and tone devoid of any indication of an ulterior motive. However, Charlotte's apprehensions persisted. She couldn't shake off the memory of one incident involving the "borrowed" key that had seemingly slipped under the radar. Yet, she couldn't help but wonder if there were other actions by Lord Carrington that might have raised red flags for Miss Hargrove, compelling her to implore Doctor Thomas to expedite Lord Carrington's recovery.

Eager to gather any useful information, Charlotte lowered her voice and asked Lord Wharton, "Did you learn anything from Miss Hargrove that could help us?"

"Are you planning to finish your game?" Lord Wharton glanced at the chessboard.

Charlotte exchanged a brief glance with Lord Carrington to confirm their mutual understanding. "Next time," she responded, speaking on behalf of both of them.

"Very well, then. Allow me to share what I have discovered," Lord Wharton began. "Doctor Thomas assumed control of the hospital in 1940, following the resignation of his predecessor. At that time, Miss Hargrove was a young and inexperienced nurse who had recently joined the staff. Westling Hospital had a smaller patient population and fewer nurses back then. The nurses were women, and according to Miss Hargrove, they were infatuated with the young and handsome doctor. Despite their attempts, ranging from subtle flirtation to more overt advances, he paid no attention to any of them. His dedication was solely focused on his work."

Lord Carrington leaned in, listening intently as Lord Wharton continued. "The nurses resided on the third floor, while Doctor Hurst's quarters were conveniently situated on the first floor, adjacent to his office. This arrangement suited him well, as he often worked late into the night, sometimes remaining in his office past midnight."

"Wait," Charlotte interrupted Lord Wharton. "Did you say Doctor Hurst?"

Lord Wharton confirmed, "Yes, Doctor James Hurst."

Disbelief etched across Charlotte's face as she glanced at Lord Carrington. After all the efforts they had gone through to uncover the doctor's name, it turned out that Lord Wharton had simply learned it through a casual conversation with Miss Hargrove.

"Please continue," Charlotte urged.

Lord Wharton delved deeper into the hospital's history, remarking, "During that period, there were only a few patients, predominantly hailing from affluent families. Doctor Hurst excelled in attending to their needs, and as a result, generous donations flowed into the hospital's fund from grateful relatives. Doctor Hurst's reputation soared, earning him celebrity status. His name was all over the newspaper articles, and he received invitations to present at prestigious conferences both in England and abroad. However, one day, everything came crashing down, and that's where the story becomes murky."

Pausing for a moment, Lord Wharton allowed Charlotte and Lord Carrington to absorb the information. Then, he continued, "Something happened between Doctor Hurst and a female patient. It's difficult to ascertain whether Miss Hargrove doesn't know the entire truth or if she's deliberately withholding something. From what I've gathered, a stunning young lady was admitted to Westling Hospital against her will. She despised being confined here and made life miserable for everyone involved. She kicked, screamed, and even attempted to harm the nurses who transported her. In order to prevent self-inflicted harm, Doctor Hurst had no choice but to confine her in an empty room. She was closely monitored for several days before he could even approach her. She resisted eating, screamed incessantly like a deranged individual, and even resorted to banging her head against the wall. Medication was administered to help her regain composure. Over time, she started to show signs of settling down and even participated in conversations with Doctor Hurst. It seemed as if she was making progress, successfully deceiving everyone around her. However, her true nature revealed itself when she craftily launched an attack on a female nurse during her rounds, and then tried to make her escape by disguising herself in the nurse's attire. It was Miss Hargrove who stumbled upon the injured nurse, promptly sounding the alarm. The young lady was placed under heightened surveillance, while the nurse received medical attention. For a while, Doctor Hurst could only meet with her when she was restrained to a chair. Once her stability was deemed satisfactory, he began meeting with her initially in her room without security present, and eventually in his office. The young lady seemed to show signs of improvement. Her family visited on several occasions, and their presence did not elicit any violent outbursts. However, it fueled her desire to flee the hospital once again. She made a few unsuccessful attempts to escape. Concerned for her well-being, the family requested a dedicated nurse to be assigned to her. They believed that having a consistent caregiver might help stabilize her mood and make her stay at Westling Hospital more manageable. Many staff members were fearful of her, with several refusing to go near her room. Doctor Hurst accommodated the family's request and allowed them to participate in the hiring process. After some time, they managed to find a middle-aged woman willing to provide care for the young lady, albeit at double the usual pay."

Lord Wharton paused again before proceeding, "The young lady possessed an uncanny talent for manipulation. She skillfully played the role of a devoted patient, once again deceiving everyone around her. She ceased her attempts to escape and remained confined to her room, seemingly engrossed in reading. However, on one fateful day, she unleashed her fury upon Doctor Hurst."

Intrigued, Lord Carrington's curiosity prompted him to ask, "What triggered her violent outburst?"

"I'm uncertain," Lord Wharton admitted. "Miss Hargrove refused to disclose specific details. She maintains that she is unaware of the events that unfolded behind closed doors, leading to the sudden eruption of violence directed at Doctor Hurst. All she knows is that the patient attacked him."

Charlotte interjected, seeking further clarification. Her voice trembled slightly as she asked, "But how did she attack him?"

Lord Wharton's words hung heavily in the air, each syllable carrying a weight of shock and horror. "She thrust a chess piece into his eye, causing partial blindness."

Disbelief imprinted on Charlotte's face as her eyes widened in shock. Lord Carrington's gaze fell upon the chess set before him, his expression a mixture of astonishment and profound horror.

Granting them a moment to process the weight of the revelation, Lord Wharton resumed his narrative. "The young lady purposefully wielded the White Queen as her chosen weapon. It is rumored that her selection of the chess piece was deliberate, symbolizing the power and dominance associated with the queen on the chessboard. Whether it was a calculated statement or simply a matter of convenience, we cannot say for certain. The incident prompted police involvement, and shortly thereafter, Doctor Hurst resigned from his position at Westling Hospital. Doctor Thomas assumed the role of the new psychiatrist."

Lord Carrington muttered in disbelief, struggling to comprehend the shocking turn of events. "But why was she allowed to have a chess set in the first place?"

"I don't have an answer to that," Lord Wharton admitted. "Miss Hargrove did not disclose any details about the day of the attack, despite being present during her shift."

Seeking closure and further understanding, Charlotte pressed for additional information. "What became of Doctor Hurst? What happened to him?"

Lord Wharton relayed what he had learned from Miss Hargrove. "Doctor Hurst relocated to live with his mother, who cared for him during his time of need. The loss of eyesight and the shattered confidence in his medical abilities had a profound effect on him. Consequently, he never resumed his medical career."

Contemplating the fragments of the story they had uncovered, Charlotte pondered aloud, "There must be more to this story. We need to dig deeper."

"Do you suspect there are hidden depths yet to be revealed?" Lord Carrington inquired.

"I cannot say with absolute certainty," Charlotte responded thoughtfully. "Yet, I have a strong intuition that there is more to uncover."

Undeterred, Lord Wharton retrieved a slip of paper from his suit pocket and declared, Miss Hargrove has graciously provided me with Doctor Hurst's mother's address. However, she could not guarantee his current residence. It has been almost twenty years since the incident took place."

"How did you manage to convince her to share the address with you?" Charlotte asked.

"A promise to increase my donation can go a long way," Lord Wharton commended.

Lord Carrington's attention shifted back to the topic of restructuring as he queried, "And what about the hospital's restructuring?"

"Miss Hargrove took great pride in the restructuring efforts. Her contributions played a pivotal role in the transformation. Male nurses were hired, security was heightened, and patients with severe mental disorders were allocated to the third floor, attended to by a specially trained nursing staff. Additionally, bars were installed on the windows. It appears that Miss Hargrove's recommendations led to enhanced patient care and propelled her career advancement."

Still seeking answers, Lord Carrington persisted, "And Rachel Offley? What role does she play in all of this?"

Lord Wharton's response was unequivocal, "None. Miss Hargrove made no mention of her. It seems Rachel holds no significance in this particular narrative."

"Does Miss Hargrove even remember her?" Lord Carrington remained determined not to abandon the thread of inquiry just yet.

"I asked about Rachel, and it took Miss Hargrove a moment to recall who she was," Lord Wharton recounted. "To her, Rachel was known as Rachel Davenport. Although they were hired simultaneously, their paths only intersected in the kitchen. They never formed a close bond. Nevertheless, Miss Hargrove remembers Rachel as a compassionate and caring individual who forged connections with many patients. She also described her as a loving soul and an exceptional cook, but we were already aware of that," Lord Wharton added.

Lord Carrington's curiosity persisted, and he wondered aloud, "Do you think Rachel ever crossed paths with the young woman who attacked Doctor Hurst?"

"It's possible but unlikely," Lord Wharton replied. "As far as I understand, the young lady was relocated to the third floor. Food delivery to the patients on that floor was handled separately, and Rachel's role was primarily that of a cook, not a server."

"Did Miss Hargrove provide any information regarding her current whereabouts?"

Lord Wharton pondered the earlier conversation before responding, "I don't believe she did. I can't recall her mentioning what became of her."

"I see, I see," Lord Carrington uttered, a hint of disappointment in his voice. He began tidying up the chess pieces, indicating his waning interest in both the game and the ongoing conversation.

A prolonged silence enveloped the room, signaling the conclusion of their exchange.

Chapter Thirty-Three

"**I can't believe I'm in Old Brompton**," Charlotte exclaimed, marveling at the magnificent homes that stood proudly on both sides of the street. The fact that Doctor Hurst resided in this neighborhood came as a pleasant surprise, as it provided her with an opportunity to explore this part of London. Brompton was known to be the home of many esteemed writers and intellectuals whom Charlotte admired, such as Muzio Clementi, the Italian-born composer and pianist, Caroline Clive, the English writer, and Stéphane Mallarmé, the French poet. Lost in her admiration for the architecture, Charlotte almost collided with Lord Wharton when he abruptly halted in front of an old yet well-maintained red-brick home.

"Here we are," he announced, knocking on the weathered, dark brown door. After a few anxious minutes, an elderly lady cautiously peered through the narrow slot created by the door chain, casting a wary glance at Lord Wharton and Charlotte.

"We're here to see Doctor Hurst," Lord Wharton stated respectfully, trying to convey their purpose.

"And you are?" she asked, her voice carrying a raspy undertone.

Lord Wharton proceeded to introduce himself and Charlotte, their warm greetings met with a chilling reception as an icy glare emanated from the old lady, who remained steadfastly positioned inside the house. In a sudden and unexpected gesture, she forcefully slammed the door shut, the resonating bang shattering the stillness of the air.

"I'm not quite sure what went wrong, but that encounter didn't go as planned," Lord Wharton remarked, his brow furrowed with confusion.

"Perhaps we should give it another try," Charlotte suggested. "After all, we have nothing to lose."

Lord Wharton nodded, raising his hand to knock once more, but before he could make contact, the door unexpectedly swung open. Standing in the doorway was a frail, petite woman in her seventies, bearing a striking resemblance to their earlier encounter. However, her almond-shaped eyes and beautifully arched eyebrows carried a gentler expression, softening the tension in the air.

"What can I do for you?" she inquired, her voice carrying a mix of curiosity and caution.

"We are in need of Doctor Hurst's assistance regarding a personal matter," Lord Wharton responded carefully, aware of the delicate nature of their request.

The mistress of the house hesitated, caught between the decision to either continue the conversation inside or conclude it at the front door. Charlotte's mind meandered to a passage from George Eliot's *The Mill on the Floss*, serving as a gentle reminder not to judge the worth of something solely based on appearances. However, in this particular moment, the weight of first impressions couldn't be disregarded. Charlotte clung to a glimmer of hope, yearning for their genuine intentions to shine through, persuading the lady to grant them entry.

"I offer my apologies on behalf of my sister," she finally spoke. "Eleanor can be quite overprotective. Please, do come in."

"Thank you," Charlotte and Lord Wharton accepted the invitation and followed their hostess into a living room filled with bouquets of vibrant red roses. The sweet fragrance permeated the air, creating an unusually calming atmosphere. Charlotte found herself drawn to the beauty of the flowers and felt their presence was far from overwhelming.

"Your sister's actions speak of her love for you," Charlotte remarked.

"Perhaps," the old lady sighed. "Many of our actions are driven by a genuine desire to protect or support, but there is always a slight chance that selfishness lurks beneath. My relationship with my sister is quite complex." She leaned closer to a bouquet of red roses and inhaled their scent.

"You can see my fondness for roses," she attempted a smile, but only one corner of her mouth moved upwards. "Archaeologists have discovered rose fossils dating back thirty-five million years. It is one of the oldest flowers on Earth. My late husband used to give me a bouquet of roses every week, and after his passing, my son carried on the tradition. How did you know James?" Mrs. Hurst asked, causing Charlotte to exchange a glance with Lord Wharton. The use of the past tense caused her heart to sink.

"We don't have a personal relationship with him," Lord Wharton replied. "However, a friend of ours worked alongside Doctor Hurst at Westling Hospital in the past. We were hoping to discuss our friend with him if he happens to recall her."

Mrs. Hurst's voice turned somber as she quietly responded, "I'm afraid my son won't be able to assist you. He is no longer with us."

Lord Wharton, though taken aback by the news, managed to express his genuine condolences with practiced composure. "Please accept our deepest sympathies for your loss," he conveyed, his shock expertly veiled.

Mrs. Hurst nodded sadly and then inquired, "Was your friend a nurse or a patient at Westling Hospital?"

"She was a cook," Lord Wharton replied. "Her name was Rachel Davenport."

Doctor Hurst's mother fell silent for a while. "Rachel is a beautiful name. If I had a daughter, I might have named her Rachel. But

I was only blessed with one son. James never mentioned anyone by the name Rachel; otherwise, I would have remembered it," Mrs. Hurst rubbed her temples. "I believe you may have already mentioned it, but my memory is failing me. Could you please remind me . . . What happened to Rachel?"

Lord Wharton hesitated, and Charlotte could sense his internal struggle between protecting Mrs. Hurst's delicate state of mind and revealing the truth.

"My husband had the assumption that roses are fragile. He treated me as one, and I didn't mind it. But if you think about it, roses are resilient. They have to be to survive for thirty-five million years on Earth. They aren't as delicate as they appear. There's a large rose bush growing on the wall of the Cathedral of Hildesheim in Germany that has thrived for almost 1,000 years," Mrs. Hurst reflected. "Young man, don't worry about my well-being. Look at me—both my husband and my son are gone, yet I'm still here. I can handle more than you might think."

Lord Wharton nodded, acknowledging her strength.

"She was poisoned," he finally revealed.

Mrs. Hurst closed her eyes, deep in thought. "Death is devastating. It inflicts unbearable pain on those left behind. I know that if James were alive, he would have wanted to help. Despite what people say, he was a good doctor and cared deeply about his patients and employees." Mrs. Hurst called out for her sister, but there was no response.

"Eleanor!" she called out louder. "I know you can hear me."

Silence lingered in the air.

"I suppose she's ignoring me. Once again, I apologize for my sister's behavior. Eleanor seeks someone to blame. James's death devastated her and filled her with anger," Mrs. Hurst wiped away a tear.

"I am struggling to convince myself that James is now in a better and happier place, but I'm not doing a good job of it. My son lived like a recluse for years, and no one cared to visit or check on him. It's as if the whole world wrote him off. He made one mistake and was condemned to a lifetime of misery. People can be cruel and unforgiving, but don't we all make mistakes? What would life be like if no one ever erred? I refuse to allow anger into my life. This world doesn't need more negativity, as there is already plenty out there. What this world needs is to learn how to forgive! Each of us must begin by forgiving ourselves first and then learn to forgive others."

Charlotte observed a flicker of fire in the old lady's eyes, but it quickly faded, leaving Mrs. Hurst looking utterly exhausted.

"Please wait here," she said, reaching for a cane with a sterling silver handle. "I don't believe Eleanor will be of any help to me. I'll be right back."

Charlotte watched as Mrs. Hurst left the room. Instead of relying on the cane for support, she carried it in her left hand, indicating that its purpose was more for reaching things than assisting with mobility.

Something Mrs. Hurst had mentioned bothered Charlotte, but she decided to keep it to herself until after their visit. Eleanor could have been lurking in the adjacent room, listening to their conversation. Charlotte chose to exercise caution and waited for Mrs. Hurst's return in silence. Lord Wharton seemed to have reached the same conclusion, as he absentmindedly flipped through a magazine on the table.

Charlotte's thoughts continued to circle back to Mrs. Hurst's comment about a mistake her son had made. Miss Hargrove had never hinted at any errors on the part of the young doctor. According to her, Doctor Hurst had voluntarily left Westling Hospital after receiving medical assistance for his eye injury.

Mrs. Hurst returned to the room, slightly breathless, and handed Lord Wharton a stack of leather-bound notebooks.

"James kept a diary during his time at the hospital," she explained. "I don't believe he documented everything in here, but you might find answers to your questions within his notes.

However, I would like them back once you're finished reading," she added softly. "Perhaps someday, I'll find the strength to read them myself . . . Maybe they'll help me understand why he did it."

"I'm sorry?" Lord Wharton looked bewildered.

"Oh, you didn't know," Mrs. Hurst revealed. "My son took his own life. It was completely out of character for him. He had endured so much, and it simply doesn't make any sense that he would do this now . . . But then again, we never truly know the inner torment someone else may be experiencing, do we?" She pulled out a handkerchief and dabbed at her eyes.

Chapter Thirty-Four

Lord Wharton departed for London on work-related matters after dropping off Charlotte at Haddonford Manor. With a farewell wave from her right hand, she tightly clutched the leather-bound diaries with her left, determined to hide them until she could devote her attention to them without any interruptions. The Manor's interior seemed strangely deserted, which worked in Charlotte's favor. She had no desire for anyone to catch sight of the contents in her hands and subject her to unwanted inquiries about the notebooks.

Charlotte quickly climbed the staircase, her steps almost silent. As she grasped the doorknob to her bedroom, muffled conversations drifted from Lady Beatrice's quarters. The anguish in Lady Beatrice's voice revealed her agitation, contrasted with the soothing, deep tones of Frank, who persistently responded with, "I don't believe so."

Conscious of the inappropriateness in eavesdropping, Charlotte entered her room briskly, aiming to shut the door quickly behind her, yet found herself unexpectedly immobile. A peculiar shiver traveled up her spine, challenging her efforts to prevent it from overwhelming her completely. Following her arrival at Haddonford Manor and notable interactions with

Frank, securing her door had become a meticulous routine. A thorough inspection of the bedroom revealed everything to be undisturbed, precisely as she had arranged earlier, with the sole exception of her missing key. She painstakingly reviewed her day's activities in her mind, from the early morning awakening, the act of dressing, and the neat arrangement of her bed. She distinctly remembered the moment she searched for her hairbrush, the subsequent hair styling, and the definitive action of locking her door as she left. Yet, now, the key was absent from its customary location. Proceeding with caution, Charlotte advanced towards the curtains, diligently drawing each aside in an effort to ensure no presence was concealed behind them. Following this, she checked beneath her bed, confirming everything was as it should be, with no anomalies detected. Weary, she eventually settled into a chair and produced from her pocket a little key—this one was designated for the lower drawer of her desk, a secure space for her personal diary. Feeling fortunate for keeping it with her, Charlotte placed Doctor Hurst's diaries atop her own within the drawer and fastened the lock securely, ensuring the confidentiality of their contents.

Just then, Lady Beatrice appeared in the doorway.

"Charlotte, I'm glad you're back. Inspector Sinclair is on his way to speak with you. Is there anything I should know?"

Surprised by the news, Charlotte responded, "No, Lady Beatrice. I'm puzzled as to why the inspector wants to meet with me personally."

Lady Beatrice scowled, her expression filled with concern. "Have you heard from Henry? How long does he intend to visit his friends? It's a ridiculous notion. He must have completely lost his mind to leave Haddonford in the midst of the investigation. I would have expected that from Lady Isabelle, but not him."

"Lord Carrington had a fondness for Mrs. Offley," Charlotte replied cautiously, "and he has been trying to assist in finding the person responsible for her murder."

"And that's why he left?" Lady Beatrice's confusion deepened.

"Yes," Charlotte affirmed, avoiding direct eye contact. "I'm certain he will return as soon as he can."

Lady Beatrice frowned, frustration evident on her face. "Nothing seems to make sense anymore. Richard keeps me in the dark, Henry disappears, and I find myself taking on Margaret and Frank's duties—responding to phone calls and delivering messages. What is happening?" she threw her hands up in exasperation before retreating to her room.

Inspector Sinclair arrived promptly, refusing to keep himself waiting.

The piercing screech of brakes and the subsequent slam of a car door reached Charlotte's ears from her bedroom. Within a minute, Margaret's voice welcomed Inspector Sinclair at the front door. As Charlotte stepped into the Blue Room, she found him already settled in a plush chair, nonchalantly crossing one leg over the other. A deep furrow etched his forehead, while his small, piercing eyes remained fixed on Charlotte without a hint of a blink.

"I see you're keeping yourself busy," he remarked, skipping any formal greetings.

"Good afternoon, Inspector Sinclair," Charlotte replied, maintaining a friendly smile despite the inspector's cold demeanor. "I've been assisting Lord Wharton. If I had known you were looking for me, I would have made it a priority to meet with you."

"I was informed that you've been conducting your own investigation," he said, his tone frosty.

"May I inquire who alerted you?" Charlotte asked, immediately regretting her words. It was clear that the inspector had no intention of sharing information with her and was irritated by her presence.

"I understand that Lord Wharton feels sympathy for you, which, in my opinion, clouds his judgment," the inspector retorted. "He has given you too much freedom, which I intend to revoke for the sake of this investigation, of course."

"What do you mean?" Charlotte asked, her voice barely above a whisper.

"What I mean is that I forbid you from meddling in this investigation. You are a suspect, just like anyone else, and your involvement could cause significant delays in solving this case. You're leading Lord Wharton on a wild goose chase."

Charlotte stood silently, feeling vulnerable and unprotected. Someone had taken her bedroom key, and now someone was using the inspector to halt her efforts. Were these actions orchestrated by the same person, or were there two different individuals involved?

"Did you hear me?" Inspector Sinclair stood up and approached Charlotte. "Your arrival at Haddonford Manor set off a chain of unfortunate events that culminated in Rachel Offley's death. You are a suspect in this case, not the lead investigator," he enunciated each word carefully, as if assuming she had trouble understanding.

"I disagree," Charlotte said firmly.

The inspector's eyebrows arched, and his eyes darkened with anger. "Disagree with what?" he demanded.

"I beg to differ that everything began with my arrival," Charlotte countered. "It was actually on the day of my hiring when I coincidentally crossed paths with Frank Offley in the hallway. It marked our first encounter. I was in search of my bedroom, and Mr. Offley graciously guided me to its location. Moreover, he offered a piece of advice—urging me to keep my doors locked and windows tightly shut," Charlotte explained.

"And?" Inspector Sinclair smirked, a corner of his mouth curling upward.

"And I found it to be an unusual piece of advice, leading me to believe that something must have happened at Haddonford Manor to warrant such a warning," Charlotte continued.

"Did he mention that something had indeed occurred?" the inspector inquired.

"No," Charlotte shook her head.

"Did you inquire further about his meaning?" he pressed.

"No," Charlotte replied softly. "Since that fateful night, numerous events have unfolded, and I've never had the chance to engage in a conversation with Mr. Offley."

"It seems evident that you failed to take his words seriously back then; otherwise, you would have exerted a greater effort to comprehend the rationale behind his warning," the inspector remarked with a touch of sarcasm permeating his voice.

Charlotte recognized the futility of continuing the conversation and decided to bring it to a close. "Is there anything else you would like to discuss with me?" she inquired, hoping to conclude the interaction.

"For today, we are finished," Inspector Sinclair coldly responded. "Remember, you are strictly forbidden from involving yourself in the investigation. I will be closely monitoring your actions," he added.

Charlotte pondered the identity of Inspector Sinclair's informant at Haddonford, but at present, she had no inkling as to who that person might be. While she wanted to trust Lady Beatrice, she couldn't dismiss the possibility that Margaret, Samuel, or even Lady Isabelle could be obstructing her progress. Even Lord Carrington, with his own hidden agenda, might have been in contact with the inspector. Charlotte still had yet to uncover the true reason behind Lord Carrington's visit to Westling Hospital.

"When the sky grows cloudy and your mood begins to change, seek out things you can control," echoed the words of Mother Superior in Charlotte's mind. Her simple advice had helped Charlotte endure numerous difficult times. She realized that she had no control over Inspector Sinclair's decisions or the missing key to her bedroom. However, what she could control was the fact that she possessed several of Doctor Hurst's diaries, generously shared by his mother. Determined not to waste any more time, Charlotte made her way up to her room and wedged a chair against the handle as a makeshift security measure. Although not as secure as a lock, it would have to suffice for the time being. Settling into her bed, Charlotte arranged the leather-bound notebooks in front of her. They all possessed an identical appearance, crafted from luxurious, hand-selected dark brown leather that felt velvety under her fingertips. A total of five notebooks lay before her, devoid of any distinguishing marks indicating which one was Doctor Hurst's initial diary. Selecting one at random, Charlotte opened it and read the inscription on the first page: "There is only one good, knowledge, and one evil, ignorance" - Socrates, #II. Intrigued, she ventured to open another notebook, revealing the words "The only true wisdom is in knowing you know nothing" - Socrates, #I. Setting that notebook aside, she peered into the next one. Above Roman Numeral IV, she discovered the quote, "Every action has its pleasures and its price." Moving on to the subsequent diary, she read the attributed words of Socrates, "Be kind, for everyone you meet is fighting a hard battle." The final notebook contained a considerably longer quote: "If you don't get what you want, you suffer; if you get what you don't want, you suffer; even when you get exactly what you want, you still suffer because you can't hold on to it forever." Methodically arranging the diaries in the correct order, Charlotte occupied herself with the captivating contents, engrossed in her reading.

CHAPTER THIRTY-FIVE

CHARLOTTE STIRRED FROM HER SLUMBER, SHE stretched and gradually became aware of her surroundings. She had dozed off on top of her duvet, amidst a sea of scattered notebooks. A twinge of stiffness in her neck and a faint headache lingered, likely the result of straining her eyes to decipher Doctor Hurst's meticulous yet minuscule handwriting. The more she delved into his diaries, the blurrier the words on the pages seemed to become. Immersed in the content, she had lost track of time, unable to recall when sleep had finally claimed her. The glimpse of the clock before drifting off had shown three in the morning, and now it was almost six. Pulling the covers up to her shoulders in an attempt to ward off the chill that made her shiver, Charlotte realized that she had finished reading the first three diaries. She longed for both, time to digest the information she had absorbed and a way to visit Westling Hospital. Unfortunately, neither option was currently within her reach.

Charlotte's senses heightened as the distinct sound of Lady Beatrice's footsteps echoed outside her door—a surprising deviation from her recent preference to remain in her room until later hours. Startled into action, Charlotte swiftly threw off the comforting embrace of her blanket and hastily dressed herself. After securing the diary, she left the room to greet Lady Beatrice.

In the Blue Room, Margaret extended a silver tray, bearing a cup of steaming coffee, while Samuel held a stack of letters in his hands. A peculiar sense of déjà vu washed over Charlotte. The sensation unsettled her, transporting her back to the earliest days of her employment, when Mrs. Offley's lively spirit still graced the household. Despite being aware that déjà vu was a common experience, Charlotte couldn't shake off the unease it evoked within her.

"Did you manage to get some sleep?" Lady Beatrice scrutinized Charlotte with a shrewd gaze.

"I was up late reading," Charlotte replied.

"I see. There have been a few urgent matters that have been keeping me awake. The sooner we address them, the better chance I have of finding some relief," Lady Beatrice said.

"First and foremost, we should go over the list of candidates for the cook position and discuss the possibility of hiring a new maid."

Lady Beatrice made it clear, "It's not that Margaret isn't excelling in her current role. In fact, she has shown a hidden talent. Margaret has been diligently carrying out her duties and even taking on Rachel's responsibilities with great success. However, I was pleasantly surprised to discover her remarkable culinary skills," Lady Beatrice praised Margaret with a warm smile.

"I learned from Mrs. Offley," Margaret replied proudly. "She graciously allowed me to observe her in the kitchen while I assisted with the dishes."

Charlotte wholeheartedly agreed with Lady Beatrice's assessment—Margaret's cooking was indeed fantastic. Mrs. Offley's skills were a perfect ten on a scale of zero to ten, while Margaret's abilities easily earned her a solid seven. Charlotte vividly remembered the days when Mrs. Offley skillfully maneuvered a ladle, expertly stirring vegetables in an iron skillet, with Margaret quietly watching her, absorbing the culinary techniques and spice combinations. Their time spent together naturally led to Margaret acquiring some of Mrs. Offley's culinary secrets, which, combined with her innate talent, significantly elevated the quality of her dishes.

"What I mean to say, my dear," Lady Beatrice turned her attention to Charlotte, "is that unless one of the candidates for Rachel's position proves to be exceptionally superior to Margaret, I would prefer to offer Margaret the cook position and hire a new maid. There are advantages for Margaret in taking on this role. Firstly, it provides her with more stability, and she will earn a higher salary as a cook. You see, when I hire maids, I require them to remain single as long as they work for me," Lady Beatrice explained. "I am more lenient when it comes to a cook."

Charlotte noticed Margaret blushing. If the young man Charlotte had seen Margaret with at the pub a few nights ago was a serious love interest, she might prefer to seize the opportunity to become Mrs. Offley's successor while the position was still available. Even if Margaret wished to remain single for some time, working as a cook offered more future possibilities compared to her current role. One question remained—did Margaret genuinely desire to work as a cook? Lady Beatrice seemed to have neglected to ask the maid, and Margaret had not made her intentions clear.

Charlotte observed Margaret carefully refilling Lady Beatrice's coffee cup, then her gaze shifted to Samuel standing to Lady Beatrice's right, neatly holding a stack of envelopes.

"Let's see what the mail has brought us today," Charlotte remarked, reaching out for the envelopes with an air of routine.

Samuel handed them over, his demeanor calm and professional.

Charlotte methodically scanned the return addresses on each envelope. Among the day's correspondence, she noticed a letter from the staffing agency Lady Beatrice often utilized. Opening it, she quickly reviewed the list of potential hires.

Sipping her coffee, Lady Beatrice asked, "Any standout candidates there?"

"A few seem quite promising," Charlotte replied, her attention absorbed by the summaries attached to each name, reflecting on the suitability of each candidate for Lady Beatrice's requirements.

"Could you provide some insight into the applicants?" Lady Beatrice inquired, her voice laced with a subtle hint of impatience.

"Absolutely," Charlotte began. "The agency has outdone itself this time, offering an in-depth analysis that aligns precisely with your requirements. Among the candidates, three particularly stand out. The first two, both in their forties and unmarried, have garnered extensive experience in distinguished households. Despite differing circumstances leading them to seek new employment, their reasons are thoroughly justifiable. The first is looking for a position due to the relocation of her previous employer, while the second has recently become available following the demise of her last employer from old age."

"And the third?" probed Lady Beatrice, her interest piqued.

"The third candidate presents a different profile," Charlotte continued. "She's considerably younger, a widow hailing from Wales with an upbringing in an orphanage. She has no children of her own."

As she relayed this information, Charlotte couldn't help but notice Margaret and Samuel's focused attention, possibly connecting her words to her earlier speculation about Lady Beatrice's seeming inclination towards hiring orphans.

Seeing an opportunity, Charlotte ventured, "Would you like me to arrange interviews with these candidates?"

"Yes, please do. The sooner we can meet them, the better," Lady Beatrice responded decisively before gracefully exiting the room.

"What's the purpose of interviews, really?" Margaret mused aloud, her tone skeptical. "It seems quite clear who Lady Beatrice will likely choose."

"You, of course," Samuel responded with a light chuckle.

Margaret glanced around cautiously to ensure Lady Beatrice wasn't within earshot. "I wouldn't be too certain," she replied thoughtfully. "That third candidate, with her orphan and widow background, might outshine me in the kitchen. Her story does tug at the heartstrings."

Samuel offered a differing view. "Your track record here speaks volumes, Margaret. You have seniority, after all. If you truly desire this position, it's essential to make your intentions known to Lady Beatrice. She seems ready to offer it to you."

Charlotte, observing their exchange, asked, "Do you even want the position, Margaret?"

Margaret let out a heavy sigh. "It's an honor to be considered, especially given Lady Beatrice's high regard for my cooking. But with all that's happened at Haddonford Manor, my feelings are mixed. The nights here unsettle me—the creaking floors, the howling wind, the rustling leaves outside—it all leaves me on edge. I'm constantly anxious. I wonder, do any of you feel the same way at night?"

"I wouldn't say I'm afraid," Samuel admitted. "But it does keep me more vigilant."

"That's easy for you to say, being a man," Margaret retorted. Turning to Charlotte, she inquired, "What about you, Charlotte? How do you cope?"

"I used to lock my door for a sense of security. But since I've lost my key, that's no longer an option," Charlotte shared, a hint of frustration in her voice.

"Lost your key?" Margaret asked, surprised. "But how is it possible?"

"I don't have any idea," Charlotte replied. "It seems to have vanished."

Margaret firmly shook her head. "I haven't seen it for sure. It is odd, though. Who would have a reason to take your key?"

Charlotte responded with a shrug. "It's a mystery."

Samuel voiced his worry, "I hope you locate it swiftly. Moreover, Margaret, I sincerely wish you'd think again about leaving. Our team synergy at Haddonford is exceptional. Perhaps all you require is a short break."

Margaret sighed. "Even if I took time off, I don't have anywhere else to go. By the way, does anyone know where Lord Carrington is and when he's expected back?"

"Yes, he should be returning shortly. Is there a problem?" Charlotte asked, noting Margaret's troubled expression.

Margaret hesitated before revealing, "He got a call yesterday about some birth record inquiry. I answered it in Frank's absence. The caller was vague but mentioned a birth record and asked Lord Carrington to call him back."

Charlotte asked, "Did he leave a contact number?"

"No, he just said he would know how to reach him," Margaret replied.

Charlotte pondered over Lord Carrington's recent activities, her mind teeming with questions. What was he involved in? She resolved to stay alert, keeping a watchful eye on the unfolding events. Despite wanting to trust him, she couldn't help but consider Lord Carrington a potential suspect in the mysteries at Haddonford Manor.

Chapter Thirty-Six

"Are you quite certain Margaret overheard a mention of birth records?" Lord Wharton inquired, bringing his convertible to a steady halt outside the imposing façade of Westling Hospital.

"Quite certain," Charlotte affirmed with conviction. "She distinctly heard a reference to 'birth records.'"

"A curious matter, indeed," Lord Wharton mused, his gaze lingering on the hospital's entrance. "Of late, have you noticed anything . . . out of the ordinary with Lord Carrington? Especially considering your recent encounters," he pressed, a note of concern threading through his voice.

Charlotte pondered Lord Carrington's mysterious frequentations of the West Wing and the archives. Nodding slowly, she admitted, "His recent activities have been peculiar, to say the least. Yet how they tie to the matter of birth records escapes me."

"Perhaps a direct conversation is in order?" Lord Wharton proposed, stepping out and offering a hand to assist Charlotte. "You are due to meet him shortly, are you not?"

As she alighted from the car, Charlotte straightened her attire, "My visit today bears no relation to Lord Carrington," she clarified with a hint of finality. However, before she could ascend the steps,

Lord Wharton gently grasped her arm, his expression earnest, seeking to understand more.

"Then, what brings you here today?" he inquired.

"I've come to chase down a personal suspicion," Charlotte replied, her tone intentionally ambiguous but firm.

"Is this related to something you discovered in the diary? You've been unusually tight-lipped about it. You've looked into it, haven't you?" Lord Wharton probed further.

Letting out a soft sigh, Charlotte conceded, "I've started to delve into it, but much remains to be sifted through. I'll share my findings with you later, perhaps after you've come to collect me."

"Am I to pick you up, then?" he queried, a shade of uncertainty in his voice.

"If it isn't too much trouble. Otherwise, I can take a cab back to Haddonford Manor," she suggested diplomatically.

"And when shall I return for you?"

"Around 8:00 PM, should everything go as planned. Will that work for you?"

"That will do, but be prepared for an in-depth conversation tonight," Lord Wharton noted, his tone carrying a mixture of skepticism and anticipation. He then let go of her arm, signaling her to continue on her way.

Upon her entry, Charlotte acknowledged a nurse stationed at the entrance and continued her way towards the recreational area. She harbored no expectations of encountering Lord Carrington here at this time. The room presented a picture of tranquility, with a select few patients deeply engrossed in their peaceful activities. From the corner of her eye, Charlotte noticed another nurse overseeing the space. This nurse's gaze met hers, prompting Charlotte to respond with a warm, acknowledging smile.

Beside the window, Charlotte noticed Emily guiding a wheelchair in which Mrs. Dale, a sweet old lady who was a patient at the hospital, relished the fading sunlight. This practice had grown into a cherished ritual between the two, and Charlotte frequently found herself observing these gentle scenes, weather permitting.

As the afternoon progressed towards evening, the sun embarked on its descent, elongating shadows and infusing the environment with a resplendent mix of orange and pink hues. The onset of cooler air induced Emily to wrap a blanket around Mrs. Dale with gentle care, ensuring her warmth. Mrs. Dale's face lit up with a smile of deep appreciation, her expression a silent expression of thanks. Following their final leisurely circuit of the garden, they made their return to the building.

Charlotte observed their silhouettes as they disappeared through the front entrance, only to reappear in the recreational room a short while later. Emily's greeting, "Hello, Charlotte," was infused with the radiance of someone who had just spent a rejuvenating period outdoors, her smile broad and inviting.

"It seems like a perfect day for a walk, doesn't it?" Charlotte said, bending down to Mrs. Dale's level in her wheelchair. "And how are you today, Mrs. Dale?"

"Very well, thank you, my dear," Mrs. Dale replied, her expression brightening with a heartfelt smile.

"And how is Lord Carrington today?" Emily inquired with a cheerful tone.

"I haven't had the chance to see him yet," Charlotte explained. "I was brought here by a friend a little while ago, and I expect Lord Carrington to join shortly," she added, her eyes briefly flicking towards the clock.

"Oh, then you're here just in time," Mrs. Dale chimed in with enthusiasm. "Would you care to join me for a cup of tea?"

"I'd be delighted," Charlotte responded, her voice conveying genuine pleasure at the invitation.

Emily slightly adjusted Mrs. Dale's wheelchair closer to the fireplace, making sure she was comfortably nestled in the cozy warmth radiating from the flickering flames.

"The crackling sound of the wood is quite comforting," Mrs.

Dale observed, her face softening into a smile tinged with nostalgia. "It takes me back to my childhood days – a period filled with innocence and exploration, free from the complexities of life." Her eyes gently closed as she savored the memory, the fireplace's warmth mirroring the fondness of her recollections.

As the soft light from the fire played across her features, Mrs. Dale gradually opened her eyes, the shift from her reminiscent state to the present momentarily disorienting her. Her gaze, which had been lost in distant thoughts, now slowly moved towards Charlotte, revealing a hint of bewilderment.

"Emily, dear, why are we here again?" she inquired, her voice soft and uncertain.

Emily gently responded, "Charlotte is here to meet Lord Carrington, and you invited her for tea." She added softly for clarification, "I'm Emily, and she's Charlotte."

Mrs. Dale relaxed into her chair, her sigh bridging the gap between her memories and the present. "Ah, thank you, dear," she murmured, her attention returning. "But where is our tea?"

"Right here in your hand," Emily responded as she gestured to the elegant Churchill cup Mrs. Dale held.

With a look of surprise, Mrs. Dale glanced at the cup, then extended it outward, inadvertently prompting both Charlotte and Emily to react. Charlotte, positioned nearer, relieved Mrs. Dale of the cup. Simultaneously, Emily, in her eagerness to help, slightly jostled Charlotte, resulting in tea spilling onto Charlotte's blouse.

Emily's face filled with concern. "Oh dear, I'm terribly sorry," she uttered, visibly upset.

Charlotte quickly rose, lightly dabbing at the damp fabric. "Don't worry, it's completely fine," she reassured Emily, even as she felt the warmth of the spilled tea against her skin.

Emily's concern deepened as she noticed the spreading stain on Charlotte's white top.

"You might have scalded yourself and I've completely spoiled your blouse," she added, her face a portrait of regret.

Charlotte, seeking to ease Emily's distress, said. "It's only tea. It'll dry soon enough."

"But the stain," Emily fretted, her eyes fixed on the blotch. "I could help remove it quickly if you don't mind changing into a nurse's uniform while your blouse dries."

"That's very kind of you, I don't mind at all," Charlotte responded, grateful for the offer. "Who should I ask for the uniform?"

"There's no need to ask anyone," Emily replied, her tone reassuring. "I'll fetch it for you."

As Charlotte watched Mrs. Dale, who seemed lost in her own world, her expression weary and distant, Emily noticed Charlotte's gaze.

"Actually, maybe I should first take Mrs. Dale back to her room to help her prepare for the night," she reconsidered. "Here, take my key. Turn right as you leave this room, and the closet you need is the fifth door on the right. You can't miss it. I'll meet you there in a few minutes."

The storage room was akin to a large walk-in closet, its shelves meticulously organized with stacks of towels, sheets, and uniforms. Charlotte, upon entering, quickly deduced the deliberate absence of medical supplies. Such items, she reasoned, would be under stricter security than mere linens. She attentively sifted through the garments, keen to find one that would fit her unobtrusively.

Her attention was soon captured by a light teal uniform, identical to those worn by the nurses on the hospital's third floor. It was tantalizingly out of reach, perched atop the highest shelf. Scanning the room for a solution, Charlotte's gaze landed on an industrial leather swivel stool secluded in the corner. Although clearly not meant to be a makeshift ladder, it was her only viable option given the urgency of her situation.

With a mix of caution and haste, Charlotte removed her shoes and ascended the stool, using its backrest for stability. She stretched upwards, fingertips grazing the desired uniform. After a tense moment, she secured the garment, quickly checking its size before carefully stepping down. Ensuring the stool was replaced exactly as she found it, she left no trace of her intrusion.

Charlotte then quickly donned the nurse's attire and cautiously cracked open the storage room door, scanning the hallway to ensure its emptiness. Moving toward the staircase, her heart raced from a blend of excitement and nerves. Though she had never ventured to the third floor, Charlotte's familiarity with it stemmed from Doctor Hurst's thorough narratives in his journals. Navigating the passageways of Westling Hospital, she found herself astounded by the congruence between her surroundings and his detailed recollections.

Following Doctor Hurst's precisely outlined floor plan, Charlotte ascended the stairs. Her fingers stretched out, reaching for the handle of the heavy metal door that separated her from the third-floor hallway. Pausing briefly to steady her nerves, she took in a deep breath and pulled the handle, relieved to find it yielding smoothly, without any telltale squeaks.

Although adequately lit, the hallway lacked the vibrant brightness that graced the lower floors. Patient rooms lined the left side, their closed doors forming a silent barrier to their occupants. Under different circumstances, Charlotte would have been captivated by the historical architecture of the place. However, her current mission allowed no room for distractions; her sole focus was on locating the room described in Doctor Hurst's diaries.

Setting foot on the soft carpeting, Charlotte braved the oppressive silence that clung to the hallway. Each door had a small window at eye level; some were shut leaving her unable to discern whether the rooms were occupied or not. Charlotte hurried past each door, moving with a measured caution. Despite her haste, time seemed to stretch and warp, elongating the search into what felt like an eternity. Finally, her eyes settled on a golden plate engraved with the number 309—her destination. Drawing in another fortifying breath, Charlotte approached the door, mentally preparing herself before stealing a quick glimpse through the small window.

As Charlotte cautiously glanced into the chamber, a soft, inviting glow bathed the meticulously arranged interior. The heart of the room was occupied by a woman of dignified demeanor, her silhouette outlined against the luminance. Unaware of Charlotte's gaze, she was absorbed in the ritual of combing her long, silver locks that fell down her back in a display of timeless elegance.

In an unexpected motion, the woman ceased her grooming and turned, her movements beautiful yet deliberate. Rising from her seat, she advanced towards the doorway where Charlotte stood transfixed. A spark of intense interest illuminated her eyes, compelling her to scrutinize the unexpected visitor more closely.

Charlotte, caught in the unexpected encounter, felt a surge of fear immobilize her. Her heart stuttered, a frigid shiver coursing through her veins. She was ensnared in a web of dread, her eyes locked with those of the woman before her, unable to move or divert her gaze. The air between them seemed charged with an electric tension, leaving Charlotte caught in a moment that seemed to stretch into eternity.

A towering male nurse suddenly strode towards Charlotte. Dressed in a pale teal uniform, his eyes were masked by a shroud of suspicion, and his voice carried a tinge of skepticism. He addressed her directly, "Are you new here? I don't recall ever seeing you before."

Caught off guard, Charlotte weighed her options carefully. Outmaneuvering the nurse seemed implausible, as he obstructed her path to the staircase, leaving little chance for escape. Persuading him of her recent employment held a slim possibility of success. However, Charlotte had already obtained the crucial information she sought from Westling Hospital, rendering the prospect of being caught and subsequently expelled from the premises inconsequential. Her purpose had been fulfilled.

Before Charlotte could reach a decision, an alarm shattered

the tranquility, piercing the air with its urgent cry. The male nurse briefly averted his gaze towards the source—an alarm positioned above the staircase door. Seizing the precious opportunity, Charlotte sprang into action. Like a gazelle in full stride, she swiftly propelled herself towards the exit, quickly descending the stairs and bounding over each step to sustain her momentum. Only when she reached the first floor did she come to an abrupt halt, taking a moment to collect herself. As Charlotte paused to regain her composure, a flurry of passing nurses scurried by, their minds consumed by the hospital's demands. Charlotte took a moment to steady her racing heartbeat, then briskly made her way to the closet where she had stashed her clothes.

Chapter Thirty-Seven

"WHAT HAVE YOU GOTTEN YOURSELF INTO, Miss Reinford?" Inspector Sinclair asked, occupying Miss Hargrove's chair. His weariness and displeasure were evident after having to make the journey to Westling Hospital at the end of his shift. Although Charlotte sensed his reluctance, she was grateful that he had responded to her call.

Examining her attire, the inspector gestured toward the teal uniform Charlotte was wearing. "Why are you dressed like this? And what were you doing in the restricted area of the hospital, meant only for authorized personnel? Moreover, why are you even here in the first place?"

Miss Hargrove, standing to the right of the inspector, seethed with anger. "I allowed you to use the phone out of respect for Lord Carrington. You were trespassing, and I could have reported you to the police."

"I am the police," Inspector Sinclair reminded Miss Hargrove, looking puzzled. "What does Lord Carrington have to do with all of this?"

Charlotte spoke quietly, revealing her purpose. "I have been visiting him."

The inspector's eyes widened in astonishment. "You have been visiting him where? Here?"

Charlotte nodded, affirming his understanding.

Attempting to grasp the situation, Inspector Sinclair stepped away from the chair and approached Charlotte. "Let me make sure I understand correctly. You're saying that Lord Carrington is at Westling Hospital?"

Once again, Charlotte nodded in confirmation.

The inspector closed his eyes briefly, trying to regain control of his emotions. Just as he was about to pose another question, the door to Miss Hargrove's office swung open, and Lord Wharton entered. Glancing at the wall clock, Charlotte noted that it was precisely eight o'clock. Lord Wharton greeted everyone present, and a sense of relief washed over Charlotte as he smiled warmly in her direction.

"I must say, this is quite an unusual gathering," Lord Wharton remarked calmly.

"Indeed," agreed the inspector. "Do you have any idea what led to this impromptu meeting?"

Lord Wharton shook his head sincerely. "I'm afraid I have no clue."

"Miss Reinford, please enlighten us and start from the very beginning," the inspector requested.

Charlotte understood that telling the truth was in her best interest, despite her discomfort. The presence of Miss Hargrove added a layer of complexity, requiring Charlotte to be cautious about the information she revealed.

"Lord Carrington checked into Westling Hospital a few weeks ago," Charlotte began, pausing to assess the inspector's approach. It seemed he opted to let her tell the whole story before questioning it. Encouraged, she continued, "I frequently visit him, and during our time together, we engage in chess matches and discuss books."

Miss Hargrove emitted a choking sound, betraying her reaction.

"I've had the chance to meet other patients during my visits to Westling Hospital, including Mrs. Dale," Charlotte recounted.

"Today, she kindly invited me for a cup of tea and a brief conversation, which I gratefully accepted. However, as we chatted, I accidentally spilled tea on my blouse. Mrs. Dale's nurse, Emily, assisted her to her room while I hurried to a nearby closet to change into dry clothes. The closet happened to be located beside the staircase leading upstairs. I couldn't resist the temptation to explore the mysterious third floor. But my inquisitive endeavor was short-lived, as one of the male nurses discovered me. Then the alarm went off. Hoping that my visit to the third floor would remain inconsequential and swiftly forgotten, I was taken aback when two security guards awaited me near the linen closet, promptly escorting me to this room. Miss Hargrove threatened to involve the police, so I implored her to allow me to contact you."

Charlotte shifted her gaze to Inspector Sinclair, who leaned against Miss Hargrove's desk lost in contemplation.

"Why did the alarm sound?" he inquired.

"Every patient was accounted for, so I'm perplexed as to what triggered it," Miss Hargrove responded. "It must have been a malfunction."

"I see. It's all very peculiar, indeed," Inspector Sinclair said, drawing out his words thoughtfully. He then turned his attention to Miss Hargrove. "Please, Miss Hargrove, could you give us a few moments alone?" he requested politely yet firmly.

Miss Hargrove, surprised by this request, sought clarification, "I beg your pardon, are you asking me to leave the room?"

"That's correct," confirmed Inspector Sinclair.

Miss Hargrove's expression flickered with a mix of annoyance and resignation, but she maintained her professionalism. Without further objection, she quietly exited the room.

Once they were left alone, the inspector fixed a penetrating gaze on Charlotte. His expression conveyed a resolute determination to no longer entertain any further nonsense.

"Let's have the full story, Miss Reinford. What brought you here? And what specifically drew you to the third floor? I trust this isn't related to the Rachel Offley murder case, as your involvement was clearly prohibited. You must remember, you're still on our list of suspects," Inspector Sinclair stated with firmness.

Charlotte responded, her eyes flickering between Inspector Sinclair and Lord Wharton, who was silently observing from the wall. "The full picture isn't clear to me yet," she admitted cautiously. "However, I can tell you the main reason I'm here. I needed to confirm a theory. A diary came into our hands, revealing insights into several past incidents and potentially answering some of my questions," she clarified.

Inspector Sinclair, looking perplexed, interjected, "Miss Reinford, your being here at Westling Hospital, particularly your actions on the third floor, remains a puzzle to me. Which diary are you talking about, and how does it tie into our current investigation?"

He then pulled a chair from behind his desk, placing it opposite Charlotte, and sat down, crossing his legs. With a composed demeanor, he asked, "Let's go back to the start. Explain your arrival at Westling Hospital, Miss Reinford."

"I persuaded Lord Carrington to check himself into the hospital, creating a chance for me to get inside," Charlotte disclosed. "The passing of Mrs. Offley affected him deeply, and a short stay here seemed beneficial for his mental health."

Acknowledging her response, the inspector seemed to ponder for a moment before shifting the topic.

"Moving on, the only link we have at Westling Hospital to Rachel Offley is Miss Hargrove," he stated. "During my interview with her, she could offer only a limited perspective. However, what she did share was largely positive. Her direct encounters with Mrs. Offley were few, but she formed her opinions from the sentiments expressed by patients, nurses, and a particular doctor."

"Doctor Hurst?" Charlotte asked.

"Indeed, Doctor Hurst," Inspector Sinclair affirmed. "I'm well-informed about the tragic occurrence at Westling Hospital.

However, I'm attempting to discern how this episode is related to my current investigation."

Charlotte observed his emphasis on 'my investigation' but proceeded, "We were also seeking that answer, but regrettably, we discovered that the doctor recently ended his own life," Charlotte said. "Doctor Hurst's mother observed no suicidal inclinations in his demeanor. No farewell note was left, though such an absence isn't unusual. It was his diary, entrusted to us by his mother, that has led me here this evening."

Inspector Sinclair paused, clearly taken aback by the news.

"That's deeply unfortunate and unexpected," he said, processing the information. Then, refocusing on Charlotte, he asked, "You mentioned 'we' and 'us' several times. Who exactly are you referring to in this context?"

"Miss Reinford and myself," Lord Wharton stepped in, clarifying his involvement.

Inspector Sinclair's eyebrow arched, his face registering both surprise and a hint of disapproval, yet he held back any immediate comments.

Charlotte, sensing the need to continue, added, "With Lord Carrington nearing discharge from Westling Hospital, I had to act quickly. Today's attempt was crucial; had it failed, any future opportunities would be slim."

This revelation sparked further interest in both Inspector Sinclair and Lord Wharton. "Today's attempt? What exactly were you planning to do, and what were you hoping to find?" Inspector Sinclair asked.

"I brainstormed several methods to access the third floor, but none were without risk. My actions were fueled more by emotion and a determination to prove my theories than by a carefully crafted plan," Charlotte admitted, revealing her impulsive approach.

Still puzzled, Inspector Sinclair sought further clarification. "But what exactly were you looking for on the hospital's third floor?" he reiterated.

Charlotte hesitated for a moment, then answered, "It's not about what, but who I was searching for."

Inspector Sinclair's patience began to wane. "Miss Reinford, I need a straight answer. Who were you looking for?"

After a brief, meaningful glance at Lord Wharton, Charlotte responded, "The individual mentioned in Doctor Hurst's diary—Lady Adelle."

"And who might this Lady Adelle be?" the inspector inquired, his interest clearly piqued.

"She is none other than Lady Beatrice's younger sister, Lady Adelle Haddonford—Lord Wharton's aunt," Charlotte disclosed.

CHAPTER THIRTY-EIGHT

Inspector Sinclair called for the prompt confiscation of Doctor Hurst's diaries immediately upon gathering at Haddonford Manor. However, Lord Wharton, desiring a brief respite, requested additional time to ensure Lord Carrington's discharge from Westling Hospital and to discuss a recently revealed family secret privately with his mother. He also promised to deliver the journals himself by the following day, thereby granting Charlotte more time to peruse the yet-to-be-read sections. The inspector, though hesitant, consented to Lord Wharton's plea.

Sequestered in her room, Charlotte deemed herself lucky to delve into the journals' untouched pages. She keenly recalled the captivating tales spun in the preceding volumes. Each book began with an insightful quotation from the philosopher Socrates, reflecting Doctor Hurst's deep admiration for the legendary thinker. Doctor Hurst's intentional pairing of these quotations with the journals' individual themes suggested a meticulous effort to align his insights with Socrates' enduring wisdom.

The initial journal, bearing the inscription "The only true wisdom is in knowing you know nothing," offered a profound exploration of Doctor Hurst's personal and professional journey.

It provided a captivating glimpse into his intellectual evolution, revealing the challenges he encountered and conquered along the way. The second diary commenced with the declaration, "There is only one good, knowledge, and one evil, ignorance," accentuating the importance of well-informed decision-making rooted in diligent investigation. Within its pages, Doctor Hurst chronicled a series of cases, recounting instances where he met opposition from colleagues, yet emerged triumphant through his groundbreaking research and exceptional expertise in the field.

In his next journal, with meticulous attention to detail, Doctor Hurst described the case of his latest patient, initially referred to as Lady A. H., but eventually revealed as Adelle. The change in nomenclature immediately caught Charlotte's attention, hinting at a shift from a formal association to a potentially more intimate and personal connection. Intrigued by the revelations contained within the diary, Charlotte felt a compulsion to meet Lady Adelle, assuming she was still alive.

With very little time left, Charlotte delved into the fourth journal. The embossed quote on the supple leather cover, "Every action has its pleasures and its price," only served to intensify Charlotte's premonitions, reinforcing her belief that the truth lay tantalizingly within her reach. As time elapsed, she found herself rapidly progressing through the final, fifth diary, which notably appeared slimmer than its predecessors.

Upon reaching the concluding page, a sense of urgency washed over Charlotte, compelling her to acknowledge the importance of engaging in a conversation with Lord Carrington. Furthermore, she realized the necessity of making a series of phone calls. Charlotte reluctantly set aside the notion of seeking assistance from Lord Wharton. One factor weighed heavily on this decision: Lord Wharton's need for private time with his mother. After careful consideration, Charlotte concluded that relying solely on Inspector Sinclair for transportation was the most pragmatic option.

After securely stowing the diaries in the bottom drawer of her writing table, Charlotte slipped into a fresh dress and made her way down the hallway. Faint sounds of Margaret bustling about in the kitchen reached her ears, but she couldn't help but notice the absence of Frank and Samuel. Determined, Charlotte proceeded towards the telephone, fully aware of the inspector's initial resistance to her request. True to form, he hesitated and even uttered a few regrettable words, though he later expressed his apologies. Eventually, he reluctantly agreed to pick her up in a few hours. As Charlotte hung up the phone, her eyes happened to catch Lord Wharton making his way towards the Blue Room, with Lady Beatrice following closely behind. Lady Beatrice's alabaster-white complexion bore the weight of weariness, accentuated by dark circles under her eyes. Leaning on a cane, she shuffled slowly across the parquet floor, briefly meeting Charlotte's gaze before disappearing into the room.

Around noon, Lord Carrington arrived at Haddonford Manor. Lord Wharton must have dispatched Frank to pick him up in Lady Beatrice's opulent Rolls Royce. Lord Carrington appeared slightly flustered, and Charlotte surmised that his mood had been affected by an unforeseen discharge from Westling Hospital. Although Lord Carrington knew that his stay was drawing to a close, he hadn't anticipated its abrupt termination that morning.

"I deeply regret the distress caused by last night's incident," Charlotte sincerely expressed, sensing Lord Carrington's troubled state of mind.

"Which incident are you referring to, my child?" he inquired.

"Did anyone inform you about the reason for your discharge, apart from the doctor's belief that you were ready to leave the hospital?" Charlotte inquired.

Lord Carrington pursed his lips and shook his head in response.

"I must confess that it was because of my own actions," Charlotte admitted. "I ventured onto the third floor without permission and was apprehended. Although I encountered a male nurse who questioned my affiliation with Westling Hospital, he was not the one responsible for my capture."

Curiosity sparked in Lord Carrington's eyes as he inquired, "Then who was?"

"Lord Carrington, your initial question should have been, *what were you doing on the third floor?*" Charlotte remarked.

A sense of unease gripped Lord Carrington as he shivered in his chair.

"I apologize that I am the cause of your early discharge. I know that you had hoped for a few extra days at Westling Hospital, and I know the reasons why . . . I am also aware that your motive for going to Westling Hospital is unrelated to Mrs. Offley's death. You probably believe that what you're grappling with is an entirely separate matter. However, you must trust me when I say there is an undeniable connection between the events at Haddonford Manor and the answers you seek. By the way, last night the alarm went off, even though all the patients were being attended to. Have you heard anything about that incident? Was it a topic of discussion, and if so, what were people saying?"

Lord Carrington furrowed his brow, visibly straining to recall the events of the previous night.

"I remember going downstairs, hoping to find you in the recreation room. It quickly filled up with patients and a few visitors, but you were nowhere to be seen. Just as I was about to return to my room, the alarm went off. We were not allowed to leave until the situation settled. I don't think anyone discussed the cause of the commotion. Truth be told, everyone seems accustomed to such occurrences. The wretched alarm goes off often, and people learn to ignore it but why does last night's incident interest you?"

"Because I believe that someone was watching me," Charlotte revealed. "I wore the light teal uniform to blend in with the nurses on the third floor, intending to follow up on some clues from Doctor Hurst's diary."

Lord Carrington interjected, "Who is Doctor Hurst?"

"He was a psychiatrist who worked at Westling Hospital years ago," Charlotte explained, noting Lord Carrington's lack of recognition.

"When I reached room 309, a male nurse saw me and inquired if I was new to the hospital," Charlotte continued.

"Before I could respond, the alarm went off, causing confusion. I fled the scene, initially thinking he was pursuing me, but I now believe he attended to his duties, ensuring the safety of his assigned patients. When I reached the closet to change back into my regular attire, the security guards were already at the door. How did they know to wait for me there? Initially, I suspected you of triggering the alarm and alerting Miss Hargrove but this morning, I realized my mistake. Your reaction to my mention of the incident confirmed my assumption that it was someone else. Lord Carrington, I need your assistance in identifying that person."

"Of course, my friend. Anything you need," he said.

"I need you to tell me the truth," Charlotte implored. "Begin from the day you first met Lady Beatrice."

CHAPTER THIRTY-NINE

THE EAGERLY AWAITED DAY TO MEET with Inspector Sinclair had finally dawned. Lady Isabelle, having ventured the longest way back to Haddonford Manor from her family visit, elegantly made her way into the Blue Room, being the earliest to arrive. Dressed in an alluring warm peach gown, she presented a striking figure; however, her magnificent entry was greeted by the room's solitude, causing a hint of displeasure to cross her features. Feeling a touch of letdown, she gracefully took a seat on the couch.

Not long after, Lord Carrington entered, his silver locks perfectly groomed, lending him an air of seasoned wisdom. His stride was confident, yet a slight quiver in his hand subtly revealed the anxious excitement within his elder frame.

Lady Beatrice followed, bringing her refined elegance to the room. Her understated black attire contrasted with her fair complexion, and the pearls around her neck glinted with a mix of uncertainty, mirroring the tumult of feelings within her.

Frank Offley was next, positioning himself beside Lady Beatrice, providing a pillar of support. Tucked away in a corner, Margaret and Samuel lingered, almost blending into the backdrop of expectant faces. Margaret, in her neatly fastened apron, gently ironed out any wrinkles with hands that quivered, echoing Mrs.

Offley's gestures in times of stress. Samuel, meanwhile, fidgeted, his restless movements betraying his discomfort.

At precisely five o'clock, Inspector Sinclair and Lord Wharton made their entrance. The inspector's cold expression and confident demeanor sent a clear message to all present—a warning that this gathering transcended the realms of mere questioning and investigation updates.

It was an announcement, silently conveyed, that this important moment would draw the curtains on the case, finally revealing the elusive killer's identity. The weight of this message hung in the air, capturing the attention of every person in the room. Even Samuel, who had previously kept his gaze lowered to the floor, now fixed his eyes upon Inspector Sinclair. Sensing the gravity of the situation, Lady Isabelle swallowed hard, wisely choosing to withhold her acerbic comments.

Charlotte noticed that Inspector Sinclair had arrived accompanied by two police officers. Positioned near the entrance of the Blue Room, they stood as silent sentinels, adding an undercurrent of authority to the proceedings. One of them was George. From a distance, Charlotte noticed a fresh scratch extending across his left cheek. It seemed he had reopened a barely healed wound, as a droplet of blood slowly trickled down. George tried to stem the bleeding by wiping it away with his uniform sleeve, but the coarse fabric only aggravated the wound further. Just as Charlotte prepared to approach him and offer her assistance, she saw Lord Wharton reaching into his suit pocket. With a gesture of kindness, he retrieved a pristine white handkerchief, which he extended to George.

As the room brimmed with anticipation, Inspector Sinclair's voice pierced through the hushed atmosphere. His gaze swept across the gathered individuals, commanding their attention.

"I am pleased to announce that we have indeed solved the case," he declared, his words carrying a sense of accomplishment.

"I must admit, it was no easy task. Not only because some of you misled me during the investigation, but also due to the truths that were deliberately concealed. In my view, withholding the truth is akin to lying. Had we not been burdened by these hidden secrets, we would have resolved Rachel Offley's murder earlier, thus potentially preventing another tragic loss of life."

Charlotte anticipated the impact of Inspector Sinclair's words as they rippled through the room. The mention of another murder elicited a range of reactions from the audience. Lady Beatrice and Margaret let out audible gasps, their concern evident. Lady Isabelle, on the other hand, inclined her head, a glimmer of suspicion flickering in her eyes. Frank, Lord Carrington, and Samuel appeared genuinely perplexed, eager for further explanations that the inspector seemed in no haste to provide.

"Now, I'm sure you are all brimming with curiosity regarding my statement," Inspector Sinclair finally continued. "To shed light on the matter, I believe it would be best if Miss Reinford herself elucidates the details."

All eyes swiftly turned towards Charlotte, who felt the encouraging nod from Inspector Sinclair. Taking a deep breath, she composed herself, gathering her thoughts before stepping forward to address the expectant audience.

Charlotte began with a steady voice.

"Many of you are already aware that I was left on the steps of St. Helen's when I was a mere few days old. While I am eternally grateful for the care bestowed upon me by Mother Superior and the nuns, I always harbored a deep sense that my life was destined to extend beyond the confinements of the monastery. For eighteen years, my path was predetermined, but a part of me knew that someday I would break free from those walls and embark upon a new journey elsewhere. When the opportunity finally presented itself, I was fortunate enough to secure a position as Lady Beatrice's companion, and I will forever be grateful for her kindness and generosity. I could not have asked for a more compassionate employer or a more welcoming place to call home."

Pausing briefly to gather her thoughts, Charlotte continued. "However, there has always been one aspect that troubled me deeply from the moment I crossed the threshold of Haddonford Manor. It was the disconcerting ease with which I obtained the position. Lady Beatrice never asked for reference letters, even though there were other young ladies who had applied before me and were turned away. It struck me as peculiar, but at the time, my excitement over having a roof over my head and a steady income overshadowed any concerns regarding these seemingly inconsequential details."

"Mrs. Offley, may she rest in peace, was a delightful and caring woman," Charlotte said, her gaze shifting to Frank.

"From the moment I met her, she made me feel welcomed, and the same could be said for her husband, Mr. Offley. It was on my first night at Haddonford Manor that I encountered Mr. Offley while I was lost, trying to find my way to my bedroom. He kindly pointed me in the right direction and advised me to keep my windows shut and my door locked. I found his advice rather peculiar for a newly hired employee, but I heeded his words faithfully. Every night before bed, I would ensure that my windows were securely latched, and my door locked. At the time, I was unaware of the events that preceded that night, events that I believe Mr. Offley kept secret from the other residents of Haddonford, and now I believe I understand why."

Charlotte locked eyes with Frank, then turned her gaze towards Inspector Sinclair, who nodded approvingly. Gathering herself, she continued, her voice steady and filled with determination.

"The longer I resided at Haddonford, the more I began to observe things that puzzled me. The West Wing, with its breathtaking beauty, remained unused for years. At first, I assumed it was because Haddonford Manor was simply too vast for Lady Beatrice, and she chose to confine herself to a single wing. However, the absence of any family portraits in the East Wing struck me as unusual. Almost every other room in the West Wing bore reminders of Lady Beatrice's past, yet there wasn't a single portrait of her family in the East Wing of the Manor. It intrigued me, and I couldn't shake off the feeling that something was amiss."

Charlotte paused briefly, collecting her thoughts before continuing, "I admit, curiosity got the better of me, and I ventured into the West Wing on several occasions. There was something about it that unsettled me, although I couldn't quite put my finger on it until one day, it finally clicked. It was the arrangement of the paintings, particularly in a room that bore a striking resemblance to the Blue Room we are gathered in now. What caught my attention was the family portrait adorning the wall—an exquisite depiction of Lord Haddonford, resplendent and dignified, alongside his radiant wife cradling an infant in her arms.

"I recognized Lady Beatrice as the precious little girl in the painting, posing comfortably before the artist. Her contented and carefree demeanor was apparent, accompanied by the comforting presence of both parents. Lord Haddonford must have commissioned a remarkable painter for the family portrait, as every detail, including Lady Haddonford's dress, was masterfully captured. I should have noticed it immediately, but it wasn't until I stumbled upon another painting in the West Wing that I truly comprehended its significance. This time, it was a full-length portrait of Lord Haddonford, dressed entirely in black. He appeared to be around the same age as in the family portrait, but it was his expression that caught my attention—an expression wrought with grief and sorrow," Charlotte paused briefly catching her breath.

"There was another aspect that troubled me greatly. It was the empty space on the wall adjacent to the family portrait. Positioned in the center of the room, the family portrait commanded attention, flanked on the right by a smaller painting of a young Lady Beatrice. However, to the left, there was nothing. It struck me as strange that someone would decorate the room in such a manner. Initially, I assumed the space was left for a future painting, yet upon closer examination, I discovered that the wall was not even.

There were clear indications of a previous nail or hook, suggesting that there had been a painting present at some point."

Charlotte paused, allowing the weight of her words to settle, before continuing with growing clarity, "It seemed implausible to leave a space for a painting that may or may not come into existence. Instead, it appeared more likely that there had been a painting already present—an artwork intentionally removed from view. It was then that I began to appreciate the brilliance of the artist commissioned to create the family portrait. The pieces started to fit together. Lady Haddonford, depicted in her pregnancy, tragically passed away while giving birth to a baby girl—Adelle."

Charlotte scanned the room, her gaze focused on those present. Aside from the two policemen stationed by the door, only three individuals should have been unaware of Lady Beatrice's younger sister. With keen observation, Charlotte examined each face before proceeding.

"Lady Beatrice," Charlotte's voice softened, "you commanded the concealment of your sister's portrait and the eradication of any reminders within this house. Not because her birth led to your mother's demise, but because of the person she ultimately became. You kept her very existence hidden, even from your own son, due to the immense pain she inflicted upon you. Tell us, when did you discover her struggle with mental illness? Did she appear normal as a child, only for her behavior to gradually change as she grew older?"

Lady Beatrice's hands trembled as she nervously rubbed them, a clear sign of her unease. "After our mother's death, Father rejected Adelle, but I was too young to understand the reasons behind it," Lady Beatrice began, her voice filled with sadness.

"I have vivid memories of spending time with Father, accompanying him to social events, riding horses, and visiting friends. But Adelle was always kept at home with the nanny. As a child, I didn't notice anything unusual about her, but Father must have seen something, for he sought to shelter her from the world." Lady Beatrice paused, deep in thought.

"Please continue," said Inspector Sinclair, taking charge of the conversation.

"When Adelle turned twelve, she became overly interested in boys," Lady Beatrice continued.

"At first, I was oblivious to the reasons behind my exclusion from my friends' birthday parties, especially those with older brothers. I was confused and deeply hurt. No one explained what was happening, and I blamed myself, convinced I had done something to deserve the exclusion. The pain consumed me, and I withdrew into my bedroom, spending countless hours alone."

Lady Beatrice cast a glance at her trembling hands, her gaze filled with a sorrow.

"During the sporadic periods when Father did not travel and stayed home, he could sense that something was wrong. He questioned me about the reasons behind my seclusion and closely watched Adelle's behavior. As a result, he made the decision to bring in a psychiatrist to reside with us at Haddonford Manor, with the sole purpose of assessing my sister's condition. The psychiatrist remained with us for what felt like an eternity, diligently observing Adelle's every move. A prescription was eventually given to alleviate her condition, and to my relief, it seemed to have a positive effect. Adelle began to behave like a normal, carefree young girl, and it brought me immeasurable joy. Finally, I had the sister I had always yearned for."

Lady Beatrice's eyes softened, her voice laced with a touch of wistfulness.

"Yes, indeed, thanks to the treatment, Adelle transformed into the most remarkable person," she reminisced. "Countless hours were spent together in the enchanting confines of the West Wing, engrossed in heartfelt conversations, sharing infectious laughter, delving into books, and pursuing our passions. The West Wing held a special place in Adelle's heart; it became her sanctuary. I, for one, cherished her presence. Adelle effortlessly surpassed me in numerous ways—her ethereal beauty, her mastery of horseback riding, writing, and art, and her incredible memory that left everyone in awe. But it was her unparalleled brilliance in chess that truly stood out, as she fearlessly defeated anyone who dared to challenge her."

"When did you realize that the medication had ceased to be effective?" Inspector Sinclair inquired with a calm yet probing tone.

Lady Beatrice let out a weary sigh. "To be perfectly honest, I'm not entirely certain if the treatment truly succeeded," she confessed. "Adelle's brilliance extended far beyond the confines of the chessboard; she possessed an uncanny talent for acting. With effortless grace, she would assume various roles, captivating those around her with a skill and brilliance entirely her own. Time and time again, I would fall into her intricately woven traps, vowing to be more cautious, only to find myself ensnared once more."

A wave of sorrow washed over Lady Beatrice. "Adelle managed to persuade me into introducing her to my then-fiancé and my best friend—a decision that will haunt me for the remainder of my days," she confessed, her head held high as she fought back the tears threatening to spill from her eyes.

Inspector Sinclair offered a compassionate pause, allowing Lady Beatrice to gather her composure before continuing her account.

With a trembling voice, Lady Beatrice turned to Lord Carrington. "I am deeply sorry, Henry," she addressed him directly. "I wish I had possessed the strength to resist my sister's demands. I wish you had never crossed paths with her."

Lord Carrington leaned forward, poised to offer comfort, yet restrained himself, acutely aware of the delicate nature of the situation.

"Beatrice," he began gently, his voice carrying a soothing tone. "You must understand that it was never your responsibility to protect me."

He rose from his seat, facing Inspector Sinclair. "From the very moment I first laid eyes on Adelle, I was swept away, irreversibly consumed by love," he confessed. "To me, she was the epitome of intelligence, daring, and captivating charm. I had even contemplated proposing to her, until that fateful spring day when I arrived unannounced at Haddonford Manor and . . ." His voice trailed off, the memories casting a heavy burden upon him.

A few minutes passed before he continued, recounting the events with a mixture of remorse and heartfelt disclosure.

"My visit had been intended as a joyous surprise. Despite Lord Haddonford's forewarning and his attempts to discourage me, I, being young and naive, brushed off his advice without due consideration. Upon my arrival, I exchanged a brief conversation with Beatrice and Lord Haddonford in the library. Adelle, however, was expected to be outdoors, and so I ventured forth to find her. Disappointment washed over me as I searched in vain through the gardens. Yet, inexplicably drawn towards the stables, despite Adelle's aversion to horses, I made my way there. The enigma of her simultaneous equestrian skill and distaste for these magnificent creatures has always perplexed me. But driven by an intangible force, whether it be spirit, intuition, or a sixth sense, I followed that path. At first, I saw no one, until a series of anguished moans reached my ears, stirring concern deep within me. Believing Adelle to be injured and in distress, I hastened towards the source of the sound, only to witness her in a state of undress, enveloped in the arms of the groom," Lord Carrington divulged, his eyes heavy with the weight of sorrow and pain.

"Was that the breaking point?" inquired Inspector Sinclair, seeking clarification.

"Do you mean if that incident served as the final catalyst prior to her admission to Westling Hospital?" Lady Beatrice asked.

"Yes," confirmed the inspector.

"Regrettably, it was not," Lady Beatrice sighed wearily. "The decision to transfer her to Westling Hospital did not occur until several years later. Adelle's insatiable hunger for . . ." Lady Beatrice trailed off, grappling to find the precise word.

"For intimacy with the opposite sex," the inspector interjected, coming to Lady Beatrice's aid.

"Thank you," Lady Beatrice expressed her gratitude. "It escalated with each passing year. Neither my father, nor I, nor my husband could rein it in. Also, her behavior grew increasingly erratic. She even attacked a maid who innocently entered Adelle's bedroom with a breakfast tray one morning. The list of unforgivable and unforgettable things my sister did could go on and on. Yet, time and again, we were willing to give her another chance."

"What brought about the change?" the inspector inquired.

Lady Beatrice turned her gaze towards Lord Wharton, her voice softening.

"Richard," she uttered quietly. "You see, we kept his birth a secret from Adelle. Initially, it wasn't challenging to do so. After my marriage, I moved away from Haddonford Manor, and as my pregnancy progressed, I visited Haddonford less frequently to conceal the changes in my body from Adelle. However, I underestimated my sister. She was far too astute not to notice my absence. I suspect she had her suspicions, as peculiar occurrences began to unfold in my new home. A maid discovered a nursery window open one day, despite her insistence that she had closed it. A toy materialized in Richard's crib, which neither my husband, the nanny, nor I could account for—no one had given it as a gift. Adelle had always possessed athleticism and a knack for scaling walls. She acquired that skill as a child, seeking to slip in and out of her bedroom unnoticed. The notion that Adelle had become aware of Richard's existence filled me with terror, yet I lacked concrete evidence. I kept telling myself that my fears were unfounded until one night, when I walked into the nursery and found the nanny fast asleep, and Adelle cradling my son. I will never forget her face when she was looking at Richard. The pure Devil in disguise ready to harm my only child to make me suffer. He meant nothing to her but a pawn in her beloved chess game. She was ready to sacrifice him as she would sacrifice anyone who stood in her way."

"What happened to the nanny?" Lord Carrington asked.

"It later came to light that Adelle had drugged the poor woman by tampering with her drink. Her trying to hurt Richard was the breaking point, and it marked the final time I laid eyes on my sister."

Lady Beatrice leaned back, her energy depleted. Lord Wharton approached his mother, and she reached out for his hand, which he gently clasped in his own.

Charlotte noticed the inspector's nod of approval, signaling for her to continue. With a determined look, she proceeded with her explanation.

"Please remember that this occurred several decades ago when both standards and medical practice were less enlightened. Lady Beatrice found the best placement for her sister at the time and never personally visited Lady Adelle at Westling Hospital. Instead, it was Frank's responsibility to make the visits and handle the financial matters for Lady Adelle's treatment. It is my belief that during one of these visits, he must have encountered Rachel. At that time, Lady Beatrice had already experienced the loss of both her husband and her father and had made the decision to return to Haddonford Manor. She closed off her sister's cherished wing and comfortably resided in the opposite wing. However, strange, and inexplicable occurrences began to unfold—such as an open window that Margaret swore, she had secured the night before, or an unsealed envelope that Lady Beatrice could not recall opening. These minor yet disconcerting incidents evoked unwelcome memories in Mr. Offley. Though he chose to keep his suspicions to himself for the time being, he recognized the significance of caution and felt compelled to offer me advice regarding the locking of doors and windows. I genuinely appreciated his timely warning."

Lady Isabelle, who had been silently absorbing the information, finally spoke up. "Why was I not given that advice?"

Inspector Sinclair attempted to interject, but she dismissed him momentarily, redirecting her focus to Charlotte.

"Never mind, Inspector. I don't care," she said icily before continuing, "So, you're suggesting that Lady Adelle somehow escaped from Westling Hospital and made frequent trips back home. And during one of these visits, she randomly decided to poison Rachel Offley?"

"No, it was not Lady Adelle this time," Charlotte clarified.

"She is no longer at an age where she could easily scale walls or find a way out of a highly secure facility like room 309. It is essentially a fortress, with no conceivable means for her to escape. Furthermore, her mental faculties have declined over time along with the progression of her illness and age," Charlotte explained.

Lady Isabelle's suspicion was evident as she questioned, "How would you know all that?"

Charlotte gestured towards a neat stack of leather-bound diaries that George had placed on an empty chair next to him. As planned, Lord Wharton handed the notebooks to the inspector, who then entrusted George with their safekeeping.

"These are Doctor Hurst's diaries. He predicted what might happen to Lady Adelle and Miss Hargrove confirmed her condition to the inspector," Charlotte explained.

Lady Isabelle's curiosity grew as she inquired, "And who are these people?"

"Miss Hargrove is the administrator of Westling Hospital, where Lady Adelle received treatment under the care of Doctor Hurst," Charlotte replied.

Lady Isabelle wasted no time, her next question striking at the heart of the matter. "If Lady Adelle is not the culprit, then who is responsible for Rachel Offley's death?"

Charlotte cast a glance at Inspector Sinclair, his confirming nod serving as a reassurance, before stating, "Lady Isabelle, I promise, I will provide you with that information in due course. The truth will be unveiled soon."

Chapter Forty

"To reveal the long-awaited answer and unveil Rachel Offley's killer, I must delve into my arrival at Haddonford," Charlotte began. It became clear to me that the swiftness of my hiring wasn't solely due to my age or skills, but rather my past. Being an orphan, I was more interesting to Lady Beatrice, who harbored a particular fondness for young adults who had grown up without knowing their true parents. This suspicion gained validation through a conversation I had with Margaret, who had apparently spent her childhood in an orphanage. I entertained the possibility that Samuel shared a similar background, but my assumption proved incorrect. Nevertheless, the notion of Lady Beatrice's inclination toward orphans lingered in my mind, leaving me to ponder its underlying reasons. For quite some time, I struggled to find a logical explanation until I stumbled upon Doctor Hurst's fourth diary entry. Its contents compelled me to question the true motives behind Lady Adelle's confinement at Westling Hospital," Charlotte turned her gaze towards Lady Beatrice, who seemed to anticipate the impending revelation.

"I must apologize, Lady Beatrice, as I need to share this information in order to unveil the person responsible for Mrs. Offley's death," Charlotte spoke gently.

Lady Beatrice, barely audible, responded, "Of course, I trust that you know what you're doing."

"On the day Lord Wharton and I visited you at the hospital, I thought I caught a glimpse of someone who resembled Mr. Offley. However, due to the distance and the brevity of the sighting, I couldn't be certain. It was only when I returned to Haddonford and spoke with Samuel that I learned Mr. Offley had indeed been in London at the exact same time Lord Wharton and I were," Charlotte revealed.

"Although my suspicions regarding Mr. Offley were plausible, I had no idea who he was meeting with until several weeks later. It was while I was engaged in the task of mailing a letter to Lady Beatrice's lawyer, containing details about a discreetly sponsored charitable event. Interestingly, the law firm's address coincidentally happened to be just a block away from the hospital where Lady Beatrice was undergoing treatment. This close proximity led me to deduce that the person Mr. Offley had encountered that day was either Lady Beatrice's lawyer or one of his associates. However, I soon realized that this encounter held little relevance in unraveling the mystery behind Mrs. Offley's murder. The true essence of the matter lay in Lady Beatrice's choice of charities and her generosity towards orphans," Charlotte paused momentarily, allowing her thoughts to settle before continuing.

"Every year, a significant amount of money was donated on Lady Beatrice's behalf to the Sisters of Charity, an organization dedicated to the care of orphans. You might wonder why she developed such a specific philanthropic passion. Out of all the charities in the world, Lady Beatrice chose to offer financial support to the one that focused on orphan care. The reason behind this is that Lady Adelle had a child."

Charlotte's revelation reverberated through the room, evoking a surge of emotions. Lord Carrington jolted from his seat, emitting a choked sound, while Lady Isabelle gasped before swiftly regaining her composure. Margaret and Samuel exchanged perplexed glances, while Frank clenched his teeth, maintaining a silence.

"Lady Beatrice," Charlotte continued gently, "I suspect that you discovered Lady Adelle's pregnancy around the same time you learned of your own expectancy. There was no way you would allow your sister to keep the child. It was evident that she was not capable of caring for anyone, and you held concerns for both the child's well-being and the family's reputation. I imagine you kept the baby's existence a secret from everyone except one person you could trust, and that person was Frank. Frank took the baby to an orphanage and left it there," Charlotte said.

Lady Beatrice nodded her head sorrowfully.

"You never forgave yourself for your actions and attempted to alleviate the guilt by generously donating substantial sums of money to Sisters of Charity and sponsoring humanitarian events that supported individuals who grew up in poverty and without knowledge of their parents," Charlotte explained.

Lady Isabelle interjected, reminding everyone of the underlying motive behind Lady Adelle's confinement in Westing Hospital. "Am I correct in assuming, Lady Beatrice, that the true reason you ultimately admitted your sister to a psychiatric facility was due to your apprehension that Lady Adelle might retaliate by harming your own son, mirroring the abandonment she experienced with her own child, or potentially eloping with him to raise Richard as her own?"

"Yes," Lady Beatrice murmured, her words barely audible. "I had to ensure Richard's safety," she added, locking eyes with her son.

"You made the right decision, Mother," Lord Wharton assured her, planting a gentle kiss on her hand.

The shrill ring of the landline phone suddenly disrupted the room's atmosphere. All eyes turned to the inspector, who swiftly gestured for them to disregard the call. The ringing ceased, allowing the conversation to resume.

"Please continue, Miss Reinford," Inspector Sinclair urged Charlotte.

"Numerous details puzzled me, including Lord Carrington's peculiar behavior," Charlotte recounted. "He arrived a day earlier than anticipated and appeared to have a heated discussion with Lady Beatrice that afternoon. On the night Lady Isabelle believed she had encountered an intruder in her room, only Lord Carrington and Lord Wharton remained fully dressed in their suits in the middle of the night. While Lord Wharton was occupied in the library, Lord Carrington should have retired to bed, yet he was still awake when Lady Isabelle called for help. It became evident to me that something weighed heavily on his mind, although the nature of his concerns eluded me at the time.

"After the passing of Mrs. Offley, I made a request for Lord Carrington's voluntary admission to Westling Hospital. Initially, he required professional assistance, and I sincerely apologize, Lord Carrington," Charlotte addressed the elderly gentleman, "for taking advantage of your vulnerable emotional state and needing unrestricted access to the hospital. My intention as a visitor was to gather crucial information to solve this case. To my surprise, you readily agreed to assist me. It seemed as though you were just as eager as I was to enter the hospital. Moreover, I found it rather curious that on the day I illicitly entered the hospital's file room," Charlotte paused, turning towards the inspector, "I apologize to you as well," she said, noticing the raised eyebrow on the inspector's face, before continuing, "Lord Carrington was right by my side with a key, leading me to suspect careful premeditation on his part. He feigned ignorance and followed my lead, but Lord Carrington lacks the skill of deception, and it didn't take long for me to discern that his motive for breaking into the file room differed from mine. Our paths unexpectedly intersected, forcing him to revise his plans. Additionally, Lord Carrington claimed he 'borrowed' the key from the doctor," Charlotte emphasized the word 'borrowed,' conveying her skepticism. "However, I knew that acquiring the key without assistance would have posed a challenge for him," she added. "I remained unaware of the accomplice's identity until our recent visit to London with Inspector Sinclair. I'm certain all of you are eager to uncover the truth, and I will disclose it. However, first, I must explain my thought process and how I discovered the killer."

The room was silent, and Charlotte continued, "My initial plan was to employ the process of elimination, but it proved to be an impossible task. Nearly everyone here was a potential suspect, and as soon as I was ready to eliminate a name, circumstances forced me to reconsider. Let's take Margaret, for instance. Initially, it appeared that she had no motive to harm Mrs. Offley until I discovered her secret meetings with a young gentleman," Charlotte turned her gaze towards the maid, who appeared as pale as the wall she was leaning against.

"Lady Beatrice has implemented strict regulations for her staff, including a rule that maids must remain unmarried while in service at Haddonford. However, the cook enjoys more privileges, such as the freedom to start a family. Margaret would be unwise to leave Lady Beatrice and the generous stipend she receives regularly. Nevertheless, if her relationship with the person she's been seeing was serious, Rachel Offley's position would hold appeal for Margaret. It not only offers higher pay compared to her current role but also provides an opportunity for Margaret to pursue marriage," Charlotte explained.

Margaret protested, asserting her innocence. "I have a compassionate heart, and I would never wish harm upon Mrs. Offley. I am not capable of such actions."

"Indeed, we all recognize your kind heart," Charlotte acknowledged. "However, love can be a dangerous force, leading people to commit heinous acts driven by passionate emotions. Love can also blind individuals, causing them to make irrational choices. Consider Doctor Hurst, for instance. Despite his professional expertise, he succumbed to love's allure and became involved with Lady Adelle."

Charlotte anticipated the impact of her statement, as another wave of emotions swept across the room.

"For those unfamiliar with the name, let me introduce Doctor James Hurst, the psychiatrist entrusted with the care of Lady Adelle during her stay at Westling Hospital. The journey for Doctor Hurst was one of gradual descent, as he succumbed to Lady Adelle's remarkable acting skills and irresistible charm. Within the meticulously kept pages of his diaries, his inner turmoil unfolded, showcasing his desperate struggle against his own conscience as he fought to resist Adelle's persistent advances. However, her pursuit proved to be an overpowering force, gradually eroding his determination. Eventually, he found himself entangled in a passionate relationship, unable to break free from the profound bond they shared. Their secret liaison, concealed from the prying eyes of Haddonford Manor and Westling Hospital, would have likely persisted indefinitely, hidden beneath a veil of deception. Lady Adelle had achieved her deepest desire: an intimate connection with a handsome and accomplished doctor. And Doctor Hurst, despite his professional obligations, had succumbed to the allure of forbidden love. However, destiny had other intentions in mind. It was on a fateful night that Lady Adelle was unexpectedly seized by agonizing pain coursing through her back and lower abdomen. She cried out in distress, and Doctor Hurst was the first to rush to her aid. The true cause of her agony became apparent to Doctor Hurst, and in that moment, he made a choice that would forever alter the course of their lives.

With determination, Doctor Hurst orchestrated a strategic plan to ensure that nobody would come close to Lady Adelle, except for a carefully chosen nurse who collaborated with the family to tend to her needs. This nurse possessed an extensive wealth of knowledge and experience, and in exchange for additional compensation, she carried out her responsibilities impeccably, providing exceptional care for Lady Adelle. Content with her career and the generous remuneration from the Haddonford family, the nurse's personal life, unfortunately, lacked happiness. For years, she and her husband had yearned to have a child, a dream that had remained elusive. Then, the long-awaited moment arrived as Lady Adelle went into labor, her agonizing screams reverberating through the hallowed halls of Westling Hospital. The occasion was shrouded in secrecy. Fully cognizant of the dire consequences awaiting both Lady Adelle and himself, Doctor Hurst made a daring decision. He entrusted the newborn child to the nurse, extracting from her a solemn vow of absolute secrecy in return.

"For Doctor Hurst, it was a move driven by self-preservation. Allowing Lady Adelle to keep the child, or even acknowledging its existence, would spell certain ruin for his esteemed medical career. The stakes were too high, the risks too great. He believed Lady Adelle to be indifferent towards the newborn, an assumption that only added to his shock when she reacted with an unexpected intensity.

"As the nurse extended her arms to receive the bundled infant, Lady Adelle's eyes burned with a fierce determination. It was the second time her child had been taken from her, and even though the maternal bond may not have taken root, the wounds of deception ran deep within her. Lady Adelle despised being outmaneuvered, whether in a game of chess or matters of the heart. In a fit of rage and vengeful desperation, she seized a chess piece that lay within her room and thrust it savagely into Doctor Hurst's eye, forever marking him as a casualty of their clandestine affair."

"What happened to the infant?" Lady Beatrice's voice trembled with a mix of curiosity and emotional turmoil. The revelation of her sister's hidden child and the long-kept secret had shaken her to the core.

Charlotte paused for a moment, allowing the weight of the question to settle before continuing.

"The letter you received, the one that alarmed Lord Wharton and prompted his call to Inspector Sinclair, it held a cryptic message:

Everything we do has consequences.
Even your actions will have their repercussions.

Lady Beatrice nodded, her eyes clouded with the memories of that unsettling letter.

"Yes, I remember it well," she replied with a heavy sigh.

"Intriguingly, the writing style of that note reminded me of something Doctor Hurst once wrote in his diary. He had chosen a quote from Socrates: 'Every action has its pleasures and its price.' It was in his fourth diary that he detailed his relationship with Lady Adelle, and that very quote aptly captured the essence of their affair," Charlotte explained, her gaze fixed on Lady Beatrice.

"But upon investigating the date the letter was mailed, it became clear that Doctor Hurst could not have been its author. He had already passed away by then. That's when I decided to contact Inspector Sinclair. It was imperative to verify my suspicions, and without a doubt, they were substantiated. The person who had reached out to you, Lady Beatrice, turned out to be none other than the nurse who had assisted Doctor Hurst during Lady Adelle's delivery," Charlotte said. "True to her word, she had kept the secret hidden all this time. It was only after the devastating news of Doctor Hurst's suicide that she mustered the courage to come forward," Charlotte added empathetically.

Shifting her focus to Inspector Sinclair, Charlotte motioned for him to contribute his part in this complex investigation. The inspector cleared his throat before speaking.

"Miss Reinford expressed concerns regarding the sudden and unexpected demise of Doctor Hurst, which initially held little significance for me. However, recent conversations with the former nurse and Doctor Hurst's mother shed new light on the matter. It became apparent that the injury he sustained years ago, leaving him blind in one eye, would not have hindered him from continuing his research or successfully practicing medicine, albeit perhaps not at Westling Hospital, but another medical institution in England. The birth of a child was indeed kept a secret, and it seemed that nothing posed a direct threat to Doctor Hurst's career. After all, who would believe Lady Adelle's claims? She was deemed a mentally unstable woman confined within the walls of a psychiatric hospital," Inspector Sinclair continued.

"As a highly esteemed psychiatrist with an impeccable reputation and exceptional intellect, Doctor Hurst was regarded with great admiration, and his return to his professional duties was eagerly anticipated by the entire medical community. Even his own mother held high expectations for his successful comeback," Inspector Sinclair elaborated.

"However, it became increasingly apparent that Doctor Hurst had no intention of resuming his previous role. Whether driven by shame, guilt resulting from his actions, or another undisclosed burden, Doctor Hurst sought solace through self-medication, attempting to alleviate the inner turmoil that plagued him. Furthermore, he turned to writing as a means to confront and find peace amidst his torment. While I have not had the opportunity to peruse his diaries, Miss Reinford kindly shared excerpts, including his final entries that provide an insight into his tortured thoughts. It is essential to note that while Doctor Hurst experienced profound remorse, there were no explicit indications of suicidal tendencies. Hence, I am treating his untimely death as suspicious. Doctor Hurst's mother has graciously granted permission to exhume his body for further investigation—an avenue I intend to pursue once this perplexing case is fully resolved-but let's go back to the events that took place at Haddonford Manor," Inspector Sinclair said.

"Wait," Lady Isabelle interjected, "why did this nurse feel compelled to send a note to Lady Beatrice? And was the child a girl or a boy? Not that it matters."

"I believe Miss Reinford can shed light on this matter. Let's allow her to proceed and provide us with the necessary answer," Inspector Sinclair suggested.

Once again, the persistent ringing of the phone disrupted the room. George turned to the inspector, awaiting his instruction.

However, Inspector Sinclair chose to disregard the ringing, and George remained motionless, following the inspector's lead.

Maintaining her composure, Charlotte patiently waited for the phone to cease its incessant noise.

"The child was indeed a baby girl," Charlotte confirmed, breaking the suspense in the room.

Lady Beatrice, overwhelmed by the revelation, struggled to catch her breath.

"Adelle had a girl?" she gasped, her voice laced with a mix of shock and disbelief.

Charlotte nodded solemnly, "Lady Adelle led a rather eventful romantic life. However, the exact number of pregnancies she had remains undisclosed at this point," she responded, maintaining her composed demeanor despite Lady Isabelle's inappropriate laughter. A stern glance from Lord Wharton swiftly silenced his fiancée.

Lady Beatrice's concern grew, driving her to press for information.

"Can you tell us more about the child?" she inquired, her voice filled with genuine worry and compassion.

Charlotte acknowledged Lady Beatrice's request with the reassuring tone. "I promise I will provide you with the details soon. But before we delve into that, let us revisit the day Lord Carrington arrived at Haddonford," she suggested, redirecting the focus.

"Lady Beatrice, it was unexpected for you to see him on that particular day, as he deliberately arrived a few hours before Lord Wharton and Lady Isabelle. His purpose was to have a significant conversation with you."

"I am eager to hear Lady Beatrice's account of the conversation," the inspector interjected. "Could you please share with us what transpired during your discussion with Lord Carrington and why it visibly distressed you?" he inquired, directing his attention towards Lady Beatrice.

Lady Beatrice took a deep breath, mustering the courage to disclose the truth.

"He informed me about a letter he received, suggesting that he might have a child," she revealed.

Lord Carrington interjected, "It would be best to spare Beatrice any further anguish by refraining from questioning her about this affair," he stated firmly. "She has had no contact with her sister for many years, a fact that I was unaware of. I mistakenly assumed they were in touch. Moreover, I had no knowledge of the decline in Adelle's mental state. You see, Beatrice and I have been friends for a long time, but neither of us has discussed Adelle since the day she was admitted to Westling Hospital. It was Frank who shouldered the responsibility of caring for Lady Adelle and ensuring her ongoing treatment," Lord Carrington explained, expressing gratitude as he glanced at Mr. Offley.

"When I received an anonymous letter suggesting that I might be the father of Adelle's little girl, I was utterly shocked," Lord Carrington confessed.

"Initially, my instinct was to consign the letter to the fireplace and be done with it. However, upon reflection, I realized the gravity of the situation and the need to thoroughly investigate the possibility of fatherhood. Regrettably, the letter lacked specific details, leaving me in the dark about the child's age and her upbringing. All I knew was that in my youth, I allowed myself to be manipulated by Adelle like a marionette—a decision that fills me with shame. I must confess that we were together shortly before Adelle was sent to the Westling Hospital."

Lady Beatrice, feeling the weight of the situation, reached for a glass of water and hastily drank it down to steady her nerves.

The inspector connecting the dots, inquired further. "Is that why you were inquiring about a birth certificate?" he asked, seeking clarification.

Lord Carrington nodded, a mix of guilt and regret evident on his face.

"Yes, precisely. Fueled by the desire to uncover the truth, I enlisted the aid of the most adept private investigators, but alas, none could find a certificate under Adelle's name. Moreover, I undertook a personal investigation, meticulously combing through the West Wing of Haddonford Manor, hoping to find answers to my questions. However, to my dismay, the drawers of every desk were empty, and the entire wing seemed haunted, void of any life that once filled its rooms several decades ago."

Isabelle, unable to contain her curiosity, muttered, "The story keeps growing stranger by the minute. I'm eager to know the identity of this mysterious child, who must be a young lady by now," she remarked "But I am also curious about the motive and culprit behind Rachel Offley's murder."

"I am almost there," Charlotte reassured her. "Just a little more time, please. The incident you witnessed in your bedroom, Lady Isabelle, was not a mere nightmare. It involved an actual person who attempted to interfere with the letter that was sent to Lady Beatrice by the nurse who delivered Lady Adelle's child. Lady Beatrice placed the letter in the pocket of her robe before retiring to her room. The intruder used the conveniently growing ivy to climb the wall, taking advantage of the serendipitous open window, which was the only access point to Haddonford Manor and Lady Beatrice's room."

"I knew I wasn't going crazy," Lady Isabelle exclaimed.

"Yes, your experience was real. However, what intrigued me that night was Lady Beatrice's reaction to learning how the intruder entered the room. Although I didn't initially understand its significance, I later discovered that Lady Adelle, who was athletic and an excellent climber, used what is now Lady Isabelle's bedroom as an entry point during her nocturnal escapades when she lived in Haddonford."

Lady Isabelle, dripping with sarcasm, questioned, "So, you're suggesting that Lady Adelle herself scaled the wall to enter Haddonford Manor?"

Charlotte softly intervened, "No, not at all. As I previously explained, Lady Adelle couldn't possibly do that at her current stage in life. It must have been someone acquainted with her, someone who knew this window could serve as a feasible ingress."

"Someone in contact with Adelle?" Lord Carrington echoed, his confusion evident. "Now, even I am at a loss. Who could this person be?"

"It is the same person who befriended you and helped you acquire the key to the filing room at Westling Hospital," Charlotte revealed, her tone brimming with certainty.

"I am guessing that you were seeking the entrance to that room to search for Lady Adelle's files. You had a suspicion that she had a child while under the care of Doctor Hurst and took it upon yourself to find out if your hunch was true. That was the main reason behind the ease with which you agreed to be admitted to Westling Hospital. You needed access to the filing room and to Adelle. You knew she was in the same facility as you were, but you had no idea how to find a discreet way to see her. Your premature discharge was quite upsetting since you had not completed your mission, but having a co-conspirator made you feel somewhat at ease."

Everyone in the room stared at Lord Carrington who sat in complete silence. His shoulders sank, and his head hung low.

"Lord Carrington, your ability to see the positive in everyone and trust people easily is both your charm and your downfall," Charlotte continued gently.

"When you were first admitted to Westling Hospital, you needed someone familiar with the building to help you achieve your purpose for being there. On the very first day, you encountered that person, and though you believed it to be a lucky coincidence, in truth, it was not. This individual deliberately sought your friendship with ulterior motives and a hidden plan of her own. She skillfully kept her identity a secret from everyone just to be in closer proximity to her mother."

"Emily?" Lord Carrington exclaimed, taking a deep breath as realization dawned upon him.

Charlotte nodded knowingly. "Indeed, it appears that Emily learned about her true heritage from the nurse who raised her as her own daughter, the same nurse who assisted in Emily's delivery. Once Emily discovered her real mother's identity, she was determined to secure a position at the hospital. It likely didn't take long for her to establish a connection with Lady Adelle. Despite her declining condition at times, Lady Adelle still had moments of clarity, during which she saw an opportunity to conspire against her sister, whom she held responsible for her own institutionalization at Westling Hospital. The extent to which Lady Adelle coached her daughter remains uncertain, given her recent significant mental deterioration. Nevertheless, it's worth noting that Emily's adopted mother was close friends with Rachel Offley during their time working together at the hospital, one as a cook and the other as a nurse. Emily grew anxious that Mrs. Offley might possess knowledge about her birth and the involvement of Doctor Hurst with her biological mother. Fearing that potential risks might arise, Emily felt compelled to eliminate Mrs. Offley. Furthermore, she had to eliminate her birth father to advance her scheme of persuading Lord Carrington of his paternity. I suspect that Emily may have been somehow involved in Doctor Hurst's murder, although that is a matter for Inspector Sinclair to investigate further."

"So how does the letter come into the picture?" Lady Beatrice asked.

Charlotte glanced at Inspector Sinclair, and upon his nod, she continued.

"Just like your father, Lord Haddonford, began to notice that something was amiss with his younger daughter, similarly, Emily's adopted mother also became aware of the unsettling nature of her child. While I cannot definitively say that the saying 'the apple never falls far from the tree' applies universally, it does seem to hold true in Emily's case. Despite her adopted mother's earnest efforts to raise Emily as a devout and law-abiding daughter, she eventually realized that her attempts were futile. In a moment of desperation, she resorted to writing a note to Lady Beatrice, hoping to gather enough courage to divulge more in a follow-up letter. Should she lose her nerve to discuss the matter further, she hoped the contents of the letter would intrigue Lady Beatrice enough to seek out its author for an honest conversation, and thus force the former nurse to reveal the truth that had been kept secret for many years.

Lady Isabelle leaned forward, her curiosity piqued. "So, it was Emily who broke into my bedroom?" she inquired.

"That is correct," confirmed Charlotte.

"But how did she know that Lady Beatrice had the letter?" Lady Isabelle probed further.

"Because she was informed that it had arrived," Charlotte explained.

"Who informed her?" Lady Isabelle pressed for an answer.

"Her accomplice," Charlotte stated matter-of-factly.

A heavy silence fell upon the room as everyone absorbed Charlotte's words. Lady Isabelle was the first to break the silence, her voice filled with urgency.

"What do you mean by 'her accomplice'?" she demanded answers.

"Emily was unfamiliar with Haddonford Manor. Despite Lady Adelle's vivid descriptions of the place, Emily knew that she would never be able to execute her plan without help. When Inspector Sinclair and I met with Emily's mother, she expressed a desperation to save her child, but it wasn't Emily she was referring to, am I correct?" Charlotte took a few steps forward, locking eyes with Samuel.

"Love can be a beautiful thing, but it can also blind us. When you were both young, you developed romantic feelings for your sister, and Emily seemed to reciprocate, or so you believed. Your mother became concerned about the growing attraction between you. What happened, Samuel? Did your mother catch you two together? Did she notice you sneaking into Emily's bedroom at night? Although she was clearly upset, she didn't seem as devastated as you had anticipated. Was it her reaction to your relationship that made you suspect that Emily might not be your blood sister after all or was it something else?"

Samuel remained silent, eyes ablaze with intense loathing towards Charlotte.

"You recognized your mother's handwriting immediately upon seeing the envelope, didn't you? You feared she might have disclosed the truth. Immediately, you reached out to Emily, who then tried to intercept the letter before Lady Beatrice could peruse it. Alas, your and Emily's scheme didn't unfold as planned, compelling Emily to abandon her attempt to seize the letter. This marked the onset of downfall for both of you," Charlotte stated, locking eyes with Samuel.

Samuel's fists tightened, poised to lash out, but Lord Wharton promptly intervened, positioning himself protectively in front of Charlotte. Inspector Sinclair acted swiftly, subduing Samuel by twisting his arms behind his back and pinning him firmly against the wall.

"You'll have a chance to say hello to Emily soon," the inspector declared as he placed handcuffs on Samuel.

"She has been detained since yesterday. Apprehending her proved to be quite challenging," the inspector remarked, glancing at George, who instinctively touched the scratch on his face—a stark reminder of Emily's desperate bid to elude his grasp during the arrest.

"You see, I couldn't take any chances," Inspector Sinclair continued. "We can't trust her – like mother, like daughter. The world is safer when she is behind bars."

A profound silence filled the room, the enormity of the disclosures weighing heavily on everyone present.

"A few clarifications are still needed," Lady Isabelle was the first one to speak. "The note that was intended for Lady Beatrice, the one that Emily was after, sounded like a threat to me. Are you saying that it was not?"

"No," Inspector Sinclair said confidently. "Emily's adopted mother was actually referring to her own actions that had nothing to do with Lady Beatrice. She was fighting a deep battle with her emotions. Unaware of Emily's intentions and Samuel's presence at Haddonford Manor, she sent a note out of desperation, guilt, and a strong desire to save her own son, who was blessed to her a year after Emily was born. However, I must admit that her unclear message caused lots of confusion."

"Who murdered Rachel Offley? Was it Emily or Samuel?" Lady Isabelle posed another question.

"We will still have to determine that. What we know with certainty is that both were involved, and either of them could have done it. Samuel acted as Emily's eyes, ears, and hands here at Haddonford Manor. It was undoubtedly he who stole Miss Reinford's key."

"What key?" Lady Isabelle asked, confused.

"The recently vanished key to Miss Reinford's room. It's merely conjecture, but Miss Reinford's deep involvement in this case was becoming a clear hindrance to Emily. Emily's unexpected encounter with her at Westling Hospital must have been startling. She had to remain vigilant. When Miss Reinford managed to covertly access the third floor, Emily quickly triggered the alarm and alerted security, resulting in Miss Reinford's prompt removal from the premises."

Inspector Sinclair took a brief pause, then remarked with a hint of amusement, "Indeed, that was quite a remarkable night," as he recalled his own experience at Westling Hospital.

"Does anyone have any other questions?" he asked and when no one spoke, he added, "I'm sure you all have much to discuss and many relationships to mend. I'll be out of your way in a moment. Charlotte," he said, addressing her by her first name for the first time.

"I want you to know that I'm thankful for your help in resolving this quite convoluted case . . ."

Before the inspector could complete his sentence, the phone rang, causing him to roll his eyes in frustration.

"Someone answer that blasted phone!" he exclaimed, directing his annoyance toward his sergeant. Startled, George hurriedly reached for the phone. The room's occupants watched as his expression shifted while he listened to the person on the other end of the line.

"Yes, of course," George responded. "And may I ask who is calling?" he inquired, his confusion evident. "I see. I will certainly relay the message."

George hung up the phone and turned to face Charlotte, his hand absentmindedly scratching his head, a sign of his deep thought.

"That was a call for you," he said, his voice filled with concern. "It's from Mother Superior. She's been trying to reach you all night. There's an urgent issue at St. Helen needing your attention—it's about the sudden disappearance of a nun."

Charlotte's breath hitched as she stood up abruptly, her heart racing with a mix of anxiety and anticipation. She cast a quick glance around the room, keenly feeling the weight of inquisitive and troubled stares directed at her, their eyes brimming with unvoiced inquiries about the sudden shift in events.

Lord Wharton moved closer, his expression one of sincere concern.

"I'd be honored to escort you to the train station," he proposed.

"And while I don't wish to intrude, perhaps view this as a chance to unravel your own past. I suspect Mother Superior might hold the key to unlocking the mysteries you've been pondering," he suggested.

Charlotte gave a thoughtful nod, her mind a whirlwind of emotions—sadness at pausing her current journey and uneasiness about the reason behind her abrupt departure. Her gaze lingered on the familiar faces around her, etching their features into her memory. As she prepared to leave, she realized this wasn't just a goodbye; it was the end of one chapter and the beginning of another in her complex narrative.

Irina McGrath, Ph.D., was born in St. Petersburg, Russia and immigrated to the United States nearly three decades ago. Since then, she has worked in various educational roles within a public school district and higher education institutions. Alongside her educational career, Irina has developed a deep passion for writing. Her novel, Murder at Haddonford Manor, is the first in the "Charlotte Reinford Mysteries" series. As a writer, Irina brings a distinctive voice to her cozy murder mysteries drawing on her diverse experiences and rich cultural background to create narratives that captivate readers' attention.